BEFORE A MILLION UNIVERSES

T.W.R. SHELTON

BEFORE A MILLION UNIVERSES

Before a Million Universes

T.W.R. SHELTON

For information, contact twrshelton.wix.com/bluesirensbooks.

Book and Cover design by T.W.R. Shelton

ISBN: 978-0692515952

First Edition: September 2015

T.W.R. SHELTON

For Hayley

CONTENTS

"Let your soul stand cool and composed before a million universes."
-    Walt Whitman, "Song of Myself"

PROLOGUE

2160

MAXWELL ODYSSEY COULDN'T SLEEP. Her eyes were open, fixed toward the wall, with its yellowed, peeling wallpaper. But the wall was not what she saw. Instead, she saw her parents, nooses tied tightly around their necks as they jerked grotesquely, their feet searching for purchase, some saving grace. Their faces slowly turned purple and then blue. Their eyes bulged. And then they died. She saw the mixed reactions of the crowd. The sadness in the eyes of some and the wonder in the small children who watched but who had no awareness of their own personal mortality.

She smelled the sweat of the crowd, amplified by the nervous excitement that a hanging with such publicity contained. The event was broadcast live, of utmost importance. After all, it wasn't every day that figures of such high political status were tried for acts of mutiny against their country.

She couldn't hear a thing outside of her own voice, screaming as she reached for them while the barrel of a soldier's gun stared her down.

Maxwell turned over in her bed and pressed the heels of her palms into her eyelids. She yearned to erase the images from her mind, but they were burned into her brain with such vibrant realism that she doubted she would ever be able to forget. She let out a breath of hot air and swiped her hand across her face. The heat in the attic wasn't helping. Hot, heavy air surrounded her, suffocating her and causing her nightgown to stick to her slender form.

Bear shifted beside her. He turned to face her, eyes opening drowsily. He took a deep breath and reached out, brushing a sticky lock of dirty blonde hair from her face. "Still up?" he murmured, voice rough with sleep.

She looked toward the ceiling. "Don't think I'll ever sleep again."

He frowned in sympathy and, ignoring the heat, slid his arm around her. At thirteen, he was merely a year older than Maxwell and her very best friend. Maxwell's grandmother had adopted him as a young child years prior, saving him from life in an orphanage. He and Max had grown up together and were as close as two people could possibly be.

Max turned her gaze to Bear and focused on the spattering of freckles across his nose. They were coming out more in the recent sunshine. She counted them slowly. One. Two. Three. Four. Five. Six. Seven.

"Someday it'll be easier to breathe," he whispered.

Eight. Nine. Ten. Eleven. Twelve. Thirteen. Fourteen. Fifteen.

"I promise."

Sixteen.

Seventeen.

Eighteen.

Nineteen.

Twenty.

Twenty-o –

A crash downstairs frightened her to her feet. It was well past midnight; nobody should have been awake. She looked at Bear, eyes wide with fear, and then padded to the hatch in the floor. She opened it a crack and watched as the lantern lights turned on downstairs.

Bear tiptoed over to her quietly, trying hard to prevent the old attic floor from groaning and alerting Gran that they were awake. She'd be furious to know that they were out of bed at this hour. "Max, come back to bed."

Max listened to her Gran gasp and whisper frantically to an unidentified other. Although she was unable to make out the words, she could tell that something was very wrong.

"Max…"

But Max had already swung the hatch wide open and lowered the ladder. She was on her way down before Bear could further protest.

Her feet had barely hit the battered hardwood floor when she saw what was happening.

Gran was speaking in low tones to Max's Uncle Vic, who was holding a young girl in his arms. His face was streaked with tears. Further examination led Maxwell to realize that the girl had been beaten to unconsciousness. Blood matted her hair and stuck to her face. Her eyes were closed.

Max hurried over. "Gran! Uncle Vic! What's happened?"

Bear followed close behind, and he grabbed Max's sleeve to keep her from approaching any closer. She slapped his hand away impatiently and moved forward.

Gran frowned. "What are you doing out of bed? Bear, go grab towels and the first aid kit right away. Maxwell, put a pot of water on to boil!"

Bear took off to do as he was told, as per usual. Maxwell stood, transfixed.

Uncle Vic turned his eyes toward Maxwell, his expression softening. "Come along with me, Max. Your presence will be a comfort."

Maxwell tailed him as he turned and walked to her Gran's room. He lay the girl down on the bed and moved back. Max immediately took his place and dropped to her knees beside the bed.

Vic left the room for a moment and came back with a bowl of water and a cloth. He handed it to her. "Be careful now," he instructed. "I need to speak with your Gran."

She took a deep breath and nodded. She pressed the cloth gently to the girl's forehead and began to wipe away the excess of blood that streaked her dirty cheeks.

The girl let out a quiet whimper and flinched at the contact. Her breath rattled scarily in and out of her chest.

"I won't hurt you," Maxwell breathed, afraid to speak too loudly for fear that she would cause further upset. "I promise. You're safe now."

The girl's eyes opened and Maxwell was greeted by the greenest eyes she'd ever seen. Like fresh-cut summer grass. She was momentarily struck by their beauty.

She sucked in a breath and continued washing away the gore and grime from the girl's face, being especially careful around a large wound near her hairline. "My name is Maxwell, and I won't ever let anyone touch you like this again," she promised, reaching for her hand.

The moment their hands touched, the world went too bright for words and Maxwell's head flew back, eyes widening in shock as she was swallowed in heat and her world changed forever.

PART I

2147

CIRCLING THE STARS AND GALAXIES was one of Gabriel's favorite activities. Allowing himself to soar, uninterrupted, through valleys of color and also through places void of all color, all light, was very pleasant. It allowed him escape from his siblings and the strict rules set in place at his home in Heaven.

But nothing could compare to freefalling. Gabriel hadn't done it in so long. He hadn't allowed himself the freedom. Because with freedom came free will, which was something he wasn't very familiar with.

Earth was a very special place to him. He enjoyed exploring it, especially since his father had created the very first humans. They were funny creatures, emotional and greedy and not altogether very self-sufficient. But there was something about them beside the mere entertainment factor. Something he just couldn't shake.

Very few of his brothers understood his affections for the poor planet, but he was closest to the ones who did. Uriel, for instance, was very fond of Earth. He had gone so far as to stay inside of his human vessel for years at a time, creating a second life for himself on the planet. Gabriel found the idea fascinating, but he didn't want to create the same rift with his brothers that Uriel had by making that decision. As an archangel, he would be severely looked down upon for spending any amount of time on Earth for purposes of personal pleasure. There were just too many other responsibilities in Heaven for him to deal with.

And besides that, angels who made lives among humans were considered distasteful.

He hadn't been to Earth in ages. Last time he'd been there had been during the Vietnam War, when he'd temporarily lost his faith in humanity. Human bodies were strange, disorienting, and it had been a terrifying experience. His brothers sometimes liked to participate in wars, but Gabriel couldn't fathom why. Everything was so overwhelming already— strange and new. Being down on Earth during a war made everything so much more alarming. Hearing young men screaming for their mothers, crimson blood spilling out from beneath their clothing— it had been too much, and it had made him want to stay away for years.

This would be the first time he would descend alone. He wasn't bored, exactly. Angels didn't get bored. But it had been awhile, and chasing the same old stars wasn't holding the same appeal it always had.

He started his journey to Earth and allowed himself to bask in the sudden warmth that enveloped him. He altered his course a bit to be sure he wouldn't slam into any large bodies of water. He'd learned through trial and error that it was impossible to breathe underwater as a human. They had shed their gills shortly after acquiring the two legs that allowed them to wander around the Earth.

Color and light and heat flew past him and he fell faster, through clouds as he quickly neared land.

He'd chosen his spot well—a plot of land free of any buildings—he noticed, just before his wings flew out, a second too late to keep him from slamming into the ground. It quaked under his feet. He took a moment to gather himself, legs shaking beneath him. He stretched his wings experimentally and took a deep breath of air, feeling the rush of it deep into his lungs as his human heart thudded in his chest.

A gasp came from just in front of him, and he looked up quickly, eyes wide.

A woman sat there, a streak of red paint on her dress from where she'd dropped her brush in surprise at his sudden arrival. Her hair was what humans refer to as blonde, but which is really much more than that. A million different shades and lights reflected from her hair, creating a golden halo around her head. It was long and fell past her shoulders in wavy curls, like a waterfall of golden, dancing light.

Her eyes were strange. One was a beautiful, copper color, with soft pigments of barely-there red throughout. The other was as blue as the sky on a sunny, cloudless day. Gabriel briefly remembered a silly human fable he'd heard before about eyes like hers. It said that a human with eyes like hers could see realms of both Heaven and Earth. It was a falsity, naturally, but a charming story, he supposed.

This girl—this woman, looked as though she could belong to Heaven.

He straightened self-consciously, shoulders pulling back so he could stand tall in front of her. Good posture was important to humans. He stretched his wings briefly before pulling them in and folding them tidily against his back. He was unsure what to do, seeing the open-mouthed shock on the woman's face. He reached a hand out to help her up. "Do not be afraid..." he murmured.

She stared at him for a long moment before taking his hand and getting to her feet. Her hand was soft and warm, and he enjoyed the contact very much. He took a breath, flustered. "I am Gabriel, Angel of the Lord."

The woman stared back at him for a long moment before covering her mouth in an attempt to smother astonished giggles.

His cheeks reddened. "I do not understand what is amusing," he said, hands going to rest on his waist.

"A naked angel just landed in front of me. I'm sorry, I'm having difficulty processing this."

He frowned deeply. "Excuse me?"

She laughed again, and though the sound was glorious, it made him turn a deeper shade of crimson and look down at his feet.

"Here." She pulled her blanket from the ground wrapped it around his waist. She tied it expertly into a knot and took a deep breath. "There are clothes at my house. My papa's. They might be a bit snug, but..."

He nodded quickly. "Yes. Okay."

"Alright. We can leave these here for now. I'll come back for them," she gestured toward her painting and various supplies that were spread among the dozens of wildflowers that decorated the field.

"Thank you, erm?"

"Aubrey." She grinned over at him as she grabbed a key from her pile of things. "Come on." She jerked her head in the direction of a small, white house with a large garden to its right.

Gabriel followed because he didn't know what else to do.

"So." she said, rather casually, as she walked toward her home. "An angel, huh?"

"You're taking it quite well," he admitted quietly, watching her.

"I might be in shock. I don't really believe in a higher power, but here you are."

"Yes. Here I am." Gabriel watched her, a small smile pulling at the corners of his mouth.

Aubrey watched him, a dark brow quirking up. "So. God?"

"What about Him?"

"Is He real, too?"

Gabriel nodded. "Of course. Very real. He's the reason why you and I exist. The reason for everything."

"Hm. I've got to say, that's pretty disappointing to hear." She kicked at a flower as they walked. "He doesn't seem to care much."

Gabriel's brows pulled together in confusion. "Of course he does. My father is very fond of this planet. Of you humans. Of *all* the life he has created."

"Have you been here before?" she asked softly, turning her eyes up to his once more.

He nodded. "Not in many years, but yes. I used to come down quite frequently."

"Why'd you stop coming?"

"The last time I was here was during the Vietnam War. It left me with many questions, and I was uncomfortable visiting for a time. I usually visit with my brothers, but this time I decided to come alone."

She watched him. "You'll find things have changed. A lot. World War III hit, and ever since, it's been hell."

"I highly doubt that." Gabriel frowned disapprovingly. "Although I agree that war is certainly crippling and uncalled for, it could never leave results as bad as Hell."

Aubrey swung around in front of him and planted her bare feet, staring up at him. "They took my papa. He came back, but he couldn't face what he'd seen. What he'd done. He put a bullet through his skull." She looked toward the sky. "I thought the world of him, you know? But after everything happened, we changed. Our whole world changed. Our country cut all ties of friendship. We destroyed so many people, so many families and lives and ways of life. And now we're alone. Nobody is allowed in or out. We're stuck at a standstill, and I honestly don't see any way of making it better.

"Washington D.C., New York City, and Los Angeles were main targets in the war. They were all destroyed. Our government was in ruins. The people with money took over. Our capital was moved to Chicago. They use the city square cathedral for all their dirty work. Separation of church and state has been overruled. If you don't believe now, you have to keep your silence or it's game over. The church preaches love and harmony and forgiveness, but soldiers are out every day struggling with the overpopulation problem and dealing with it by murdering homeless people. It's disgusting. And this whole time, nobody has ever bothered to come to our rescue. Nobody from up in your little kingdom in the sky gives a single shit about us."

Gabriel took in the scene before him. Aubrey had a paint-splattered hand in her hair, raking it back away from her face. She looked frustrated, hurt. He could understand. He knew firsthand how difficult it was to lose faith. "You're wrong."

She snorted and began walking again. "Can you hide those things?"

"What?"

"Your enormous wings. They might cause unnecessary attention."

"Oh." He frowned and then let them fade away from human view. "I apologize."

They climbed a small staircase that led to the front door of the tiny house, and Aubrey unlocked the door.

He followed her inside and looked around. It wasn't much. He quickly deduced they were a poor family, and it made sense if Aubrey's father had passed away. The family would be left without a second income.

"It's not much," Aubrey murmured, voicing Gabriel's thoughts aloud. "But it's home. And I intend to make it better as soon as I can get a job." She led Gabriel through the kitchen and living room back to a small, dark room. "Mom isn't home yet. I don't think she'd mind if you wear his things, but I don't like to remind her."

Gabriel looked around the room as she rummaged through a dresser for clothing. Old, slightly tattered pink curtains hung on the windows. The ancient pink quilt on the bed was fringed with yellowed lace. A bible sat on the cracked headboard of the bed. He picked it up and sat down on the bed, flipping it open to the first page of the Gospel of Saint Luke.

The bed shifted with Aubrey's weight as she sat down beside him, clothing in her hands. She leaned closer, reading over his shoulder. "How accurate is it?"

He smiled. "Not very. It's always been a source of entertainment among my brothers."

"Are you in there?"

"Yes, unfortunately. It's been a cause for much teasing throughout the centuries. Have you read it?"

She shrugged, leaning forward so her elbows rested on her knees. "Not in ages. Wait." Her back straightened and she eyed him suspiciously. "Gabriel as in *Archangel Gabriel*?"

He shifted uncomfortably, the back of his neck growing hot. "The messenger of God. Yes."

"Holy shit."

Gabriel winced. He closed the bible and set it back on the headboard. "It's not a big deal."

Aubrey patted his knee. "Maybe not to you, but there's a supernatural celebrity sitting on my mother's bed. It doesn't get much more exciting than this." She set a pile of clothing on his lap and smirked. "Here. It's not the most angelic dress, but you won't shock the neighbors anymore."

"Thank you." He stood, letting the blanket around his waist fall to the ground. He pulled the pants on first and then tugged on the shirt, stopping to look up at her as he felt her eyes on him. He flushed, flustered, and fumbled with the buttons on the shirt.

Aubrey stood and pushed his hands away gently, doing up the buttons easily for him. "Gee, Angel, not very accomplished at fine motor skills, are you?" she teased, looking up at him. A small smile turned up the corners of her mouth.

Gabriel licked his lips and watched her, flushing deeply. "I'm unused to this body."

"Sure." She smiled and rolled her eyes.

Gabriel took a deep breath and stepped back, relieving himself of her scent, which reminded him of cedar and the sea, even in the middle of the poor Chicago outskirts. Unfamiliar bumps rose along his arms, and the hair at the back of his neck stood up.

He cleared his throat and rubbed the side of his neck, ducking his head. "Thank you, Aubrey."

"You're so bashful. Are all angels this nervous around humans?"

"I don't think most humans are quite as intimidating as you are," he admitted in a gruff voice.

She laughed and shook her head. "Come on, Angel. You hungry or anything?"

He took another deep breath and looked down at his stomach, setting his hand to it. He looked back up at her, chocolate brown eyes meeting hers uncertainly. "I think I could eat."

She nodded. "Alright. I'll pack a picnic, if that's okay. I'd like to get back to my painting. Do you have any big plans for your visit that you need to be getting to?"

He followed her to the tiny kitchen and stood at the sink as she began rummaging through cupboards. "No. I just wanted to look around. I thought I might visit my brother, Uriel. He's been here for quite a while. I'm beginning to think maybe he won't come back."

"Can he do that?" She raised her brows at him as she pulled a picnic basket from a bottom cupboard.

Gabriel shrugged his shoulders. "I don't think so. He's going to be in a lot of trouble when he gets back. For shirking his duties. He's an archangel, too, so there's a lot riding on him in Heaven."

"Hm. Well, here," she said, placing an apple in his hands. "You can be in charge of washing the fruit while I prepare everything else. Might as well make yourself useful, huh?" she bumped her hip to his teasingly, and he flushed deeply, nearly dropping the fruit.

She pretended not to notice, turning her attention to the sandwiches that she was preparing. "Hey, Gabriel?"

"Yes?"

"Was Mary really a virgin?"

Gabriel's cheeks burned as he purposefully avoided her gaze. "What do you think?"

Aubrey tipped her head back and laughed, joyous. "I knew it!"

2165

"MAXWELL!"

I pull my headphones tighter around my head and increase the volume, hoping to drown out the sound of my Gran. The music pumps through my entire body as I lay on my bed, a well-worn copy of *Leaves of Grass* in my hand. It's my favorite. A million times my favorite.

"Maxwell!"

Jesus Christ. She is *loud.*

I mutter a small grumble of defeat I know she won't be able to hear and get slowly to my feet, boots scuffing slowly along the dusty floor as I make my way to the hatch door.

"MA—"

"I'm coming!" I yell back, pulling open the door and begrudgingly making my way slowly down to the main floor of our home.

"Don't you yell at me," Gran chides, looking over at me. She smiles anyway. She looks exhausted, and I feel a little guilty for making her wait.

"Sorry," I mutter.

"Set the table."

"Yes, Gran."

I set out a plate at each setting, admiring them as I go. These plates have been here since before I can remember. Gran says they belonged to my mother, a wedding gift given to her by the President himself.

My parents used to be hot shit around here. Unfortunately, around here, being regarded as such generally comes to an end in death and the subsequent devastation and shaming of family and friends.

Our family name is forever tainted. I am Maxwell Odyssey, daughter of traitors. I have a brother, Matty, but he was taken away four months ago to become a soldier, and I don't expect to see him again. At least not while he's still breathing.

The plates on the table are a reminder of how things used to be. They're beautiful china, painted in flowing blue and purple lines. We've taken great care with them, since they're the most valuable things we own. There are no cracks, no chips, or scratches in their delicate design. Gran makes me polish them on a regular basis. We would sell them if it weren't for her stubborn pride. The woman is a goddamned lioness, I swear to God.

Aside from her very obvious bark, Gran is an inherently good person. She can never turn a soul away, even when they're low on cash, which is *always*. It's been especially hard since Matty was taken. Before he left, he and I worked out of Gran's garage, fixing and maintaining hovercrafts. Our family had a tiny second income and we were able to scrimp by. But after Matty left, so did our business. Customers were reminded of our bad luck and decided that even though I'm a fantastic mechanic, the risks weren't worth it. It's just as well because the garage is lonely without him, and I don't need the constant reminder of his absence.

Gran and I have never gotten on too spectacularly, but Matty was the glue that stuck our family together. When he was taken, Gran fell apart on the inside while keeping her shit together on the outside. She grew harder than before, but she stuck around and commanded her ship as though our very lives depended on it – which they do. She shut down her laundry business in favor of opening our home up to boarders.

I sit down in my usual place at the end of the table. It's where my papa would sit if he were still with us. Now I sit here, partly to feel close to his spirit, but mostly so I don't have to sit beside our boarders.

Right now we have a widow, Mrs. Timothy, and her snotty daughter, Ethel. I don't know who names their damned kid Ethel, but I'm willing to bet that her hideous name contributes to her equally atrocious attitude problem. Mrs. T and her daughter share Matty's old room.

We also keep Mr. Davis, a bachelor who I doubt will ever settle down and marry. He's considered very handsome around our community, but I have a difficult time seeing past the monster I know he is. He's been blackmailing me since he got here. He sleeps in the room that used to be our front room, but which has since been converted because our house was originally only a two-bedroom.

Mr. and Mrs. Barnaby are our final paying boarders. They're crotchety and mean. They sleep in Gran's old room while she has been reduced to a small room in the mildew-filled basement where I know she damn-well near freezes at night. I sleep in the attic with Bear, which always feels hollow, but I don't mind so much as long as I can keep away from everyone else.

My Uncle Vic and his adopted daughter, Jamie, moved in when I was twelve. He helped Gran split the basement into two additional bedrooms and he sleeps there while Jamie sleeps on the couch most nights. She used to sleep in the attic with Bear and I, but it got awkward as we grew older.

"I'm not late, am I?"

I feel myself smile immediately at the voice, despite myself.

"Theodore!" Gran smiles, too. My best friend is quite the charmer.

His face lights up. "Bear, Gran," he corrects gently, leaning down to kiss her weathered cheek.

"Oh, I don't know why you still insist on using that silly nickname. You're all grown now, Teddy."

Ethel sniffs and turns up her nose. "Bear seems to fit that grisly scruff he's been trying to grow on his face."

"Nobody asked you, Ethel!" I growl as Bear laughs, unaffected. He swoops down and kisses my cheek affectionately before settling down at the seat to my left.

Jamie looks up at us and smiles knowingly. I watch her for a moment before turning my attention back to Bear.

"How's your day be—"

Mrs. Timothy interrupts by clearing her throat. "Perhaps we could say grace before we have the pleasure of hearing about Theodore's exciting endeavors for the day?"

I snort, and Bear kicks me lightly under the table in warning.

Mrs. Timothy shoots me a look before beginning grace in her ugly, pinched voice.

I'm zoning out almost immediately, drifting.

It's dangerous to criticize prayer or show any sort of disrespect toward God. Prayer is fully expected before each meal and at set times each day and night.

I'm reminded again of Matty. He held great hope in prayer.

We used to have a shed in our backyard. Dad built it years before his death. Matty installed a tiny window in the roof shortly after our parents' passing. It was so small that the officers on patrol every evening wouldn't be able to tell we were there as long as we were quiet.

That was how I viewed the night sky for the very first time since the curfew laws came into effect in 2160.

Every night at 7:00 pm, our doors close, our windows and shutters are locked, and curfew is in full operation. We are forbidden from viewing the night sky. It's against the new set of commandments. From what I can understand, it's because a long time ago, scientists called astronomers were seeking information about life on other planets. This kind of thinking is greatly discouraged. The scientists were terminated when our new commandments were installed. The curfew didn't come into effect until years later, when a new interest in space arose.

Gran was furious when she found out what we'd been doing, sure that we'd be caught. She burned the shed the very next day. Matty and I both cried.

Matty said the stars made him feel closer to God. Closer to our dead parents.

He said they were in a place called Heaven.

I didn't have the heart to tell him there was no such thing.

I guess I've always been skeptical because if there really is a God, he's a shitty one anyway. He allowed my parents to be murdered by a corrupt government, he let my brother be taken from me, he holds no regard for the hundreds of homeless who are slaughtered every day for population control—the list is endless.

Mrs. Timothy finally shuts up, and we're allowed to eat.

I look up at Bear expectantly.

He smiles gently. "Same old shit, different day."

Gran swats at the back of his head as she approaches with a pitcher of newly purified water. "Theodore! Watch your mouth."

He nearly chokes on the biscuit in his mouth. "Yes, ma'am." He coughs out a laugh.

She smiles kindly and leans down to give him a one-armed hug as she hands him an extra biscuit. He's got her wrapped around his finger. Bear has always had that kind of impression on people. He's genuine and compassionate and it creates a warm glow that follows him everywhere he goes.

"Have you heard anything about your interview at the shelter?" I ask. Bear has recently applied to a housing center for orphaned children. They seem to need all of the help they can get, and I'm positive Bear will get hired. He's been volunteering there for years.

At eighteen, all men are required to find a job or they are automatically drafted into the army, if they haven't already volunteered. Bear has been lucky enough to escape the draft so far, but if he doesn't secure a stable job soon, they'll pull him away and he'll be lucky to come back alive.

After ten years of service, men are allowed to leave and return to society to find work. They have first priority. Their job is to find stable employment, take wives, and raise a small family with no more than two children.

"Uh, no. Not yet, but I'm sure I will soon." His tone is pleasant, but something in his eyes has changed.

"They'd be crazy not to pick you," I say quietly, looking down at my plate.

"The competition is a little crazy these days. No one wants to be drafted, you know?"

I nod quietly.

"Nothing wrong with going into the service," Mrs. Barnaby barks from her place at the table. "Did my Jonathon well."

Oh yes. Because coming back from the service touched in the head is what every man dreams of, I think. Mr. Barnaby doesn't say much of anything, but he always looks so sad. It's like living with a ghost.

I only glare at her.

"It's honorable," she continues, dabbing at her wrinkled mouth with her napkin. "If you're chosen, you should be glad to die for your country. For your religion."

There's a horrible sniffling from the other end of the table, and I don't need to look up to see who it's coming from. Mrs. Timothy, as awful as she is, has lost a son to the service. It's probably what makes her such a wretched person.

"Oh quit your sniveling, Tanya. You should be proud."

"Excuse me." Mrs. Timothy stands quickly, bumping the table in her haste. She hurries to the bathroom and slams the door just as a loud sob erupts from deep within her.

Ethel stands silently and takes her and her mother's plates and dumps them in the garbage before setting them in the sink. She hurries to the bathroom to console her mother.

I chew my lower lip and stare at my plate.

Bear has stopped eating as well. He reaches out and sets his hand over mine.

I look up and see that Gran is silently pushing her food around her plate. I stare at her for a while, but she never looks up to meet my eyes. I can't stand the silence.

I drop my fork. "I appear to have lost my appetite as well," I murmur, standing. Instead of being wasteful, I opt for wrapping my meal in foil and placing it in the refrigerator. Bear follows suit, setting his plate on top of mine.

Gran looks up at us and gestures us over.

I pull him over to her and sigh. "Yes?"

She pulls me down into a hug, burrowing her face in my hair for a moment. I'm surprised by the gesture, but I wrap my arms around her tightly and kiss her weathered cheek. "Goodnight, Gran," I murmur softly.

"Goodnight, Maxwell. I love you."

She hugs Bear, too, and wishes him a goodnight.

I take him by his shirtsleeve and pull him to the ladder. He takes a deep breath and follows after me. We climb up to my room and then close the hatch door.

Bear looks up at me when we've brushed ourselves off, and then he steps closer to me and takes my chin in his hand, leaning down and kissing me hard.

I melt into him but pull back after a moment to look up at him, suspicion obvious on my face. "You're eager tonight. What's going on?"

"Nothing, Max. Don't worry about it, okay?"

I grit my teeth. "What is it?"

He swallows audibly and looks up at me, his cerulean eyes becoming sad. "I received a letter today, and it just – I don't know how to tell you…" His shoulders slump.

"A letter from who, Bear?" I hear my voice tighten, ready to snap. I know it can't be good if he's trying to hide it from me.

He bites his lip and pulls a letter from his pocket. He hands it over quietly.

I look down at it and read.

The President of the United States,
August 7, 2165

    To: Theodore B. Mitchell
    209 W. McKimmy St
    Chicago, IL 61019

Greetings:
    You are hereby ordered for induction into the Armed Forces of the United States, and to report to the Lobby of the U.S. Chicago Library, Chicago, IL. on September 5, 2165 at 07:00 a.m. for forwarding to an Armed Forces Induction Station.
    May God always be with you.
                        Franklin M. Shumaker
                        Member of Local Board

IMPORTANT NOTICE
IF YOU HAVE HAD PREVIOUS MILITARY SERVICE, OR ARE NOW A MEMBER OF THE NATIONAL GUARD OR A RESERVE COMPONENT OF THE ARMED FORCES, BE PREPARED TO SUPPLY EVIDENCE. IF YOU WEAR VISION CORRECTION TECHNOLOGY, BRING IT. IF YOU HAVE A JOB, BRING PROOF OF YOUR JOB. IF YOU HAVE ANY PHYSICAL OR MENTAL CONDITION WHICH, IN YOUR OPINION, MAY DISQUALIFY YOU FOR SERVICE IN THE ARMED FORCES, BRING A PHYSICIAN'S CERTIFICATE

DESCRIBING THAT CONDITION, IF NOT ALREADY FURNISHED
TO YOUR LOCAL BOARD.

I don't bother reading the rest of the draft letter. Instead, I let it drop to the floor, feeling sick to my stomach. "They can't do this. No."

Bear takes a step closer and sets his hands on my shoulders. "They can, Max." He sighs shakily, biting his lip. "I didn't want to tell you..."

I slap his hands away. "You didn't want to tell me? What, were you just going to leave me without saying anything?"

"No. No, listen. I didn't want to worry you."

"Oh, that's rich." My voice is thick with tears, and I hate myself for it. "That's rich. Don't want to worry me, so just leave without a word. Just don't even say a fucking *thing*!"

"Max, please..." his voice breaks and I finally look back up at him, my lower lip trembling dangerously. "Listen to me."

I stare up at him, quivering. My eyes are hot with unshed tears, but I hold fast, unwilling to let them fall.

"I'm sorry, Max. I know it's going to be hard. Really hard. But I know it'll be okay. I'll come back." His hands find my shoulders again, and I feel them slowly sink.

I shake my head back and forth slowly. "No you won't. Don't promise me that, Bear. Nobody comes back."

"They do! People come back every day."

"It's ten years, Bear! *Ten*!"

"I'll come back."

"You won't!" My fists flail out before I can stop them and I'm hitting his shoulders, his chest, anything I can come in contact with. "You won't come back! You won't!"

Bear stands still and takes his beating, only reaching forward to catch me when I become weak with shock and a sadness that threatens to bring me to my knees.

"I promise I'll come back for you." He buries his face in my hair and I can feel his beard scratch at my forehead as he presses kisses along the top of my head.

I don't respond. There's nothing left for me to say; I know he won't be coming back.

"Max," Bear murmurs in a soft, sad voice. "Maxwell..."

"Stop," I growl, turning my face up to stare at him, tears wet on my face. "Just stop talking." I take his face in my hands and I kiss him just as eagerly as he'd kissed me earlier.

He makes a soft, surprised sound, and then he's kissing me back. Our teeth click together roughly. I'm desperate to feel something, *anything* other than the agony that his news has brought into my chest. I kiss him hard and jerk him back to our cot by the collar of his shirt. The side of the cot catches the back of my knees and I fall back onto it with a gasp, pulling Bear down with me.

"Fuck, Maxwell," Bear breathes, arms sliding around me.

"Shut up," I murmur, closing my eyes against more tears as I tug at his shirt and pull it away so I can feel his skin. "Just shut up and kiss me."

"Please tell me you're not *really* going to go volunteer today."

Bear smiles sadly. "The kids will miss me, Max."

A miserable lump grows in my throat. "*I* will miss you."

He strokes a gentle finger along the bare skin of my shoulder. "I know," he murmurs. "I'll miss you, too."

"They'll make you cut your hair. Shave your face. You'll look like a child. And you won't be allowed letters. Or phone calls. Or—or..." my voice trembles and catches, refusing to work properly.

I don't know why I'm trying so hard to punish him. It isn't his fault he's been drafted.

His jaw tightens as he strokes my hair, but he doesn't respond.

"I won't wait for you," I mutter, shoving my invisible dagger deeper into his chest and giving it a twist.

"I don't expect you to," he finally replies. "Ten years is a long time."

My eyes fill again and my gaze wanders toward the ceiling. I put my hands over my face and blow out a shaky breath of air.

The skin of my cheek tickles as Bear sprinkles gentle kisses along it. "But, if you're still here—if no one's snatched you up, I'd be happy to have you."

I sniff and look up at him. "Okay."

He smiles, sad and sweet. "I love you, Maxwell." His warm hand slides slowly through my hair and down my back, enveloping me in his precious heat.

"Be careful, okay?"

He nods.

"Don't let it change you."

Selfishly, I think what scares me the most is the possibility that he will come back ruined, that he will lose his beautiful, carefree nature. His smile.

"You know that's something I can't promise," he replies quietly. "It's an unfair request. But I'll try my damnedest."

I nod slowly and climb over him, wrapping my limbs around him like an octopus. He tucks his face against my neck and sighs.

"Maxwell!" It's Gran.

I groan and shake my head.

Bear huffs out a laugh and pokes my sides gently, making me squirm. "Breakfast time."

"*Maxwell!*"

"Jesus Christ, I'm coming!"

I'm alone with Gran. We're working on the wash together while Bear is out volunteering and our various boarders are off living their own lives. The constant, familiar scratching noise of the laundry in the machine is a comfort. It reminds me of my childhood, of helping—or hindering— my mother, in her efforts to do our laundry.

"Is there anything you want to tell me?" Gran asks hesitantly, looking over at me. She has an annoying habit of always knowing when something is wrong.

I wrinkle my nose and shake my head, scrubbing harder to work at a questionable stain on Mr. Davis's shirt.

"No?"

"You already know."

She nods once. "Bear is leaving."

My teeth dig into my lower lip and I look down at my washing.

"I'm sorry." Her hand lands on my shoulder, but I shrug it off.

"It's no big deal. I think I always knew it was going to happen. It's fine."

She frowns deeply and folds her laundry carefully. "Maxwell."

"I don't want to talk about it, okay? I told him I don't want to discuss it. It's not important right now; he's not leaving until next month."

Gran grows very quiet, continuing on with her folding.

My eyes fill and my nose stings with the threat of oncoming tears. I blink rapidly, turning my face toward the ceiling. "I'm tired of everyone leaving me behind."

"Maxwell." She takes my hand gently. "I know things seem unfair. They are. But we've got to make the best of what we have."

I nod slowly and swallow hard past a lump in my throat. "I love him, you know?"

She nods. "Of course I do. And he knows it, too. That'll help him, honey. Everyone that's drafted needs a piece of love from home to hold onto while they're away. To keep them sane. He will always be a part of our family, and he will always be welcomed back home."

"I hate the rules," I murmur. "They're so stupid. Ten years is too long. Bear isn't qualified for warfare. He wouldn't hurt a fly. He *couldn't*. He's so sweet. He won't come back the same."

"He won't," she agrees, "and that's why it's going to be even more important for you to be here waiting for him when he gets back, to accept him for who he has become, but to remind him of who he used to be. Remind him how to smile again. Take care of him like he's taken care of you all these years."

There's a rustling in the doorway and I wipe at my eyes quickly before looking up to see who it is. Jamie stands there, looking a little embarrassed. "Am I interrupting?" she asks quietly.

Gran smiles and shakes her head. "Not at all, honey. What can I do for you?"

Jamie stands taller. "I finished weeding. What else can I do?"

"You can take over here for me while I get supper on. Max could use the company."

"Okay." Jamie nods and walks over to me. "Vic is going to be late for dinner tonight. The Anderson girl down the street has fallen very ill. He's doing his best to help, but he says there's not much more he can do for her. He's trying to make her passing as comfortable as possible."

Gran nods sadly and stands. "I'll keep a plate warm for him. He'd better get himself home before curfew, though."

Jamie nods. "Of course."

I listen to Gran's retreating footsteps and look back over at Jamie. "How's it going?"

She shrugs and looks up at me, green eyes wide. "I heard you talking. About Bear. I'm so sorry, Max."

I throw the shirt I'm folding back down into the basket carelessly. "I don't want to dwell on it."

She nods and reaches out, taking my hand in hers. She squeezes tightly and I'm immediately comforted. She's always had that effect on me. It's like I'm a storm and she's a calming wind, blowing the bad parts of me away so I can breathe again.

"It looks like laundry is almost done. Can I braid your hair?" she asks, thankfully dropping the subject.

I nod and move to the cool, concrete floor in front of her, setting my back to her knees. Her fingers begin to comb carefully through my long hair, never tugging or breaking it, despite its constant wild state.

I swallow hard and look back down at the laundry basket near my knees. I begin folding again while Jamie's fingers work an intricate braid into my hair.

The radio crackles near us. It's old. Older than me. Older than my parents would be if they were still alive. It doesn't even have hologram capabilities. I'm not sure why Gran keeps it, but she insists it works just fine. I suppose we wouldn't be able to afford a better one even if we wanted to upgrade. The afternoon hanging schedule is read by the announcer. Nothing too exciting; just population control.

I hate the hangings. They're grotesque. I can't think of a more gruesome and horrible way to die.

They're public for a reason, to make an example. In criminal cases, like my parents, the public usually gets pretty riled up, sometimes even in defense of the offenders. My parents' case was enormous and a lot of people were upset about their death sentence, seeing them more as messengers of knowledge rather than dangerous rebels.

The homeless hangings are something else entirely. They're all about population control. There are too many of us, so pretty much any chance they can get, they terminate as many of us as possible. Hangings are favored because they're cheap and efficient. Homeless families are split up. Those eighteen and older are hanged, and the rest are sent to facilities like the one Bear volunteers at, taking care of orphans. Those children are forced to get jobs immediately upon turning eighteen. If after six months they haven't found jobs or been drafted, they are disposed of as well.

"Max?"

"Yeah?" I look up, my thoughts interrupted.

"Do you ever think about how it could be if things were different?"

"They can't be different."

"But if they could."

"I don't understand why you're thinking about something that can never be."

She sighs and her fingers pause in my hair. "I just think there's got to be something better out there. I can't live the same old story every single day and pretend nothing is wrong. What about the rest of the world? How are they doing? We send our men out every day and never hear from them again. Where are they going? What are they doing, and why can't we ever speak to them?"

I shake my head. "I don't know. We can't talk about this here, okay? Keep your voice down. If anyone heard us..."

She sets the side of her cheek to the top of my head. "What if Bear didn't have to join the service? We could all leave together. We could fight."

"Fight for what?"

"For our freedom. For the rest of our people."

"They don't want our help, Jamie."

"They need to know the truth. This can't be all there is."

"Don't bring this into Gran's house. Please. We've had enough trouble as it is."

"Gran is a part of a bigger picture. You'll see."

I close my mouth and refuse to say anything more.

"You do like the idea of him not having to leave, though."

"Who, Bear? Of course I do."

She smiles. "It could be fun. An adventure."

"A never ending nightmare, more like. I don't understand where you think we would be going."

She finishes off my braid. "I've heard of these places underground. There are hundreds of rebels down there, maybe thousands, all waiting for their chance to rise up and take back the city. They just need leaders to show them how to do it."

I scoff and roll my eyes, turning to face her. "Who's going to be stupid enough to do that?"

She stares at me, eyes wide and innocent, as though she isn't committing mutiny by speaking her dangerous thoughts aloud. "We are."

"Were you and Jamie able to finish the laundry?"

Gran is adding the finishing touches to our dinner, a creamy tomato basil soup from scratch with some garlic grilled cheese sandwiches. The boarders will probably bitch about the lack of meat, but we're struggling right now just like everybody else, and quite frankly, for as little as Gran is charging them to be here, they're lucky she's feeding them at all.

"Yes."

"Is something wrong?"

"Sometimes Jamie speaks dangerously," I mutter, busying myself by setting the table.

"She's a leader."

I look up at her in surprise, nearly dropping the stack of china in my hands. "Wha—"

The door opens and Mr. Davis walks in. Gran shoots me a pointed stare, obviously letting me know it's time to shut up. She looks back over at him and smiles. "Hello, Jonathon."

He smiles and gives her a nod. "Mind if I steal Maxwell away for a moment? I've got something for her to see in the garage. Possible upgrades for that hoverbike of hers."

God damnit.

"Be back in no more than ten minutes," Gran replies, not looking away from her soup. "We've got people to feed."

I give her a look but allow myself to be steered toward the garage.

"We haven't had any alone time in quite a while," he murmurs, hands locking around my wrists as soon as we've made it to the garage.

I'm disgusted by my predicament, and in my garage, too! This is my sacred space. My safe haven.

I exhale, tipping my head away from him. "I haven't been too bothered by it," I mutter, refusing to look at him.

He laughs and leans down, pressing his nose to my collarbone. "I'll just bet you haven't."

"I thought maybe you'd gotten bored with me."

"With you? Never?" I can hear the creepy smile in his voice as I fight the urge to throw up all over him. His hands slide up my shirt and then tug the buttons apart easily. I don't fight him on it.

He's got dirt on my family. He knows Gran isn't allowed so many boarders and has used his advantage to threaten calling the authorities. With the amount of shit my family has been in the news for, I'm sure it would end badly. On top of everything else, I know Gran still has some of mom and dad's things hidden away in her room that could get us into a *lot* of trouble. If our house were to be searched, we would be completely screwed. He's disgusting and pervy, but if I have to let him hump my leg and feel me up a little to get him to keep his mouth shut about our dirty laundry, I'll do it. I'm not willing to risk her life.

I stare silently at the wall as he drags his filthy tongue down to my breast. My arms hang useless at my sides.

He huffs out a laugh. "You're in a foul mood today," He murmurs, slamming his hips up against mine and effectively knocking me back against the wall. His hands reach for the button on my jeans and I squirm, shaking my head.

"No. You know I won't let you," I snap, slapping his hand away.

He laughed again and kissed me hard, slamming my head back against the wall with a low thud. "I can do whatever the fuck I want, you little slut. What's stopping me? I heard you and Jamie talking today. What are the police going to say when I tell them Mary is harboring rebels?"

I'm horrified. I'm going to *kill* Jamie the next time I see her!

He's trying to drown me in his putrid saliva, I swear to God. He licks across my mouth and it's the most disgusting thing I've ever let myself be subjected to.

His hands slide back to my jeans and undo them. I shake my head, but he pins me harder to the wall, kissing me sloppily.

Panic shakes me to my core and I begin to push at his shoulders, but it does nothing to deter him. He's got his mind set on this and things do not look good for me, so I do the only other thing I can think of while I'm pinned against the dirty garage wall. My teeth sink so far into his lower lip that I can feel the skin break and taste a warm gush of blood on my tongue.

Mr. Davis howls in pain and jerks backward, eyes furious. Blood streams down his chin.

I zip my pants, turning toward the door. I stop abruptly, seeing Jamie's horrified expression as she stands in the doorway. Her mouth is open in confusion, eyes wide. I push past her quickly, buttoning up my flannel as I go.

"Max." She grabs my shirt sleeve, but I shove her away.

I don't look back at her as I hurry into the house.

2165

"YOU'RE LATE," GRAN SCOLDS when we walk in, not looking up from where she's busy ladling soup into bowls. "I said ten minutes."

I take a shaky breath and shake my head quickly. "Sorry, Gran. Got distracted."

She looks up, frowning, and then her eyes widen. "Maxwell! You've got blood on your face!"

I reach up to wipe at my mouth. Sure enough, my fingers come back red. I shrug and laugh without humor. "Whatever. It's not mine."

She frowns. "What on Earth?"

Mr. Davis comes in after me, scowling. He pushes past me and heads to the bathroom, muttering something about how much of a bitch I am and how we're going to pay.

Gran's eyes widen. "Max."

I shake my head. "I took care of it. Don't worry."

But I *am* worried about it. If he says something about Gran harboring rebels because he's angry with me, we're fucked. The system is not forgiving, and they won't let anything slide.

She walks to me and wipes at my mouth with her dishcloth. "I knew he was trouble."

I shrug and look away. "I'm fine. Like I said, I took care of it. Don't worry about me, okay?"

"I'll throw him out."

"You can't. He knows things."

She laughs without humor. "Oh, he's playing that game, is he? Well, I know enough about him that I can have him taken care of if I need to."

"Gran…"

"End of discussion. I'm not going to have some lowlife pervert messing around with my granddaughter as blackmail."

I know fighting with her is worthless. She's tough. She won't put up with any bullshit. She won't allow me to be hurt anymore.

"How long has this gone on for, Maxwell?"

I look away as I hear Bear come in. "Gran."

She can't take a hint, either.

"How long?"

"Long enough. Not now, okay? Please."

She frowns and nods slowly. She looks over at Bear and gives him a tiny smile. "Hello, Sweetheart." She pulls him into a big hug.

He smiles. "Hey, Gran. Good day?"

"Not the best, but tomorrow is a new start." She takes my hand and gives it a squeeze. "Sit at the table now, you two. Dinner is ready."

Bear slides an arm around my waist and leads me over to the table. "What's going on?"

"It's not important. Just a little sad today, that's all."

He kisses my cheek. "We'll talk after dinner."

I nod. "Yeah, okay." He probably thinks I'm going to attack him again about being drafted, which I honestly feel pretty shitty about. I know it isn't his fault. I felt bad while I was doing it, but I've felt progressively worse about the whole thing throughout the day because I know he's probably been thinking about my outburst, too.

Maybe I should bring up what Jamie said about the rebels underground. Maybe I could, for a moment, just entertain the fact that we could get away and Bear wouldn't be robbed of his innocence.

Maybe.

I take his hand during dinner and hold it tight.

Mr. Davis doesn't return from the bathroom. I'm not bothered, and apparently neither is anybody else. Jamie doesn't come to dinner, either.

"Do they have to be so loud? They're going to get into trouble." Gran stands and peers out the window over the kitchen sink. Our neighbors are throwing a party outdoors. They're cutting it really close to curfew, and their laughter is really loud. I don't blame them, though. It's nice to be outside in the warm air. They're having a cookout, from the smell of it. Hot dogs. The cheapest and most readily available meat there is. Also one of the most delicious, to be honest.

I stand and look out the window beside her. I squint a little. "Gran. What is that?" There's a huge mass in the sky.

"I'm not sure."

"It looks really close."

A screeching consumes the sky. "What the hell?"

By now we're all gathered around the window, staring. There's a huge plane, and it's flying way too low to the ground. Soon I'm unable to see it anymore, but I can hear it as it lands just outside the city with a huge crash and burst of light. There's fire and screaming in the distance.

I'm running outside before I fully realize what's even happened.

To the North, the cathedral that lies in the city square is still, and the sky has turned a brilliant orange. The enormous cross in front of the church hangs black in the sky around it.

"Maxwell, curfew!" Bear yells from somewhere behind me. It's funny, by now I'm far from the house, but I don't remember getting here so quickly.

There is more screeching as another plane falls from the sky. What is *happening*?

"Oh my god," I mutter, watching another piece of my city burst into flames.

I turn to Bear. He's standing beside me. He takes my hand. "We're going to be in big trouble if we're out past curfew."

"*Look*, Bear!" I gesture in front of me with my free hand. "What's happening?!"

He shakes his head, frowning deeply. "I don't know, but it can't be good. We should probably get to the basement."

There's a ringing in the sky that has me down on my knees in no time at all, pressing my hands to my ears and gasping. Bear is unaffected. He stares down at me in confusion as I writhe in pain, fearing my eardrums will burst at any moment. It stops just as quickly as it began, and I get back up to my feet on shaky legs.

Another high-pitched noise shoots across the atmosphere. I look up and take a deep breath. There are balls of fire falling from the sky. The noise from the fire is accompanied by hundreds of people screaming. We're all out in the street trying to figure out what's going on.

"What *are* those things?!"

"Max, let's go inside!" Bear pulls on my hand, but I jerk away and begin to run.

Thunder cracks, and lightning strikes, hard and fast. My heart thuds nearly as loud as the thunder does, pounding in my ears. My feet are hitting the pavement hard.

I'm not sure where I'm headed until I get there. I have to stop at the bridge to the old city because there's so much traffic that there's nowhere to go. I gasp at the scene before me. There's a hole in the bridge. Cars are falling deep into a pit that is filled with what looks like fire. There must be a downed plane there. I swallow hard. "What's going on?"

A huge ball of flames hits the ground only feet from where we're standing, and I'm face down on the concrete before I can even take a look to see what it is that landed.

CITIZENS. RETURN TO YOUR HOMES IMMEDIATELY. CURFEW IS IN PLACE. ANYONE WHO REFUSES TO COMPLY WILL BE PROMPTLY TERMINATED.

CITIZENS. RETURN TO YOUR HOMES IMMEDIATELY. CURFEW IS IN PLACE. ANYONE WHO REFUSES TO COMPY WILL BE PROMPTLY TERMINATED.

CITIZENS...

The message drones on, blaring through the emergency speakers placed throughout the city. My ears tune the sound out as I get to my knees, the tangy taste of blood in my mouth. I look up and stare at the creature that has fallen in front of me. I stand on shaky legs and take a step toward it.

"Maxwell!"

Bear grips my hand and pulls me back.

"What is it?" My voice is breathy in my own ears. I've never seen such a magnificent creature in my entire life. It stands. It looks almost human, but it is far too glorious. It is radiating a light that is far too bright to allow me to see its features. Its huge wings span more than double the length of its body on each side. If I believed in Heaven and God and that sort of thing, I would think it was an angel. But angels don't exist. They can't. God is fiction. The whole idea is *ridiculous*.

So why is my throat tightening? Why can't I breathe? Why is the gloriousness of this creature threatening to bring me to my knees? I choke and now I've even lost the ability to move.

The spell is broken as the shouting from citizens around me grows louder. There's the sound of shots firing, and I hear a woman scream from beside me as she's hit through her chest, blood spraying out into the street.

The soldiers are on their hoverbikes, shooting everyone left in sight. And there are a lot of us. Humans are curious by nature, and tonight it looks like we're going to be paying permanently for it.

"Maxwell!" Bear gasps from my side. "Max, we've gotta get out of here or we're going to die!"

I gasp and jerk forward as a bullet hits the back of my shoulder.

"Max!" It's a different voice this time. Jamie's. Funny how I never noticed her before. "Grab her, Theodore. Follow me!"

Bear makes a strangled noise and scoops me up.

The pain is excruciating. My face screws up in pain, and I close my eyes. "Bear..."

"I know. I know. It's going to be okay."

"They shot me." My voice sounds faraway.

"Yeah. Yeah, but you're gonna be fine. Max? Ma—"

The urgent tone in his voice is lost to me as the lines around my vision blur and then it slowly fades away completely.

PART II

2165

WHEN MY EYES FINALLY FLUTTER OPEN, it's hard to know if I'm actually awake because it's so *dark*. My head explodes with the pain of a thousand sharp needles, all pressed to the same spot at the back of my skull.

"Bear?" I murmur, trying to sit up.

Shit. Pain stabs through my shoulder and I whimper, letting myself lie back down. "Owowow…"

"Maxwell?" It's Jamie. She squeezes my hand.

"Where's Bear? Is he okay?"

"He's fine. Just took a bathroom break. You've been out for a while."

"Where are we? Why is it so dark?"

There's a scratch and a flicker as Jamie strikes a match, illuminating a small patch of light around her. She sets the flame to a lantern wick, which immediately catches fire and casts a dim glow around the room. "We have electricity, but only as long as it's available topside. When they shut down, we're cut off, too."

"What?"

"We're underground."

"*What?*"

Jamie brushes her fingertips over the top of my hand in slow, soothing strokes. "We had to come here to hide. There are loads of people down here. Luckily for you, there are a couple of doctors. They were able to remove the bullet from your shoulder and sew you up."

I take a deep breath. "Help me sit up."

She nods and helps me, allowing me to pause for a moment to control myself. My entire shoulder is on fire.

I take a look at my surroundings. I'm on a small cot, covered in a thin sheet. The floor and walls look like concrete. A tiny metal table is to my left. It holds a bottle of water and an extra lantern. There's a bookcase in front of me, but I can't tell what's on it in the dim lighting.

"They've never heard of pain killers down here, huh?" I mutter grumpily.

Jamie sighs, shooting me an exasperated look. "Frankly, you should just be thankful someone was here who could help you at all. If that had gotten infected, you could have lost your entire arm."

Yikes. I know she's right, but the pain is making me even more disagreeable than normal. "Guess you got your wish, huh?"

"What do you mean?"

"We're underground, aren't we?"

She frowns and watches me. "It wasn't supposed to happen this way, with angels falling from the sky."

"Angels!" I scoff. "What's gotten into you lately?"

She narrows her eyes at me. "I'm sorry. Did you not see the flaming angels shooting down to Earth? You were almost hit by one. Maybe you should get your eyes checked."

"Yeah, right. It's probably just some idiot stunt from the President to instill fear and belief in his poor, stupid people," I mutter, looking away. "There are no such thing as angels. And if there were, they wouldn't give a damn about coming down to Earth with how screwed up it is."

The door opens and Bear steps inside. I reach for him with my uninjured arm.

He sits beside me and pulls me into his lap. He presses soft kisses against my face, and I take comfort in how soothing and familiar they are. I close my eyes and lean my head against his shoulder.

"I'm so glad you're alive," he murmurs. They told me you would be and I only mostly believed them. God, Max, you scared the hell out of me."

I swallow hard and tuck my face into the fabric of his shirt. It smells like Gran's house, and it brings up a lot of feelings. I'm so worried. Is she okay? Did she stay inside, or did she come after me?

"Sorry. I should have listened," I mumble, clinging tighter to him. His warm embrace will have to be enough to get me through today. "I'm so sorry, Bear."

He shakes his head and strokes his fingers through my hair. "We're okay."

"What about Gran?"

"I told her to stay inside. She's a smart woman. I'm sure she's fine."

"But what if she's not? Even if she stayed inside, those— things—they were everywhere. What if they hurt her?"

"Angels would never hurt anybody," he says softly, watching me. "That's silly."

"There are no such thing as angels, Bear."

"Then what were they, Max? You saw the one that fell in front of us. His wingspan was enormous. He wasn't human, obviously. He wasn't a machine. He was living, breathing. Alive, but not from Earth."

"I can't believe either of you. This religious paranoia is going a little overboard."

He sighs. "Yeah. Listen. I'm sure it's fine. The Angels, or whatever they were, they're not going to hurt her. She's smart. She'll know how to protect herself. She's a tough old bat."

I know he's right, but I have no idea what those things are capable of. None of us do. They're foreign to us. The only obvious thing about them is that they're much, much more powerful than we are. If not for the tremors they caused or the very real heat of their fires, I would have guessed they were holograms. If they're droids sent by President Byron, they could probably do about as much damage as a supernatural creature could. I've heard rumors of droid-powered destruction during WWIII and our President is all about ruling with intimidation and fear.

But why would President Byron waste so much time and extra money on a night of fear factor? Maybe it was a ruse to further the efforts of population control. Our city is sick with people. Although the laws have changed to control how many children a family can have, and although homeless hangings are a daily occurrence, it's still a problem. Maybe by putting on his little show, he was hoping to lure people from their homes so he could exterminate them via the curfew law. It kind of makes sense. After all, it's easier to explain than lining up a bunch of random civilians and shooting them for no reason.

"When can we leave here?"

Bear scratches absently at his arm. "I'm hoping we can step out for a while tomorrow— check on Gran and see how things are up there. Don't know how the government will handle the aftershocks of a slaughter like that. The rebellion will probably be causing chaos. More and more people might join the ranks. That or go into hiding. Either way, the behavior was inexcusable and won't be written off."

I look down at my lap, thinking about the panic and confusion during the shooting. "They were going after everybody. It may have been after curfew, but they could clearly see those things falling from the sky just as obviously as we could. The repercussions will be obvious. Maybe it'll be enough to change things for good."

Jamie slams her hand down on the cot beside me. "That's what I'm hoping for! People will understand how crazy things are being run. People were content to be quiet before out of fear, but this could push them to become angry enough to actually do something about it. This is the perfect time for a revolution."

"But what about those things? They're going to get in the way."

"The administration is going to explain this as a sign from God, regardless of whether it actually is or not. The religious nuts are going to go absolutely crazy for it. It's only going to solidify their faith. If those things aren't some brilliant rouse from the government and they're actually angels," Jamie begins, staring pointedly at me. "If they aren't sweet and angelic, it'll cause an upset."

"Maybe they're not even ours," I say, looking up at her. "Maybe it's another round of mechanical warfare from an invading country. Maybe they've all finally decided to band together and finish us off. We deserve it."

"I don't think so."

"Why?"

"We would have had more of a warning. I also doubt our soldiers would be shooting at *us* if it was an enemy attack." Jamie shrugs. "That wouldn't make any sense."

"Did you notice them shooting at those things?"

"No."

"Don't you think that's a little strange?" It further solidifies my belief that the President is behind it all.

"I don't know, Maxwell. It's possible they weren't given orders to fight right away because everyone was too in shock to figure out a plan of defense. There's no way we're going to know anything more until we actually get up there to see with our own eyes how it's being handled."

I shiver and curl closer to Bear. It's too much to process right now. "How did you guys find this place, anyway?"

Jamie bites her lip and looks up at me guiltily. "Vic told me about it."

"Excuse me?"

She nods. "I've known about it for years. It's a great place. They send rebels out to recruit people all the time. It's a whole different world down here. A thriving community. They push for the greater good, but they're missing a leader. They need to generate anger from those above in order to cultivate a real difference. Without their trust, we're going to be stuck in the same place forever without making any real change."

"You're crazy," I groan, shaking my head. I look up at Bear accusatorily. "We should have stayed up there. She's going to get us killed."

Bear sucks his lower lip between his teeth. "I know how it sounds, but I think she might actually have a point." He stands and puts his hands on his hips. "And think about it, the longer we're down here, the more time we're buying for ourselves. I won't have to worry about the stupid draft, and Jamie says your grandmother knew about this place all along."

"That's a lie!"

Jamie scowls. "It's not. She knew about it. Your parents were part of this group. They wanted to fight for the greater good, so why don't you? Are you going to let their sacrifices be in vain?"

"Shut up!" I want to hit her so badly. Knock the know-it-all look right off of her face. I have *never* wanted to hurt Jamie. She's always been my security blanket, but right now I can't believe a word that's coming out of her mouth.

"Maxwell, you're—"

"Shut up! I don't want to hear about it! Leave me alone. Just for tonight. I'm tired and I don't want to know." Childishly, I cover my ears with my hands. My shoulder hurts and my nose burns with the threat of unshed tears. "I don't care about this movement. What's anybody ever done for *me*, huh? Maybe we are doomed, and maybe that's for the best. I'm tired and I don't care. Just leave me alone."

Jamie's expression softens. "I'm sorry, Max. I know it's a lot. We'll let you rest, okay? You need to relax while your shoulder heals. We'll figure it all out tomorrow."

I don't believe her, but I'm not in a place to argue. I'm in an unfamiliar environment, far from home. I'm worried about my Gran, worried about my home, and worried about what the future will hold. I'm especially worried about the winged creatures that now fill the streets of our city.

"I want to come with!"

"It's risky if we both go, Maxwell." Bear is beginning to lose patience with me. I don't care. I won't be left behind with this group of crazy revolutionaries. I want to go find my Gran. I want to see she's okay with my own eyes.

"Then *you* can stay. I don't care, Theodore. You should know by now that I refuse to be left behind."

He rolls his eyes and pinches the bridge of his nose. "Hurry up, then."

"I've been ready." It's true. I haven't been able to sleep all night. Besides my overactive brain, the throbbing in my shoulder made relaxation almost impossible.

Jamie finishes lacing up her boots. "Don't forget about me," she chastises, hopping to her feet.

"Ugh, you too?" Bear's tone grows more exasperated. "Well, fine. I guess if one of us gets killed, we may as well go together."

"Please don't talk like that," I murmur, taking his hand.

He says nothing, but his face softens just enough so I know he isn't mad at me anymore.

We're led down a dark, wet hallway made of concrete. It smells like dirt and mold. The woman who leads us is in her late twenties. She has tan skin and espresso eyes. Her wavy, dark chocolate hair is pulled back into a ponytail. She's stunning in an unconventional way.

"Let us know what you find out straight away. Make sure at least one of you makes it back now, alright? But if you suspect anyone else is following, don't lead them back here,. understand? If you bring back a spy, you'd better pray they get you first because you'll suffer a lot more than a shot to the head if you go endangering the rest of us. We clear?"

I nod. "We'll be careful. No need for the dramatics, alright?"

Her head snaps to the side as she shoots me venomous look. "You listen to me, you little brat. I don't care who your fuckin' parents were. I don't give a damn about you or your snot-nosed friends. But these people down here are my family. If you compromise them, I'll finish you. And it won't be quick."

Bear frowns deeply. "Hey! There's no need for that!"

She smirks. "You scared, sweetheart? Good. You should be. The war that's just been started is far bigger than just you or I. Our survival depends on it."

I swallow hard and look away. *Psycho.*

We're led up a ladder that climbs into the basement of an abandoned warehouse. From there we're able to sneak out the back and through the broken fence.

The sun is barely peeking over the horizon, and the hazy, smoke-filled air makes it difficult to see. Fires are spread randomly through city, but everything is freakishly quiet. I look down at my feet to avoid the scene.

Jamie clears her throat. "Well, you're great at making friends. Maybe you could give me a few pointers later."

"We don't need to go back there," I say, kicking a piece of debris from our path. "I don't want to."

"We'll see. Maybe everything will be business as usual."

"But don't get your hopes up." Bear chides, raising his brows.

I sigh and pick absently at my bandage as we get near enough to really see what's going on in the city. "Oh my god."

Smoke is still billowing from buildings that were downed by planes or hit by the falling creatures. Bodies litter the streets, but the soldiers and police droids are coming by with wagons and carelessly loading them up. The ground is damp with blood. A couple of workmen are walking by with hoses and trying to spray down the mess, but it's only spreading the gore further around.

ATTENTION CITIZENS: PLEASE TURN YOUR ATTENTION TO THE SKY ANNOUNCEMENTS.

We all look up as a hologram is projected into the sky, as is done for all important community broadcasts.

Our president, Byron King, stands at attention, looking every bit as smug as he always does during announcements. He adjusts his tie and smiles toothily.

How can he smile after all of the bloodshed last night? Hundreds, maybe thousands of his people were murdered at the hands of his stupid curfew law.

"Good morning, citizens!" he says, and my stomach turns at the chipper tone in his voice. "As you well know, we had a bit of a surprise last night. I'm here to let you know that everything is just fine. We've had visitors sent to us from our almighty God, himself!" He throws his pudgy arms out excitedly at this exclamation and then pauses to smooth his salt and pepper comb-over back over his shiny scalp.

I have to try really hard not to roll my eyes at his announcement. Bear squeezes my hand harder. It's a warning.

President King rocks back on his heels and clears his throat. "Many of you probably wondered about the strange storm we experienced last night. It was no small event. Angels have come to visit our city. They're here to help us. They've seen how sick some of our residents are, and they've come to help clean up our community and eventually our entire world."

A shiver rolls down my spine, and I move closer to Bear, holding his hand tighter. I rest my head against his arm as I look up toward the sky.

"Unfortunately, those in our community who refused to obey curfew were terminated. This can be translated as a blessing. Those of us who hold ourselves above the law can be considered a disease to our precious city. Their loss may weigh on the members of their families and friends, but I'm sure it will be realized that we can't have their sickness carrying on throughout our time of need.

"Additionally, we can't be bothered by nonbelievers. If anyone you know openly doubts our maker, they are to be immediately reported to authorities. They will be promptly dealt with." He smiled toothily once more and claps his hand excitedly.

"And now, dear citizens, I'm excited to introduce you to one of our visitors, the Angel Michael."

The camera turns to a different man. He's tall and statuesque, more beautiful than any man I've ever seen. He has golden brown hair that falls in waves to the tops of his shoulders and eyes the color of glass. He could be a painting. Or a model. He could be human, if not for the huge wings that protrude from his back.

There are gasps all around us as the rest of the people in the streets stare at the screen.

Bear trembles beside me. "My God."

"This is bad," Jamie whispers, very quiet so no one else will be able to hear her. She grabs my hand tightly in a clammy fist, shuddering.

"Angels could never be bad," Bear replies, just as softly.

The Angel Michael stares fixedly into the holocamera, effectively appearing as though he's gazing into every one of our souls. He looks so stern.

Goosebumps rise dramatically along my arms as I stare back at him, straightening.

And then he smiles, and his entire face lights up, causing more wonderstruck gasps to fill the streets around us.

"Hello, humans of Earth. I am Michael," he greets us, his voice like honey. "As your President has said, we have come to help with the disease that has overtaken Earth. This will mean cleaning up the land and revitalizing the animals and plant life that have been destroyed by centuries of carelessness. We are here to cure the sickness and to bring peace once more to my Father's beautiful creation."

He pauses and then smiles brighter. "I don't want any assumptions to be made. You may be used to taking orders from your dear President. Make no mistake, there is a higher power judging even him. For this reason, he is no longer your leader. He takes orders from us, as well. But he will be helping us to understand the nature in which you have been previously ruled.

I can only imagine the horrified expression on President King's face when he hears this news. Stupid pig.

"We are very happy to be here, to help you through this trying time in your lives. We hope to bring inspiration and hope back to your communities."

Jamie's trembling is growing. She's horrified, but I'm not sure why. I welcome the idea of our President being overthrown. And I take back what I said earlier. This creature has to be an angel. There's no other word for him. And angels can't be bad. Angels are real. God is real. I have been so wrong.

I squeeze Jamie's hand and look at her. "It's okay, Jamie. They're going to fix everything for us," I whisper.

She makes a choked noise. "You have no idea how dangerous this is."

"Hush," I whisper, squeezing her hand and looking back up at the projection in the sky.

Michael's expression grows serious. "There's one more thing," he says softly, his tone grave now. "There are creatures among you who will threaten the growth and healing of your home. They are an embarrassment to all of God's creations. Rebels, but not as you know them.

"These creatures look like any one of you. It is impossible to tell them apart from yourselves. That is because they are partly human. But they are very dangerous. They contain power strong enough to threaten us all. We are here to destroy them. If you know of anyone that you suspect may be supernatural in any way, they are to be reported immediately. They don't care for you or the health of your planet. They don't care for God. For the sake of labeling them, we will refer to them as nephilim from now on. Keep an eye out. I trust all of you will be very willing to help us in this endeavor. Your safety and future depends on their demise."

Michael stares at the camera for a moment more before smiling. "We will be updating you regularly on our progress. You will see us walking your streets and cleansing them. If you are sick, we will heal you. Do not be afraid to approach us. We love you. We were created to love you and to care for you. Thank you and God bless."

The hologram vanishes.

Jamie sways beside me for a moment before her eyes roll up in the back of her head and she collapses.

2147

"YOU'RE LIKE A BIRD, YOU KNOW? A lost little bird," Aubrey said softly as she and Gabriel lay out in the field beside her house.

"I am *not.*" Gabriel scowled over at her, frowning deeper as she grinned back at him, obviously amused.

"I don't mean it in a bad way, Angel," she promised, reaching out and tousling his hair. She rolled over onto her stomach and folded her arms so she could lay her head on them as she watched him. "I just mean…your hair is always a mess. All tousled in the wind. It's sweet. Your eyes are so wide, like everything is such a wonder to you. But you're an *angel*, so it seems like you should have seen it all already. No big deal."

Gabriel sighed and shook his head. "I don't know how to explain how strange it is to be inside of this body," he replied. "To feel things. To be emotional and confused and overwhelmed by all of the senses I've been missing. It's frightening. I'm not used to it."

Aubrey watched him and nodded slowly. "I think I can kind of grasp it." She unfolded her arms and reached out and set a hand over his, squeezing gently.

Gabriel took a deep breath and looked at their hands. The warmth that spread through his chest was nice and also frightening. He slowly entwined their fingers, not looking away from their hands. "Touch is the most amazing sensation," he murmured quietly. "I can compare it to nothing else."

Aubrey smiled and watched him as he played with her hand, rubbing his thumb slowly over the top of it. She took a deep breath and sucked her lower lip between her teeth for a moment before looking back up into his eyes. "So when are you going to go look for your brother?"

"Uriel?"

"I thought that's what you came for."

He shrugged. "I also came to explore."

She laughed quietly and rolled onto her side, facing him. "You haven't done much exploring yet, Angel. It's been three days and you haven't left my side except to hide from my mom."

"She's terrifying."

Aubrey laughed and the sound filled Gabriel with such warmth that he thought he might explode. She sobered after a moment and looked up at him. "You'll leave soon, won't you?"

He frowned, brows pulling together. "You wish for me to leave? I've overstayed my welcome."

She shook her head quickly. "No. No no no. I just don't understand why you're still here."

Gabriel glanced down at their hands. "I enjoy spending time with you, Aubrey."

For the first time since he'd met her, Aubrey's cheeks flushed in the darkness of the night. She looked down. "I don't understand. I've taken you in, but I haven't even shown you very much," she murmured, looking up at him. "You're an *angel*. I'm just a very poor, very discontent human."

Gabriel's eyes widened in shock. "You are much more than you think you are, Aubrey," he said very seriously, watching her. "Being with you is like being inside of a different universe entirely. I am content spending time with you because I am never for one second bored or wishing that I was elsewhere. I enjoy walking with you, talking with you, and I love watching you paint. You get very serious when you do, which is unlike you. I enjoy watching your concentration -- the way you put your soul into your work. And I love to watch you dance. Sing. You tease me. You are unafraid of what I am. Truthfully, you seem to be unafraid of everything. You frighten me, and I like it very much." He licked his lips nervously. "Like right now. I don't know what to do."

Aubrey's eyes had softened considerably during his speech. She reached out and touched his cheek, which was rough with stubble. She smiled and climbed over him, instantly setting Gabriel's entire body on fire. She leaned down, nudging her nose to his. "Let me show you what to do," she murmured, before pressing her soft lips to his and drowning him in flames.

It took him a moment to figure out how to reciprocate, but he learned quickly and allowed himself to let go of his fears and uncertainty, gasping into her mouth as her hands trailed down his body, pulling his shirt open.

Her lips moved from his and trailed down his neck and shoulder, nibbling and sucking marks into his skin. He tipped his head back, panting at the overwhelming rush that was consuming him. He could barely hear over the pounding of his heart and his own breath in his ears.

Aubrey pulled back for a moment and sat up on his hips, tugging her dress over her head. She tossed it to the side so it lay in a white heap beside them.

Gabriel gasped and stared up at her in wonder. He slid his hands up her sides, allowing himself to feel her soft skin. Skin that he hadn't had the pleasure of seeing until now. "I thought nudity was ill-advised when outside," he managed through quivering lips.

Aubrey laughed and set her hand over his mouth. She leaned down and pressed her lips to his ear. "Shh." She pulled her hand away and pressed another kiss to his mouth. "It can be our little secret."

He stuttered and slid a hand up into her hair. "Are you sure?" he breathed between scorching kisses, his body burning against hers.

She pulled back briefly and looked down at him, breathless. She stroked his cheek and smiled, her entire face beaming. "Of course," she replied, pushing a hand back through his floppy hair. "I've never really been one for following the rules anyway."

2165

"ARE YOU OKAY?" I stare down at Jamie, whose eyes have only just opened since her collapse on the street. Her face is contorted in fear, lips trembling violently.

She winces. "No. This is happening too fast."

Gran walks to us and sets a wet cloth to Jamie's forehead. We'd found her relatively unharmed. She was shaken up, of course, but otherwise okay. She frowns and takes her hand, squeezing. "I know you're afraid, Jamie. But everything is going to work out."

"How can you say that, Mary? You know what this means!"

I watch them in confusion. "Someone needs to tell me what's going on. Like now. Why would angels be bad?"

"Oh, so you've finally found God now, Maxwell?" Gran snaps, before her face softens and she shakes her head. "I'm sorry."

My face burns and I look toward the floor. "It's hard to believe in something that can't be seen. I should have been more faithful."

"Well, you haven't been given much reason to believe," Gran replies quietly. "Anyway, God isn't the problem here. It's the angels."

"Why the angels?"

She takes a deep breath and walks to me, setting her hands on my shoulders. "There is a lot that you don't know about our family."

"What's that supposed to mean?"

She pads across the living room, going to her trunk. She opens it and pulls out a backpack. She walks over to me and places it in my hands. "This is for you. You need to get underground as soon as possible. Don't let anyone see what's in there, do you understand?"

"But—"

"Maxwell! This is very important. Do you understand?"

I can feel myself nodding dumbly. My mouth feels like it's full of cotton.

"Will you come with?" I ask, watching her.

She smiles sadly and shakes her head minutely. "I'm sorry, Max. I have to stay to keep up appearances. The boarders have gone, but I don't want anyone to suspect our family."

My stomach sinks. "Oh."

She looks from me to Jamie. "I trust you'll watch over my girl. Inform her of everything she needs to know."

Jamie nods. "Of course, Mary."

My stomach twists in knots. "Why are you so afraid?"

Gran stares at me, unblinking. "They'll be looking for you."

Bear scowls. "What would they possibly want with Max?"

"Maxwell, you're nephilim."

"What?"

She nods, looking regretful. "Your mother… She—"

But she isn't able to finish her sentence, because as soon as she tries to explain herself, our front door crashes open and a group of soldiers bursts in, guns turned on us.

"Mary Addams, you have been charged with harboring rebels. Your sentence is immediate termination without trial."

They don't allow her to get a word in. She is forced to her knees and a gun is pressed to her forehead before I have time to process the scene before me.

"Gran?! No! What are you doing? She's done nothing wrong!"

But they don't listen. They never do. She's nothing to them. Just another body.

Gran looks up at me in fear. "Maxw—" She is cut short as the officer in front of her pulls the trigger.

Her blood sprays across my face.

Jamie is at my side in an instant. She and Bear are working together to hold me up. I turn quickly from her body, blinking gore from my lashes. "Gran…"

A rage is building in my chest. I can't think. I can barely breathe. Anger consumes me and I begin to shake. I can't possibly hold it down.

I rip away from my friends and launch myself, screaming, at the soldier.

"Maxwell, no!" Jamie yells as the rest of the soldiers turn their guns on me in surprise.

There is one single gunshot that rips through the house. I'm sprayed with warm blood once more. The soldier drops from beneath me, dead in an instant.

A multitude of gunshots follow the first, and we all drop to the ground. Bear's arms wrap around me, and I hear him gasp. The soldiers are shooting, but so is somebody else, somebody who isn't in sight. The soldiers are forced to shoot blindly.

The gunfire lasts for less than a minute, followed by an eerie, horrible silence that is only disturbed by our heavy, horrified breathing.

A man steps inside the house and looks around quickly. He is tall and dressed in dark clothing, clutching a huge gun to his chest. "Get up!" he hisses. "You need to get up! We need to get out of here! Quickly!"

Jamie is the first to stand. She pulls me up, and together we get Bear to his feet. He hisses in pain, and I see blood seeping through his jacket. "Bear..."

"S'fine." he breathes. "Let's go. We've got to get out of here."

The man jerks his head toward the door. "Quickly now."

My vision is blurred by tears. "How do we know we can trust you?"

Jamie looks over at me. "I know him. It's fine."

There is no other option at this point, so I nod, slinging my arm around Bear's waist. "Come on," I say, pulling him toward the door.

Between the two of us, Jamie and I are able to stumble quickly after the man with Bear in tow, though he's making me very nervous. His face is washed of all color and his eyes are dulling by the second. A sheen of perspiration covers his face.

"You're going to be okay, Bear. Just keep breathing," I instruct, following the man back to the old warehouse building that we came through before.

Bear's labored breathing is scaring the shit out of me. We help him down the ladder as quickly as we can, the mystery man giving us a hand whenever necessary. "He needs medical attention immediately!"

By the time we're back in the tunnel, it's getting harder to keep Bear up. His legs aren't working anymore, and there's so much blood covering his front that I'm terrified to even look at his injury.

"He's not going to make it," the man murmurs, helping us lower Bear to the ground.

"Shut up!" I snap at him, "Go get us some help! What are you standing around for?!"

I kneel down beside Bear and run my fingers back through his hair. "Bear, you're going to be just fine, okay?"

He closes his eyes with a gasp, his lips quivering. "M-Maxwell," he breathes.

"Hey, keep your eyes open, okay?" I look up at the man. "Go get a fucking doctor!" I yell at him. "Christ, what are you *waiting* for?"

He shakes his head. "I'm sorry. He's not going to make it."

I choke on a sob and shake my head, unwilling to believe it.

"No. Bear, open your eyes, okay?"

Bear's trembling is subsiding. I whimper and pull his jacket open and undo the buttons of his shirt with shaking fingers. I know when I finally see his wound that the man is right. Bear won't bounce back from this.

I clamp a hand over my mouth to keep from screaming. I can't lose Bear, too. I can't. I can't. I can't.

"Max, there's nothing you can do," Jamie murmurs softly from my left. Her hand rests heavily on my back.

I jerk away from her and touch the side of Bear's face. I lean down and rest my forehead to his. "Hey. Hey, you're okay. You're alright. Keep your eyes open. Please. Bear. Theodore, I love you, okay? Please."

His body goes still as the air leaves his lungs, and I feel myself crumbling. "Bear!" I shake him hard. His head lolls grotesquely to the side.

"Bear!"

"Maxwell, *enough*." The man pulls on my arm, but I shove him away.

"Bear, please. Pleasepleasepleasepleaseplease... Oh, God, please. Please don't be dead." My chest erupts with violent sobs and I set my forehead to Bear's, completely falling apart.

"Stop it!" The man pulls on my arm again, and he jerks me up to my knees.

I shake my head stubbornly, still clinging to Bear with my free hand. "Bear, open your eyes! Open your eyes!"

And he does.

Bear's eyes snap open and he gasps for breath, his chest rising up from the floor.

"Goddamnit!" The man curses, jerking me to my feet. "How could you?"

Jamie glares up at him. "Hey, fuck you," she spits. "Leave her alone."

He glares at her in response and then turns his attention to me. "Do you have any idea what you've done?" he growls, shaking me.

My shoulder screams in pain and I shake my head slowly. I'm so exhausted. "Let go of me," I murmur. "Please. Let me go." I feel a trickle of warm liquid run lazily down my upper lip and I wipe at it halfheartedly. My hand comes back with more blood.

Bear is sobbing on the floor. The noise is horrible. I need to take care of him. I need to clean him up and make him feel safe again.

The man glares at me. "You'll be the death of him," he hisses, before letting me drop.

I end up on my knees beside Bear. I take him into my arms and hold him tightly, closing my eyes.

He turns his face into my shoulder and clings to me, sobbing. I rock him and press my lips to his ear, whispering to him that he's okay and that he's alive and that everything is going to be okay.

Later, when I'm cleaning the blood from him, we are both unable to stop staring at the smooth skin of his stomach that is free of any indication that he's just died of a fatal gunshot wound. I don't understand what it means, but I think maybe it has to do with the fact that nephilim are real, and I am one of them.

2147

"YOUR HEART IS BEATING SO FAST," Gabriel murmured, ear resting against Aubrey's chest.

She laughed and it made him smile, wide and genuine. "Are you surprised?" she asked, fingers tangling into his hair.

"Not really," he admitted after a moment. "But I like the sound."

"Yeah, Angel?"

"Gabriel," he corrected softly, looking up at her.

Her face softened and she continued to stroke his hair. She nodded. "Gabriel."

He grinned at her, his face lighting up. "That's better. And yes, I appreciate it. I also enjoy feeling it inside my own chest. It makes me feel alive."

She smiled in confusion, raising a brow. "But you're always alive."

He nodded. "Maybe. But not like this. Not nearly as alive as I am now. Not as present and secure and happy as I am right now."

"You're really happy, huh?"

"Aren't you?"

She nodded and shifted so she could look at him. She pressed a kiss to the tip of his nose. "I'm very happy, Gabriel."

He watched her, entranced.

Aubrey yawned and curled close to him. "We will be in an outrageous amount of trouble if we're found like this. But I don't want to leave."

"I can keep watch if you'd like," he replied softly, stroking her hair slowly.

She buried her nose against his shoulder, inhaling deeply. "That's okay. We'd better get in soon anyway. It's getting chilly. I just want to lay here with you for a moment."

Gabriel nuzzled his nose into her hair, inhaling her scent. He kissed the top of her head. "I would be content to stay here forever," he admitted softly. "Just like this."

Aubrey pressed a soft kiss to his neck. "Sounds beautiful," she replied, sliding an arm over his chest.

He nodded and looked up toward the stars, thinking that maybe the obsession humans seemed to have with Heaven was a little superfluous, considering he'd found his very own version on their small planet. "Yes, it does."

2165

IT'S SO QUIET. INCREDIBLY, SCARILY QUIET. The only sound I can hear is Bear's soft breathing beside me. I sigh and pull him closer, holding him tight against me. It doesn't matter that my shoulder is screaming in pain; it's important for me to hold him and be with him and keep him safe.

He's had a rough night, twisting and turning from nightmares. I don't know what he saw when he died, but I know it scarred him deeply enough to leave a mark on his soul.

I'm having a hard time processing everything that happened. My Gran is dead, Bear died, but came back. I'm nephilim— whatever that means.

A hand comes down on my arm, and pulls me roughly to my feet. I gasp and look up, but it's too dark to make anything out.

"We need to have a little chat." It's the man from before. The man who saved us at my Gran's house.

"I can't leave Bear."

"He'll be fine. He's sleeping deeply now. The nightmares have gone."

He jerks me along, and I stumble blindly behind him. "Where are you taking me?"

"Hush, Maxwell."

"How do you know my name?"

"I know a lot about you."

"But—"

"Hush."

I scowl and follow him, not because I trust him, but because I have no choice. His grip is too tight, and even if I were to get away now, it's too dark for me to know where I'd be going. He pulls me along for a few more minutes and then stops and shuts a door. There's a familiar scratching noise as he lights a match and then sets the flame to a lantern's wick. It catches and casts a glow across the small room that we're in.

I glance around. There's not much here, just a tiny cot and a little folding table with two chairs. I look back up at the man.

"Sit down," he mutters, pulling out a chair for me.

I sit obediently and stare at him. "What's your name?"

He pulls his hood down further on his head and sits across from me, crossing his arms. "Brie."

"Hm."

He shoots me a look, frowning deeply. "I would think you would feel a little more grateful toward me. I saved your life."

"Yeah. Why?"

He takes a deep breath and watches me for a long moment. He's got brown eyes that look very familiar, but I can't quite place them. His dark hair is cut short beneath his hood. "You have a very big job to do, Maxwell."

I cross my arms. "You mean because I'm nephilim?"

"Yes."

"What does that even mean?"

He looks down at the table and scratches at a line in it with his fingernail. "Nephilim are created when a human woman conceives a child with an angel. Biblically speaking, your people believe they're giants, destroyed by the flood. Horrible, nasty creatures."

He's obviously got his facts wrong. "My dad was human. He and my mother were high school sweethearts."

"Everything you have been told about your parents' romance is likely fiction," he replies, staring back at me.

"That's impossible."

"Considering recent events, I'm surprised you are able to doubt anything," he replies. "Anyway, you're going to have to believe it. As I said before, you have a job to do. Your friend, Jamie, is nephilim as well. Fathered by the Archangel Michael."

I look up at him in surprise. "That's why she was so afraid."

"She's known about her bloodline since she was a small child. She's had to prepare for battle."

"Battle?"

"The only way to stop the apocalypse is for the nephilim to rise and fight back. You are your planet's only hope for survival."

"But the angels are helping us. They're healing the world."

He laughs. "They're healing the world by killing all of the humans. Humans are the reason for the fall of the planet. The reason for the disease. They think that by terminating them, the planet will heal itself. And maybe it will, but man is God's most brilliant creation. His favorite. The apocalypse isn't scheduled for thousands of years. It isn't time yet."

Goosebumps rise along every inch of my flesh and I shake my head back and forth. "How do you even know about all of this?"

"That's not important. What *is* important, is that you need to help Jamie raise an army. To educate people on what is at stake if we lose."

"Why me?"

For the first time since meeting him, I watch as his mouth turns up at the corners. "Because every leader needs a voice, Maxwell, and you are the daughter of the messenger of the angels. Archangel Gabriel."

I couldn't say anything even if I wanted to, so I keep my mouth closed, staring at him in disbelief.

"Jamie is meant to be a leader. A fighter. A warrior. But she isn't equipped with the skills needed to reach out to the people. That's where you come in. You are also a warrior, but you rely more on your words."

He suddenly frowns darkly. "You've already discovered another of your talents."

I suddenly feel very dizzy.

"You can bring life back to the dead, as you demonstrated on your friend out there. Gabriel was not only a messenger. He was also responsible for mercy and revenge and also death and rejuvenation."

Bile rises is in my throat and I put my hand over my mouth, willing it back down. "You're fucking crazy."

"Your vocabulary is astounding." Brie looks toward the ceiling before meeting my eyes, expression hard. "You saw what you did. He had no injury when you brought him back."

"Yeah, but—"

"But nothing. It's what you are. But you can't use that power, Maxwell, because it's very dark, very dangerous. Not only does it take away a piece of your soul when you perform the rejuvenation, it is also very unnatural. Those who have died should not live again."

I frown at him. "There's nothing wrong with what I did. Bear would have died without my help."

"He would have stayed dead. It would have been for the best. He had already passed through the veil. He had gone to Heaven. He will be different now. You pulled him back through the veil, and to do that, he had to pass through many dark places. Now he holds that darkness inside of himself. He's not the same. It would be better to kill him now, before he falls to a path of destruction and violence."

"I can't kill Bear."

He frowns deeply. "I was afraid of that. You'll have to keep a very cautious eye on him then. He will be very easily swayed."

I look down at my knees. My throat and eyes burn with the threat of unshed tears. "Bear is very important to me," I whisper. "He would never hurt anybody."

Brie watches me quietly and then reaches out and touches my hand. "I know you have suffered great loss in your life," he says quietly. "I understand how deeply that kind of loss can touch your soul. I'm sorry I was unable to save your grandmother."

I look away, sniffling miserably. "Um. Yeah."

We're both silent for a few long moments before I find my voice to speak again. "So the angels are trying to kill their own kids, huh?"

He nods slowly. "For the most part. A couple have fallen from grace to avoid destroying their own."

"Gabriel?"

"He is dead." The words come out very bitter, and I look up in surprise.

"Angels can die?"

He nods. "They tortured him. You don't want to hear about it. It was very brutal."

"How do you know?" I ask quietly.

"I am fallen," he replies softly, looking away. "I fell beside my brother. They didn't kill me, though. I didn't offend them enough."

My eyes widen in shock. "You're an angel."

"I *was* an angel. Not anymore. My grace is gone. I'm just a vessel now. As human as you." He barks out a bitter laugh and shakes his head. "No. You're not human. You're more an angel than I am."

I shiver.

He takes a deep breath and then stands and grabs a blanket from the cot. He slings it around my shoulders.

"Your father cared for you very much," he says quietly. "He died for you. He fell for you."

"What about my mother?"

"He adored your mother. The day she died was the darkest in his existence."

"Did my daddy know that I wasn't his?"

He nods. "He did. But your father was a good man. He raised you as his own."

"How many nephilim are there?"

"There's no way to know for sure. There are quite a few. Our brother Gadreel thought we were missing out on pleasures of the flesh, so he goaded many of our brothers to share in the experience. It was a weak moment. Most of my brothers realized when they found the women were pregnant that the creatures they had created would be dangerous. And it has held true. Through the centuries, angels have continued this practice and every once in a while they come down to destroy what they themselves have created. Often nephilim have no idea what they truly are. With Earth being as it is now, my brothers believe it is far too dangerous to leave you alone, as it could cause further disruption. It has been many, many years since Earth has had a visit from us."

I focus on the scratched tabletop. "I'm scared."

He reaches out and takes my chin in his hand, forcing me to look up at him. "You should be," he replies, smiling sadly.

I wet my lips, clenching my left hand in a tight fist. "Can everybody bring people back from the dead?"

He looks agitated again. He pulls his hand from my face and lets it rest heavily against the table. "No. Each nephilim has different strengths based on the angel they were fathered by. For example, Jamie is a very skilled warrior. She is also very confident, maybe too much so. You'll need to keep her grounded."

A sharp pain in my shoulder sparks an idea. "Hey, I should be able to heal my shoulder, right?"

Brie scowls and shakes his head in warning. "It's hard on your body to do that. More harm than it's worth."

I shake my head. "Not true. It's killing me."

"Maxwell, it's hardly killing you."

I ignore him and focus my attention on the pain in my shoulder. I concentrate on the wound and will the pain to go away and the tissue to heal, the skin to smooth over. Soon, I feel no pain. I grin and slide my shirt off so I can take a look. Sure enough, my shoulder is healed. There isn't even a scar.

"So cool," I mutter.

"Are you hard of hearing or just stupid? I told you not to—"

The lecture continues, but I don't hear it. I'm too busy having another sudden burst of inspiration. "I could bring Gran back!"

He slams his fist down on the table, causing me to jump in my seat. "Damnit, Maxwell, I said no. First of all, even if you tried, she would come back much worse than Bear. Her brain would be scrambled. She's been dead for far too long. Second, every time you resurrect you are leeching away a piece of your grace. That is incredibly dangerous. Put the thought out of your head at once."

I look back down at the table and don't say anything. Brie is not the boss of me and I have already lost enough. I'm willing to take my chances.

He sighs and then stands. He walks to his cot and comes back with a gun in his hand.

"Ever used one of these?"

I shake my head. "They're not allowed."

He sighs and hands it to me anyway. "You'll learn. Don't go anywhere without it. Don't let Theodore anywhere near it. Jamie already has one."

I refrain from rolling my eyes and instead nod. "Okay."

"You should try to sleep a little more. Big day tomorrow."

"Why? What's tomorrow?"

He takes a deep breath and holds it for a moment before releasing. "Tomorrow you are going to learn more than you want to about your past."

Frowning, I stand quietly. "Great," I murmur heading for the door after grabbing the lantern.

He smiles just a little. "Goodnight, Maxwell."

I nod in reply and then head back to Bear, leaving Brie alone in the dark.

2147

GABRIEL LAY WITH AUBREY in her attic room on a stormy afternoon. They'd spent most of the day outside, helping her mother with the garden but had eventually been chased back inside by heavy rain.

Aubrey laid her head on Gabriel's chest and smiled. She hummed softly along to the music on the turntable. "This is one of my favorite songs," she declared softly as the next one started.

Gabriel smiled. "Who is it by?"

"Bob Dylan. He was a really big deal in his time." Aubrey hopped up and moved to the center of the room, her still-damp dress fluttering around the tops of her thighs as she closed her eyes and swayed along to the beat of the music.

He watched, entranced, as she began to sing along, completely taken by the lyrics.

Aubrey opened her eyes and looked up at him, a smile on her face. She walked to him and took his hand, pulling him to his feet. She set her hands on his waist and swayed with him to the music.

He bit his lip, feeling silly at first but soon finding her rhythm and falling into it. He closed his eyes and held her close as they moved, allowing the words to wash over his skin.

Aubrey fell silent for the majority of the song but murmured along to the last little bit, her voice choked.

"You feel it very deeply," Gabriel murmured against her hair. "The words. The music."

"Everything is just really fucked up right now," Aubrey replied, stepping back away from him. "Feels like it's always going to be this way. They thought it was bad back then? They should see it now. If anyone knew I had this, that we were listening to this, to anything I have up here, we would be punished. Everything is banned. Censored. Our books, our music, our news. Nothing is real anymore, Gabriel. Nothing is real, and we are prisoners."

Gabriel frowned deeply, watching as her eyes filled with tears. "The worst part," she began, staring up at him, "is that people are beginning to forget how to be angry. They're forgetting how to fight back. Fear has overtaken everything that they may have once felt. They know that they've had family members killed for trivial things, that they've been oppressed and lied to, but they take it without question because it's the only way they know how to live.

"I'm going to change things. I swear I will. I'm going to be better. I'm going to become the keeper of knowledge. And I'm going to leak everything," she said fiercely. "I'm going to make sure that everyone knows the truth."

Worry twisted through Gabriel's gut, but it was accompanied by something more, a feeling he would only later come to recognize as hope. He nodded, watching her. "You will, Aubrey. You will change the world."

"You really think I can?"

He nodded. "You'll change it for the better."

2165

I SHAKE BEAR'S SHOULDER as soon as the electrical lines have been reopened and I'm able to turn on the light. It feels early, but I need to get home and back before Brie has the chance to make an appearance and ruin my plans. I've thought more about it and there's just no way I'm willing to leave my grandmother dead in a pool of her own blood on her kitchen floor. Not when I hold this kind of power. What kind of granddaughter would I be?

Bear grumbles and covers his face with his arm. "It's too early," he mumbles.

"I know, babe. But we need to leave right now, okay? It's important."

He groans but sits up anyway, rubbing at his eyes. He yawns.

I reach out and run my fingers back through his greasy hair. We're both in desperate need of baths. I lean down and press my lips to his forehead. "Have I mentioned today how grateful I am to have you?"

He pulls me into a tight hug. "I have you to thank for that, don't I?" He presses sloppy kisses all over my face and smiles wearily. "I love you, Max."

I smile and duck away. "Yeah. You, too."

"Ugh," Jamie groans from somewhere behind us. "Could you two lovebirds maybe knock it off so we can get going before it's too late?"

I look back at her, face burning "Who says you're invited?"

She shrugs. "I do. As the daughter of Michael, I reserve the right to invite myself to anything I please. I am your leader, you know."

I snort and roll my eyes.

Jamie grins and takes my hand, squeezing gently. "I've got your back, Max."

I sigh and nod, shooting her a small smile. "Alright, alright." It feels strange to know she's lied to me all these years. But it's difficult for me to be angry with her. She's still Jamie.

She laughs and rolls her eyes. "Come on."

I feel a little sick as we climb my Gran's stairs and reach the doorknob. I'm worried. What if she isn't here anymore? What if the soldiers are waiting to do me in for the deaths of their men? What if the boarders came back and took over the house? What if all of the bodies are still there and I accidentally bring them all back?

The list is endless.

I hold my gun close to my chest as I turn the knob. The door swings open easily. I take a deep breath and step inside.

The smell hits me like a ton of bricks. There is so much death in this room.

Surprisingly enough, the soldiers' bodies are still here. It's possible no one has realized they're missing yet. But surely *someone* would have let out an alarm about the shooting yesterday. Wouldn't they?

I look over at Jamie. "This doesn't feel right."

She shakes her head and grips her gun tighter, knuckles white. "We'd better be quick. Someone could come at any time." She turns to Bear. "You keep watch, alright?"

He nods.

I take a shaky breath and watch them for a moment before turning toward Gran. I walk to her and kneel beside her body, trying not to look too closely at the gore that's covering her. I set my hands down on her body and try not to gag. I concentrate hard, like I did with my shoulder, while focusing on her entire body. I close my eyes and picture her heart pumping new blood through her veins, her flesh merging back together and becoming brand new, her soul returning to her body.

There is a horrible, raspy noise coming from inside of her. I open my eyes and watch as her eyes open as well. They're dull. Something is off, and it takes me too long to realize what it is.

She opens her mouth and a thick, gelatinous black goo comes sliding out, covering her chin. She gurgles as her eyes roll up in the back of her skull.

I gasp and sit up on my knees, pulling my hands away, but she grabs my wrist in a clawed hand and jerks me back to her.

"Gran," I breathe. "Let me go."

She makes a horrible moaning sound and reaches out, grabbing my hair and pulling my face down to hers.

I feel horrible and lightheaded. A hot line drips down my lips and chin from my nose. I'm bleeding again.

Her moaning turns into a hideous shrieking and her grip on me tightens. The putrid, black goo speckles my face, and I start screaming. She won't let me go. She's not Gran.

I fumble with my gun for a moment before I can get it pointed at her. Then I shoot.

Her horrible wailing doesn't stop. I scream and kick at her. "Jamie! Jamie, help me!"

There's another gunshot and Gran, or the vessel that used to carry her soul, drops, splattering blackened blood all over my face. It is the same scene repeated twice in only two days.

I put my hands over my face and scream, scrambling backward.

Hands grip my wrists and jerk me to my feet. "What did I tell you?" Brie growls, his face so close to mine that our noses are nearly touching.

I begin to sob, my knees weak. I'm shaking like a leaf in a windstorm.

"This is what happens! You think you know it all, but you don't!" he yells furiously, shaking me.

"I'm sorry! I'm s-sorry!" I moan.

"You're damn right! What if she doesn't make it back to Heaven because you were too selfish to let her go?!"

I hadn't thought of that. I shake my head, shoulders slumping. "I didn't know!"

"I told you! I told you to leave her in peace! How are you supposed to lead if you run into things blindly?"

I sob harder, shaking my head. "I didn't know, I didn't know."

"Hey," Jamie sounds upset. "Hey, stop!"

Brie lets go of me and I fall to the ground. He turns on Jamie. "What about *you*? You're supposed to be the smart one, Jamie! Why are you encouraging this? What kind of leader are you?"

I don't hear any more of their exchange. My hands go over my ears, trying to muffle the noise as I curl up on the ground and sob into the soiled carpet, shaking my head. "I didn't know. I didn't know!"

I'm sorry. I'm sorry. I'm sorry. An anthem in my head.

Bear pulls me into his arms. "You didn't know." He sounds about as shaken up as I am.

Brie scowls. "Don't baby her!" he spits. "Don't tell her it's going to be alright, because it isn't! Not if she keeps acting against orders."

"Shut the fuck up," Bear spits in return, his entire body going rigid. "Don't you talk about her that way."

I press my palms to my eyes and shake my head back and forth. It's like a scene from a horror film. I keep thinking about the horrible noises Gran had made. The horrible smell that had come from deep within her. I shudder.

Brie stomps over and hauls Bear up by his shirt collar like it's the easiest thing in the world. "You listen to me, Theodore. You are *nothing*. I am nothing. These girls are *everything*. If they don't take some responsibility and get their shit together, the world is going to end. You and I will cease to exist. Your entire people will cease to exist. Everything your kind has built will be destroyed."

Bear opens his mouth to give a smartass response, but I reach out and tug on his hand instead.

"Don't," I murmur quietly. "Please. He's right." I stand on shaky legs.

Bear looks over at me and scowls, his brows pulling together, but he doesn't say anything. He squeezes my hand and then lets go in favor of sliding his arm around my shoulders instead.

Brie rolls his eyes. "We need to leave this place. It's going to be a target now. We'll be lucky if it wasn't rigged in the beginning. You made enough of a scene."

I nod quietly and pick up my gun.

He turns and walks out.

Jamie doesn't look at me but follows after Brie, shoulders rigid. She's clearly been affected by his harsh words. I look back up at Bear. "Let's go," I murmur softly.

He nods and lets me pull him outside.

"Are we still going to talk about my family history today?" I ask in a small voice, pretending to be suddenly very interested in the floor so I can avoid Brie's judgmental stare.

We've just made it underground. Nobody saw us, which was a miracle because I'd been sure we would run into more soldiers on our way back to the tunnel.

He sighs and pinches the bridge of his nose, looking down. "I don't know. I'm not sure you deserve it."

Can't argue with that logic. My shoulders slump in miserable defeat.

"You may want to go clean up before we start. I'll meet you back in my room. Bring the bag your grandmother left for you."

I look up at him in surprise and then nod. "Okay," I murmur softly. I take hold of Bear's hand and pull him away to clean up.

Bear keeps his head down, not looking at me.

He remains quiet as we step under the spray of the showers and scrub at the gore. I try not to think about the fact that I'm covered in Gran's guts. It doesn't work, though, and I have to step out twice to heave up the rest of what little had been in my stomach.

Bear steps out with me and holds my hair from my face. He pulls me into his arms soon after and hugs me tight. I cling to him and close my eyes, letting out a shaky breath. "I'm so sorry."

He presses his lips to the top of my head. "Don't."

I look up at him and notice for the first time that his eyes are red and wet, but not because of the stream from the shower. It makes me feel worse. I swallow hard and pull him back into the shower and finish washing up without further conversation

We part ways after dressing, and I walk slowly to Brie's room, dragging my feet. I stop at his door and knock.

I hear him clear his throat from inside the room. "Come in."

I open the door and step inside shyly. I'm a little frightened of him. I don't know him yet, but I know he doesn't think very much of me.

"Sit down," he instructs, watching me.

I walk slowly to the small table in his room. I set my backpack on the table and sit. My arm slides across my middle to rub at my injured arm. I chew my lip between my teeth.

"Oh, stop looking so wounded. I'm probably not going to yell at you again," Brie says. He sits down on the chair across from me and reaches for the bag.

"I could really have gotten us all killed, couldn't I?"

He looks back at me and then shoots a tiny smile that's probably supposed to be reassuring. "But you didn't. Last free pass, Maxwell."

I take a deep breath. "So, you're an angel."

He nods. "A strange one, but yes. More or less. Or, I *was*. My brothers teased me mercilessly about my attachment to humans, despite my status, but they had no idea how truly involved I was until recently, when I refused to help hurry along the apocalypse. I will never help them. It's an abomination. My brothers and I have been created to love and take care of humans."

I arch an eyebrow and watch him. "Sounds like they're the weird ones."

He shakes his head. "Angels were also created to keep their feelings at a distance. To protect without any real interference. I've always struggled with that." He scratches at the scruff on his face and scowls. He pulls his hood further down over his face and crosses his arms.

"Cold?" I ask quietly.

He nods. "This body is virtually useless. I can't keep my body temperature comfortable. It's either too hot or too cold. This skin itches, this eyesight is inadequate. These lips are always chapped, and my stomach is constantly aching for food. I'm always suffering mood alterations. It's very limiting."

I watch him and smile a little. It's interesting to listen to an angel bitch about the consequences of being human. "How come you fell then? You knew this would happen, right?"

He sighs and looks up at me, a serious expression on his face. "There's a certain beauty in being human. A simplicity. I'm able to view humanity in its rawest, most natural state with this body. I'm able to view the colors of the world through a set of eyes just like yours, to enjoy the taste of your food and understand the reasoning for variety. I'm able to appreciate the feeling of the sun's light on my face and the warmth that accompanies it. I'm able to feel the textures of the world…a tickle of a blade of grass, the roughness of my jeans, the soft feeling of skin on skin.

"As I have visited Earth, I have grown to enjoy the many sensations. It just takes time. I've also come to understand love. Real love that can't be pre-programmed. It's not a full, all-encompassing love of humans as a species, but a love that has stemmed from personal relationships. All by accident."

Brie bites his lower lip and raps his knuckles in an almost nervous fashion against the tabletop. I'm curious about what he could mean. I open my mouth to ask him about it, but he clears his throat suddenly and shakes his head, silencing me before I've even begun.

He turns his attention to the bag and reaches inside. I have no idea what it holds. I've been too busy with everything else to bother looking.

He pulls out a thick, black journal, and a necklace.

I freeze, staring at the necklace in his hand. My hair stands up at the back of my neck. It's a vial and it's shining brightly.

"What is that?" I blurt, unable to look away from it.

"This is very important, Maxwell." He looks up at me. "And very special. You can't misuse it. It's the purest form of your father's grace that there is. It's only a piece, mind you, but it is very valuable. You're going to have to keep it hidden. Don't tell anyone about it. Not Jamie, not Theodore. Nobody. Are we clear?"

I nod. "Can I touch it?"

He takes a deep breath. "Yes. But don't let it out. You won't get it back." He holds it out in offering.

I run my fingertips over the vial slowly and the glow burns brighter, as if it's responding to my touch. I look back up at Brie, eyes even wider than before. "It's so warm!"

"Yes. It's quite powerful."

"Why is it in the vial?"

"It was a gift for your mother. A form of protection while she was pregnant with you. It made the process a little easier on her and it eased her feelings of anxiety at having your father so far away. She had a piece of him with her always, you see."

I bite my lip and look up at him.

He watches me for a moment longer and then gets to his feet. He steps behind me and sets the vial around my neck, fastening it for me. "Just be careful with it. You won't be able to get more of it."

I pick up the tiny vial, examining it more closely. It's the most beautiful thing I've ever seen, like a galaxy of stars. An entire universe. I look up at him as I tuck it beneath my shirt. It shudders against my skin for a moment and then pulses in time with my heart. "It feels like it's alive."

"It very much is." He looks back down at the book on the table and opens it just a fraction before slamming it shut and shaking his head. "That's enough for today."

"But I just got here."

He shakes his head again quickly. "Please. No more today."

"But—"

"You need to leave!"

I flinch and get to my feet quickly, swallowing hard. I hurry to the door, ducking my head, shoulders slouched. I slam the door a little harder than necessary on my way out.

Brie is right about his mood swings. He needs to learn how to keep them in check.

2147

"BROTHER!"

Gabriel's head jerked up from the bowl of green beans he'd been busily snapping the ends off of. His eyes widened in shock as he registered the figure striding toward him, the blond hair and eyes the color of sunlight through whiskey were very welcoming to him. They were bright and full of mischief, just like Uriel was.

Uriel pulled Gabriel from his seat on the porch swing and hugged him tightly.

A smile came to Gabriel's lips as he hugged him back. He'd missed his favorite brother very much, and it brought him great joy to see him again.

"Didn't think I'd be seeing you around these parts. Rather coincidental, I'd say. Decided to check out this part of town when I heard a couple of ladies gossiping about a mysterious tall dark and handsome who showed up out of nowhere and was probably further corrupting that hooligan Aubrey Addams."

Aubrey cleared her throat and stood, hands on her hips. "Well, I'm offended. All this time I thought *I* was the one doing all of the corrupting."

Gabriel snorted. "You're right, of course. Spoiling my formerly angelic disposition."

Uriel grinned and looked over at her. "I like you already." He took her hand when she held it out for a shake, and he gave a little bow, kissing it instead. "Pleasure to meet you, Miss Aubrey. I admire your ability to bring my dear brother out of his shell. It's a task that I have tried and failed many times."

Aubrey grinned. "It's nice to meet you, too. Uriel, I'm guessing?"

He nodded and smiled wide. "I am." He wiggled his brows. "Has my dear baby brother been talking about me?"

She nodded. "A bit. I hear you're his favorite."

Gabriel shot her a look. "Shh. We don't want his head getting so big it explodes."

Uriel laughed. "That's a handy bit of information. Thank you, darling."

Aubrey laughed and set her hand on Gabriel's arm. She gave it a squeeze and looked back at Uriel. "Well, we were just getting ready to fix dinner. I'll go inside and finish, but if you've got some time, you're more than welcome to join us."

He smiled warmly and nodded. "That sounds wonderful. Thank you."

She nodded and then turned back to Gabriel and leaned up on tiptoe to press a soft kiss to his mouth. "I'll call you when it's ready."

He nodded and smiled, watching her walk back inside with the bowl of beans.

Uriel cleared his throat and grinned, watching his brother. "You're completely infatuated with that girl," he murmured. "She's got you wrapped around her finger."

Gabriel took a deep breath and looked back at him, cheeks coloring. "Well, I don't know if I would say *that*."

"She does. You've discovered love, and now you're drowning in it." When Gabriel didn't respond, he went on, "she certainly seems charming enough. How long have you been here?"

He shrugged. "A few weeks, I suppose."

Uriel's eyes widened. "You're in very deep then. Deep enough, obviously, to have decided that you don't care what our brothers think or that they will be irked by your prolonged absence."

Gabriel snorted in reply. "*My* prolonged absence? What about yours? How long has it been?"

The other angel smiled and shrugged, looking down at his feet. "Five years. Going on six, actually."

"And you're an arch."

"Yes. Just like you."

"Why did you stay? What has kept you here?"

Uriel took a deep breath and looked up at him. "Same reason as you. Plus one. I have a daughter."

Gabriel's eyes widened in shock. "They'll be *furious*, Uriel."

"Yes." Uriel's eyes lost a bit of their former shine. "Yes. They would most likely try to kill her and Lana. I would ask that you please, *please* refrain from mentioning their existence. I would be quite lost if anything happened to either of them."

His brother nodded quickly, reaching out and squeezing his shoulder. "Of course not. Never."

"Has Michael been driving you crazy about coming back yet?"

Gabriel shook his head, frowning. "No."

"That's surprising. He's not in a good place." Uriel chewed his lip.

"What do you mean? He seems as cool and level-headed as usual."

"He spent more time down here than anyone realized."

"What?"

Uriel nodded, watching his brother. "He fell in love."

"Ridiculous."

"He *did.* You remember our sister, Ananael?"

"Of course I do."

"She went through an existential crisis and decided to fall. But she's fallen in love with the atmosphere down here. She's a doctor now. Takes care of the sick and the injured."

Gabriel smiled. "I can imagine she would be very good at that."

"She is. She lives about an hour from here. She was in contact with Michael. He fell in love with a human. Her name was Adelaide."

Gabriel's brows rose in question. "Was?"

"She got pregnant. She didn't survive the birth." He watched his brother and swallowed hard. "It was very difficult for him. Ananael was there. She gave him the news and he was immediately furious." He shook his head. "Wanted to destroy his daughter. So Ana told him the child had passed away, too. He left shortly after."

Gabriel shivered. "He never mentioned anything about a romance or a child."

"He wouldn't. He's always had a chip on his shoulder about nephilim even though we haven't had any issues with them since the old days. Now he's even worse. Out for revenge."

"What happened to the child?"

"Ana is raising her."

"As her own?"

He nodded. "Yes. As a nephilim." He shook his head, looking away for a moment. "She mentioned something else."

"What?"

"She said she received a message from our Father."

Gabriel's eyes widened in shock. No one had heard from their Father in years. It had been a source of recent panic among his brothers. They weren't sure if they'd offended Him, or if He'd just given up and gone on to create bigger and better things.

Uriel squeezed his brother's shoulder. "I was just as shocked as you. She said He gave her instructions to care for the child and keep her safe. That there was another coming. She said it was vague, but that the nephilim need to be protected if humanity is to be saved."

"Another is coming? Your daughter?"

Uriel shrugged. "I'm not sure. Chloe is already five years old. She's very advanced in her abilities, but she's already here. She needs to be protected, obviously, but I'm not sure she's the one that Ana was talking about."

Gabriel swallowed hard. "What's it like?"

"What? Being a father?"

He nodded.

"Well, it was a lot like first falling in love with Lana. Immediate and overwhelming and the sweetest feeling in the entire world. The entire *universe*. Chloe is wonderful. Already so smart. She talks nonstop and is very inquisitive. She has mastered glamour, thankfully, as she was born winged. She looks like her mother, but she's got my eyes and personality. She's very rebellious— naughty, but also too sweet and sincere for words. She and Lana have lit up my life in a way previously unimaginable. I could have never dreamed of this before. This undying, all-encompassing love. It's so strong and so pure that honestly, I have been considering falling."

"Uriel, no!" Gabriel was shocked by the suggestion.

The other angel shrugged, clearly not bothered by his brother's astonishment. "I have lived for a very long time, Gabe. I've never been this content with my life. I understand our Father's obsession with humanity now. It's special. Free will and the ability to feel things so deeply and so completely are things that I'm no longer willing to go without. This is the life I want. I want to grow old with my Lana— make her happy. I want to watch my darling Chloe grow up and begin her own life. I could never do those things as an angel."

"But your responsibilities…"

"I have new responsibilities now. Heaven has done just fine without me. Michael sounds like he's just as douchey and in charge as usual. And if our Father really does have a plan for the nephilim, I should be here to watch over my daughter anyway."

Gabriel swallowed hard past a lump in his throat. "I will miss you, brother."

Uriel smiled and rolled his eyes, pulling him into another hug. "I won't do it quite yet. But soon. And who knows, maybe you'll end up making the same decision."

2165

I MISS SUNSHINE.

 Grass.

 Our garden.

 Music.

 My room.

 My garage.

 Even though we've only been here for a few days, the gray walls of the bunker already bring nothing but homesickness. I'm lying with my head in Bear's lap while he plays with my hair. There's really nothing more comforting. Gran used to—

 I can't think of her right now. I take a deep breath and look up at Bear instead. He's got his tongue poking out of the corner of his mouth, concentrating as he tries to twist my hair into a long blonde braid.

 He scowls, brows pulling together. "How do you do this? You have too much hair."

 I smirk and reach up, taking his face in my hands to pull him down for a quick kiss.

 "It's not so hard," I murmur against his mouth, feeling his lips curl into a smile against mine.

 "Give it some time, and I might be able to do yours. It's getting a little long on the top," I tease softly, working my fingers into his light brown hair.

 He chuckles and nudges his nose to mine. "No way."

 "I'll have to give you a haircut, huh?" I sit up and climb into his lap, facing him.

 He smirks. "Nah, we could leave it. I see the whole long, shoulder-length hair thing becoming a trend after Michael's speech. He was quite a looker."

 I laugh.

He kisses me gently, hands slipping to the bare skin of my lower back and pulling me closer.

I slide his arms around his neck and allow myself to bask in his warmth.

He strokes a hand through my hair. "I love you, Max."

I press a kiss to his upper lip. "Yeah. Always?"

"Always," he agrees, nosing my cheek gently.

There's a sharp knock at the door. I look over, grabbing my shirt and sliding it over my head. "What?"

Jamie peeks her head in first before she opens the door fully. "Hey, Max. There are people you need to meet before we really get started on a plan and introduce you to the entire colony."

I take a deep breath and nod. "Okay." I climb out of Bear's lap and slide my boots on, tying them up.

Bear follows suit, but Jamie shakes her head. "You should stay here for now."

He scowls, but I smile and pat his chest, leaning down to kiss the top of his head. "Sleep for a little longer, okay?"

He sighs and nods. "Alright. Be careful?"

"Always."

Jamie takes my hand. "Come on!"

"Yeah, yeah." I roll my eyes but smile as she pulls me along excitedly.

She looks back at me and beams. "You're going to meet the people who make this place run. They're all really great. And they know about nephilim already. Uriel is fallen, too. He fell around the same time as Brie."

My brows raise. "Really?"

She nods. "He was friends with your dad."

"Hm. Is he as much of a dick as Brie?"

She giggles, but it sounds wrong. Nervous. She shakes her head. "He's very excited to meet you. I promise. And Brie likes you. He just comes across kind of moody sometimes."

I look up at her, frowning. "Jamie?"

"Yeah?"

"What aren't you telling me?"

"Nothing, Maxwell."

It's bullshit, of course. I can read Jamie like a book. I've been able to since the night we met. She tugs me into a bigger room with a long table in the center. It looks like some sort of conference room. Brie is sitting at the table with the girl who led us out of the underground the other day and four other people who I kind of recognize but haven't formally met.

Jamie smiles and pulls me to the table where I shake everyone's hand in turn. I learn that Cami, the girl who led us from the underground initially, is second in command of the raiders. She doesn't look very thrilled upon meeting me formally and has a very cold and unenthusiastic handshake.

Jeremy is sitting beside her. He's the head of the raiders. His handshake is warm and firm. He's young, probably in his early twenties, with jet black dreads pulled back into a bun and dark eyes to match. He's got a charming smile. He briefly explains to me that it's his job to lead a team in search of food and supplies for the rebellion. He also recruits and introduces new rebels to the underground community and works with the head of security to ensure that everyone stays safe and secure.

Ari is next. She's the main healer. She has her long, dark brown hair in a side braid and her pretty brown eyes are incredibly sincere when she pulls me in for a hug instead of a handshake. I learn that she was the one to patch up my shoulder upon my initial arrival. Jamie jokes that I shouldn't let Ari's warm embrace fool me because really Ari is a complete badass and extremely skilled in hand-to-hand combat. She is also notoriously protective of her friends and not to be crossed.

Darren, the head of security, sits beside Ari. He's all smiles and awkward praises as he shakes my hand once, and then again, holding it far longer than is socially acceptable. I let it pass because he seems like such a nice guy. He's an older man, balding on top. His almond eyes survey me nervously but seem to warm considerably as we introduce ourselves. Darren is extraordinarily intelligent and especially skilled with technology and has cameras set up around the entire city so we're able to view what is going on from below. It's an incredible asset to the community and allows him to collaborate with the raiders as a sort of guard dog system.

I take a deep breath and try to smile, but a nervous feeling flutters in my stomach as I turn from Darren to Brie.

He nods his head toward me and smiles. "Good morning, Maxwell."

"Good morning, Brie."

"Maxwell!" My Uncle Vic's sudden presence causes me to do a double take. My eyes widen in shock before I run to him and jump on him, locking my arms around his neck.

"Uncle Vic! Oh my god, you're alive! Nobody told me you were here and safe!"

"You sure gave me a scare, kid." He presses a wet kiss to my cheek and ruffles my hair like I'm small again. I would be irritated if I wasn't so relieved to see him alive. As it is, I can't stop hugging him, clinging to another family member that is safe and here with me.

"Gran is gone," I tell him quietly.

He nods. "I know. I'm sorry, honey." He takes a deep breath. "I have something to tell you. I don't want you to get upset, okay?"

Oh, great. "What is it?" I ask nervously, taking a step back and staring up at him.

"I haven't been completely honest with you."

"Gee, that sounds new. Just spit it out, okay? I'm sick of going through this conversation over and over again." I cross my arms, staring up at him.

He rubs the back of his neck, eyes turning down for a moment before he looks back up at me. "My real name is Uriel. I fell with your father. He was my brother."

Goosebumps cover my arms as I stare at him, trying to control my facial expressions. I'm so fucking mad. Everybody knew this. Everyone but me. Gran kept it from me. Jamie kept it from me. Uncle Vic isn't even who I thought he was.

"I know you're probably upset, Maxwell, but I'm the same person I've always been to you. The only difference is my name. I'm human now. I've fallen. I have no further association with the angels."

I can't even look at Jamie as she touches my hand, trying to hold it. I pull away and shake my head quietly, looking up toward the ceiling for a moment before I look back at Vic. Uriel. I nod once. "Okay."

He arches an eyebrow disbelievingly. "Okay?"

I shrug my shoulders, staring at him. "It's not like being angry is going to change anything."

He takes a deep breath and his lips turn up into a small smile. His golden eyes crinkle at the corners.

"So, you're the angel of?"

"Oh! Wisdom. And, ironically, repentance." Uncle Vic looks down for a moment, cheeks flushing. "But uh, not anymore. I fell willingly."

"Why?"

His expression darkens and he takes a step back, looking down at his boots. "I had a daughter, Chloe. But I was unwilling to suppress her memories. She was found by Michael. I was unable to stop him."

I don't think I want to hear this story.

"She was rather advanced in her abilities. Able to fly. She had the most brilliant pair of wings I've ever seen on a nephilim. But they were ripped from her back along with her grace in front of hundreds of angels as a warning that we were not to communicate with humans in that way anymore. And if we did, we were to dispose of them before a pregnancy could occur. Michael was disgusted that some of us had grown attached to our human lovers and their children. We were falling in love, and it was not acceptable."

It's hard to look at Vic, so I turn my attention back to the others at the table. All eyes are focused on Vic except for Brie's. He's staring silently at the table. His expression is hard, resolute.

I look back at Vic to see that he's staring at me. "She died that way. Screaming for help that I could not give her. And I was forced to watch the entire display. So I fell."

My vision is swimming with unshed tears. I blink them back and clear my throat. "How could God let that happen?" My voice is no more than a whisper.

Vic's hand slams down on the table, causing everyone to jump. "There *is* no God!" he spits angrily. "He has gone missing. Doubtless disgusted by the slaughter his children are committing every day."

I stumble backward in shock, bumping back against the table.

Brie stands quickly. "Uriel. You don't know if that's true."

"Of course it is!" Uriel spits back, glaring at him. "If it wasn't, he would have stepped in by now! He would have shown us some kind of support!"

"Uriel. His message…"

Uncle Vic is shaking in fury, his entire body trembling. He slams his fist down on the table again. "Leave us!" he hisses to the rest of us before his attention turns back to Brie.

Jamie grabs my arm and pulls me out with the rest of them before there's a loud crash. It sounds as though the table has been flipped over and the two fallen angels are yelling at each other in a fury. I swallow hard and look over at Jamie as we hurry down the hallway.

She looks at me and takes a deep breath. "Sensitive subject."

I stop walking and lean back against the wall as the others file past us. I slide down slowly until I'm sitting, knees pulled to my chest. My hands reach into my hair. "What are we doing?" I moan, closing my eyes.

Jamie kneels in front of me and takes my face in her hands, setting her forehead to mine. "It'll be okay. I promise. I swear. I've got you, Max."

I'm so tired of hearing that! My face feels wet and I realize I'm crying. I gasp for breath. There are too many secrets. Too many horrible twists and turns to this already fucked up story.

I can't do this.

I can't. I can't. I can't.

I don't want to.

"I've got you," she repeats, voice like honey. She nuzzles her nose to mine and then presses a kiss to my forehead and strokes my hair until I can breathe again.

2147

GABRIEL KNEW IT COULDN'T LAST FOREVER. His long days and blissful nights spent with Aubrey, watching her paint, research, or fill out hundreds of job applications, dancing with her, making love with her, cooking with her, laughing with her, were wonderful. He felt incredibly blessed to be at her side.

Though he knew it couldn't possibly last forever, he'd also more or less forgotten about his brothers up in Heaven for the time being, allowing himself to relax and carry on in everyday activities that had become routine for him. He'd lost his brothers up in Heaven, but he had gained a family on Earth that felt more real and more genuine than anything he had ever had before. He and Aubrey kept in touch with Uriel, and they got together with him and Lana frequently. Gabriel had been absolutely charmed by little Chloe. She was as bright as Uriel had described and a truly beautiful child. He'd been on Earth for nearly six months, and he had no plans to return to his old home any time soon.

It came to him in a dream: Michael's urgent command for him to. It woke him with such force that he sat up, gasping for breath.

Aubrey opened her eyes and looked up at him, frowning. "Gabe? What's wrong?" She sat up and pressed her hand to his back, rubbing his skin in slow circles while he grasped at his chest, squeezing his eyes shut tightly and shaking his head.

"I have to leave," Gabriel finally murmured, unable to look at her. "I have been ordered back home."

He could feel her eyes on him, but he refused to look up. "I'm sorry."

Aubrey was silent for a long time before he felt the bed shift as she stood. "It's fine. I knew you wouldn't be able to stay."

Gabriel frowned deeply and looked up at her. He'd expected more of a reaction. Tears or anger. Something. Anything.

She smiled at him, but it looked strange, forced. "Don't look at me like that, Angel. Go."

He swallowed hard. "I have to go collect Uriel. He was ordered home as well. He will be very upset."

"Well, he should have known. Earth is no place for angels. You both have bigger responsibilities. You've wasted too much time here with me, being lazy and neglecting your duties. You'd better hurry back."

He stared at her, not understanding. "Aubrey…"

"Don't. You don't have to explain, really. It's been nice hanging out, but I have things I need to be doing, too. My life is supposed to be more than being an angel's tour guide. You're a distraction."

Gabriel frowned deeply and looked down at his lap. "I thought—"

"You thought what?"

"I thought you'd be upset."

"Yeah? What am I supposed to do? Lie down and cry because you're leaving? Am I supposed to try to believe you'll be back someday when I know for a fact it's been over a hundred years since you were last here? Am I supposed to be sad because by the next time you visit I'll be dead? Because I'm never going to see you again? This wasn't supposed to happen. I was trying to be your friend, Gabriel. Give you shelter. That's all. There wasn't supposed to be anything else. But you should have left earlier. You should have gone. And Uriel. He's going to leave Lana? They're practically married. He's going to leave his *daughter*?"

Gabriel's chest ached with heaviness. "He will have to. Michael is our leader. Going against his word would be like going against our Father."

"God would want a man to abandon his daughter? His family?" Aubrey asked, angrily pulling a shawl around her shoulders. "Really?"

"We *aren't* men, Aubrey. We're angels."

She pinched the bridge of her nose, frowning. She shook her head and then opened her eyes and looked back at him. "You need to go."

"Aubrey."

"What?"

"Please. Can we just talk for a moment, I—"

"What do you want me to say, Angel? That I'm upset that you came down and stayed too long and got tangled up in my life? That you became my friend, my family? Do you want me to tell you how the world seems a little less messed up when you're around because you're so innocent and sincere? Do you want me to tell you how much I'm going to miss having you around? How much I'm going to miss embarrassing you just to see your cheeks flush red? How much it sucks because for a short time I had convinced myself enough that you would be able to stay that I ended up loving you?" Her eyes were wide and full of tears. She took a step back and ran a hand back through her sleep-tangled hair.

Gabriel stood and took her hands in his own, squeezing them tight. "Aubrey. Listen to me now. I would not leave if I didn't have to. This time I have spent on Earth with you has been like nothing I have ever experienced before. I wish it did not have to be this way.

"It's true that I have many brothers up in Heaven, but I don't believe I've ever had a real family until I came to visit this place. You have made an enormous impression on my soul, Aubrey, and I don't know how to thank you enough for that. I love you. I didn't think I would ever be able to experience something like this. And I have. Because of you.

"The last time I was here, it was a very dark time. I'd lost my faith in humanity. I left and didn't come back for a long time. But now I've spent time with you, and I can understand why my Father cares so deeply for this world. You are beautiful. This place is beautiful. And you've shown me the very best parts of it."

"Then why are you leaving?" Aubrey murmured, staring at him. A couple of tears had rolled down her face and dropped onto her nightgown, dampening little spots of the fabric.

"I have no choice in the matter," he replied quietly, sadly. "But I need you to understand how much you mean to me. How much this time spent with you has meant. I need you to know how loathe I am to leave, but also that I will never forget about you. Ever."

Aubrey swallowed hard and looked up at him.

"And anyway, we both know I've always needed you more than you've needed me. You're sad that I'm leaving but you're strong, Aubrey. The strongest human I've ever met. You've got goals I know you will achieve. I can't wait for your life to become what you've always wanted it to be. You're going to change the world, remember?"

She wiped her eyes with the back of her hand. "Yeah," she said softly. "Yeah, I'm going to try."

"You *will* succeed," he promised. "I know you will." He pulled her close and wrapped his arms around her. "You're going to be the truth-teller of this world. You'll expose the monsters and lead the fight for change. You're very stubborn."

She rolled her eyes and hugged him tightly. She took a deep breath of him. "I'll miss you. I wish we would have had more time."

He nodded, setting his face in her hair. "So do I," he murmured softly. "I would have stayed forever."

"Promise?"

"I promise. I love you, Aubrey."

"Love you, too, Angel." She held him for a moment longer before pulling back and looking up at him. "You'd better go, okay? Be safe. Say goodbye to Uriel for me?"

Gabriel nodded and leaned down, pressing an unreciprocated kiss to her mouth. He straightened after a moment, a hand lingering in her hair for just a second longer before he closed his eyes and disappeared.

2165

"THIS IS WHERE EVERYONE EATS. Go ahead and grab a plate and get in line."

I stand in line between Bear and Jamie, watching Cami. She's been showing us around. We've learned she's nineteen years old and an orphan. Fearing termination upon coming of age, she'd escaped her shelter at fifteen and had been running until she met a group of rebels who showed her into their underground home. She'd been here ever since, along with hundreds of others, living in this underground safety bunker that was abandoned so long ago that it has been since forgotten.

Jamie nudges my shoulder gently and smiles at me before she grabs a plate for each of us and hands one to me.

I try to return her smile, but I'm still feeling bothered by the meeting yesterday. Afterward, Brie had come to tell us that everything was okay; Uncle Vic had just had a meltdown, which was common for fallen angels. He'd taken the loss of his daughter very hard and was understandably passionate about taking revenge on Michael.

I had gone to him later in the night and hugged him as he trembled, face damp as he snuffled into my hair. He'd told me he was sorry, and I told him there was no need. I understood.

I hold my plate and looked up at Bear. "Hungry?"

He nods. "Starving. Feels like we haven't eaten in ages."

I crack a tiny smile and nod. "I think that's because we really haven't."

Cami watches us. "Hurry up. If you guys want to address the group, you'll have to do it soon before everyone finishes up and goes off to do their own thing."

"Maybe we should eat after." I look at the buffet of food, my stomach turning. I'm not looking forward to addressing the rest of the group. There are hundreds down here. But I know I have to. Brie has made it clear that the rest of the group needs to know there are nephilim living with them in the beginning so they won't feel blindsided later on. We're also supposed to mention the tiny details of Uriel and Brie being fallen angels. I don't know how well that's going to go over.

Jamie nods. "Good idea."

Cami smiles and touches Bear's arm. "How about you and I go sit down with the others while we listen? And then when they're done, they can come back and join us."

I don't particularly like the friendly way Cami is touching Bear, but I choose to ignore it. There are more important issues at stake right now. I look down at Jamie and bite my lip. "Okay, let's go."

There is a tiny stage in the front of the room where a podium sits. It's used for group meetings. Everything underground works in an organized manner, just like upstairs. The difference is that this community works hard to make sure everyone is heard and nothing becomes corrupt.

Jamie takes my hand and gives it a squeeze, pulling me up to the podium. She looks the picture of grace. It's obvious she isn't nervous at all. In fact, as she steps up to the podium, her shoulders straighten and her confident smile grows. She switches on the microphone attached to the podium and stares out at all of the curious onlookers. I'm surprised to note that I've never noticed this side of her before.

"Hello," she says, voice ringing out clear as a bell across the room. "As most of you know, my name is Jamie. This is Maxwell. She's new and excited to be here."

A couple of cheers ring out throughout the room, and I take a deep breath and force a smile. I look around and see Brie standing near the podium with Uncle Vic, arms crossed over his chest. He's watching us intently, no sign of how he's feeling on his face.

"Angels have fallen to Earth. I know a lot of you are scoffing about that because you haven't been up there recently to see, but we have seen them with our own eyes and let me tell you, they are as real as you or I."

A collective booing rises from the crowd. I can tell they're becoming restless, annoyed.

For the first time since stepping up in front of the crowd, Jamie seems to become a little unsure of herself. "They're giving out a warning about creatures called nephilim. The government is issuing an alert with the angels that if you see these people, you need to report them immediately because they're dangerous. What they're trying to eliminate are people like Maxwell and I."

By this point in her speech, the only people who are still paying any attention to her are either cracking jokes about her or yelling for her to get offstage so everybody can get back to work.

I feel myself growing less afraid as anger sets in. How are we supposed to be leading these people if no one is going to listen? My hands ball into fists, a scowl growing on my face. I look over and see Cami chatting with Bear, who isn't even listening to Jamie anymore but now focused on his new friend. My eyes wander over to Brie, who is still staring at us, but who is beginning to look very unimpressed.

"Enough!"

The moment I speak, the ground begins shaking. It starts at my feet and moves through the ground, upsetting glasses at tables and earning the attention of everyone in the room. There's a great rush of air in my ears and I suddenly stand straighter, staring out at the astonished crowd.

"You will *listen* to me," I begin, staring out at them. I'm absolutely furious. "Because if you don't, you'll die. I am nephilim. Daughter of the Archangel Gabriel. I am what the government is afraid of. We are. There are angels above ground, and they have made it their goal to cure our world of its sickness by eradicating all humans. Their first goal is to terminate all nephilim because we are the only thing that could stop them from finishing this apocalypse.

"You will give us the respect we deserve. Jamie is the daughter of the Archangel Michael. She is your new leader. You will follow her, and you will listen to her because if you don't, there will be consequences. If you don't like it, you can leave. But let it be known that if you sell us out, you will die a traitor's death, and it will not be quick.

"Our goal is to save you. To overthrow their shithole system and bring peace to our world. To get rid of the angels who are trying to harm us. We can only do this with your cooperation."

I stare out at the crowd and they stare back, wide-eyed and speechless. There is complete silence in my pause, not even the sound of breathing. I can feel the vial of my father's grace burning against my chest.

I lick my lips and watch them. "What you need to know," I continue, "is you cannot trust an angel. Trust no one above ground. We'll try to recruit more people because we need as many warriors as we can find, but if an angel were to find this place now, without an army ready, we would all die. There is, however, one exception to this rule." I gesture toward Brie and Uncle Vic. "Brie and Vic are both fallen angels. They fell to keep us safe. They're our mentors. Vic has been your leader for a long time, and this new information about him changes nothing."

Brie and Vic stride to the stage and step up beside us, nodding. The beginnings of a smile pull at the corners of Brie's mouth.

I look up at him and then back at the crowd. "I'm not going to stand up here and spew bullshit promises about fixing *everything* and creating a utopian society, but we're going to do what we can. We won't keep you in the dark. If you have questions, we will answer them to the best of our ability. If you have concerns, let them be known. But this is how things are going to be from now on. This is the change you have been praying for. This is the war you have been waiting for, and we are going to win it."

My declaration is met with a moment of shocked silence. Very slowly, a figure in the back rises. I squint and realize its Jeremy. He lets out a yell of support and begins to clap. He's quickly followed by Darren and then Ari. People from the crowd begin to rise, filling the air with the sound of their support and applause. The roar of the noise hits me all at once and I step backward, blinking.

I look over at Jamie and see that she's watching me, eyes wide. "Damn, Max," she whispers, taking my hand and giving it a squeeze.

Brie steps behind me and sets his hands on my shoulders, squeezing. He leans down and sets his lips to my ear. "I think you're going to be just fine," he confides, and when I look up into his face, I can see that he's grinning at me.

2162

MAXWELL SAT BESIDE HER GRANDMOTHER'S GARDEN, weaving a flower crown of daisies. She'd gotten some precious alone time as she had been given leave of her chores in honor of her fourteenth birthday. She stared down at the flowers in her hand, counting the individual petals and smoothing them out carefully with her fingertips. When she was finished, she placed it atop her head and then lay back in the soft grass, staring up at the sky.

It was summer, but the weather was cool for once. A gentle wind caressed her body, light as the kiss of a butterfly landing on skin.

She took a deep breath and smiled, closing her eyes. She was in a much better place than she had been only a year earlier.

She was sleeping through the night, most nights sharing a bed snuggled between her two best friends, Bear and Jamie. They allowed her a peace and a comfort she hadn't thought possible. They chased the bad dreams away and replaced her with a wondrous calm that filled her to the brim with happiness and affection for the both of them.

"Max!"

Matty's voice jerked her from her thoughts. She sat up with a grin, spotting him immediately.

"Max, you gotta come to the garage! I have a present for you!" Matty was practically shaking with excitement, blue eyes sparkling.

She laughed and hopped up to her feet. "Matty, you shouldn't have…"

"Shut up and come here!" He grabbed her hand and pulled her to the garage quickly.

Maxwell's heart stopped the moment she stepped into the garage. A stunning, 2091 Nova Dawn stood in front of her. It was black, paint peeling. It was covered in rust, missing an entire wind turbine and only half of the seat remained, but it was the most beautiful thing she had ever seen.

"Matty," she breathed, eyes wide in shock.

He grinned. "It's in pieces and the engine is shot, but I think we can make it run if we can find all the parts for it! Maybe we'll finish it by the time you can legally drive. That'd be pretty cool, huh?"

"Oh my god, Matty!" She jumped on her big brother in a hug, squeezing him tightly. "She's beautiful! Thank you so much!"

He laughed and patted her back. "I figured we could use a side project when we aren't working on other people's vehicles. She's old, but that's what makes her special. Nobody else'll have anything like her."

Max grinned and finally let him go, walking to the bike. She ran her hand along the rusted handlebars with a tender touch. "We're gonna fix you up real pretty, Nova. Welcome home."

2165

"IT WAS THE CRAZIEST THING EVER," Jamie laughs, watching me. "Your eyes went white and filled with this huge light. Your grace. It was impossible to look away. And then these shadows rose up behind you like wings. You were stunning."

I flush and look down at my lap. "I don't know what happened. Nobody was listening to you. I got angry."

A flush rises in Jamie's cheeks. "I really appreciated it, Max. The lack of respect can be frustrating. I've known about my birthright for my entire life, understood my duty and my purpose, and it's difficult to swallow that everyone else doesn't understand its importance as well."

I feel rejuvenated. Like maybe this whole thing isn't going to suck as much as I thought it would. "I wish I'd known."

Brie walks to me. "That's your father's fault. He wanted your memories locked away to keep you safe until the time came that it would be alright for you to know."

"How will I remember?" I ask, looking up at the fallen angel.

"The journal in your bag is full of memories. It should trigger you to begin to remember as we go through it, but we need to go through it slowly so you aren't hit all at once. Your powers should begin to develop with your memory."

Jamie grins. "You'll love playing with them when they develop."

"What can you do?" I ask.

Jamie opens her mouth to respond, but Brie beats her to it. "Jamie is highly skilled in combat. She'll have to teach you hand-to-hand. It's her specialty. She's also very good with weaponry. Another specialty. She inherited her skills from Michael. Aside from that, you should both share some level of telekinetic abilities, elemental and energy manipulations, eventually teleportation, and, if you're lucky, flight."

He smiles proudly. "I'm fairly convinced you'll be able to fly, Maxwell. Your wings nearly showed themselves tonight. You were born with them, but your father locked them away from view when he took your memories. You'll need to summon them into this plane of existence in order to use them. But they won't be important yet anyway."

I watch them both with wide eyes. "Teleportation?"

"It's really difficult," Jamie cuts in, watching me. "I haven't mastered it yet. I can teleport alone, but I can't bring anyone with me. Everything I've tried to bring hasn't made it with me in one piece. And telekinesis? Forget it."

Brie smiles kindly at her. "It's impressive that you can teleport at all. It's very difficult for nephilim, and you're still quite young." He looks over at me. "We're going to start you out with hand-to-hand combat before you begin trying out your abilities. It's important that you're able to defend yourself in case you ever, God forbid, lose your grace."

Jamie smiles at me. "I'll help you out with that. I'll even go easy on you at first. Build you up."

I laugh nervously. "I'm going to embarrass myself."

"It'll be fine. Nobody is perfect at first. I can teach Bear, too."

Brie looks over at her, a shadow crossing over his features. "He can learn hand-to-hand, but I'd rather keep him away from weaponry for now."

Jamie nods. "You really think he's going to be dangerous?"

"I don't know. It's hard to tell. He seems okay, but we have to be cautious around him until we know for sure."

I frown and look down at my lap.

Jamie squeezes my shoulder. "I'm sure he'll be okay, Max. Don't worry for now, okay?"

Brie smooths my hair. It's kind of weird. "Jamie is right. No need to worry unnecessarily for now, alright? Just relax. You've had a long day. How about you two go get him and take him back to your room? You should go to bed early. Rest up so we can begin going over the journal and training tomorrow."

I nod slowly and look up at Brie. "You're being awfully friendly today."

He laughs in surprise and shakes his head. "I'm just proud, is all. Didn't know if the two of you could do it, but it appears you've proven me wrong."

Jamie winks. "I think we're going to make a pretty okay team."

I nod. "We can try, at least."

Brie smiles. "Goodnight, girls. Don't get lost on your way back to the room." He hands over a lantern. "And lock your door. The response you received tonight was overwhelmingly positive, but you never know for sure."

2148

HIS FIGHT WITH MICHAEL HAD BEEN OVERWHELMING. Getting used to Heaven's rules and the lack of free will was difficult. Gabriel couldn't blame Uriel for refusing the request to return when Michael had called, because he was sure his punishment would have been much worse, as Uriel had been gone for so much longer.

After the punishment, which had been bloody and humiliating, Gabriel found he was still thinking about Aubrey. Constantly. To the point where she was impossible to ignore. Every day he found himself wishing he could be near her. Hear her voice. See her. Touch her.

One day, as he was falling among meteors out of boredom and heartache, he thought he heard his name.

So he decided to take a page out of Uriel's book, and he left his responsibilities in order to visit her again. He knew he wouldn't be able to stay long, but he hoped a short visit would do no harm.

He landed again in her field and then walked to her house and knocked on the front door.

Mary answered the door. She gave him a very long, very hard look before stepping aside so he could come in. "She's up in her room."

"Thank you, Mary," he said gratefully, stepping forward to kiss her cheek but being rejected as she moved away, shaking her head.

He swallowed hard and looked at her for another moment before walking toward the ceiling door.

"Gabriel, wait," Mary said, holding out a blanket to him. "Wrap that around yourself. Aubrey will have some clothes in her room for you."

He nodded. "Thank you."

When she didn't respond, he pulled down the ladder and climbed up into Aubrey's room.

She was lying on her bed, fast asleep. Her golden waves lay around her head like a halo, and Gabriel thought she looked very much like an angel. She was stunning. Her summer nightgown stretched tight around her swollen middle. He stared at it in disbelief.

He rubbed the back of his neck as he walked slowly to her bed and sat down on its edge. He reached out slowly and touched her hair, brushing a few strands away from her cheeks. It was hot up in the attic, and even her multiple fans weren't enough to keep the humid Midwest heat from leaving a light sheen of perspiration on her forehead. He leaned forward and pressed his lips to her cheek for a moment before sitting back and just watching her as she stirred, eyes opening slowly.

Aubrey stared up at him for a moment, her eyes adjusting slowly in the bad lighting. She took a deep breath and her eyes widened slowly in recognition. "Angel. My Gabriel…" she breathed.

Gabriel watched her, chewing his lower lip. He smiled. "I couldn't stay away," he admitted softly, ducking his head.

She sat up and reached for him, and he acquiesced, wrapping his arms around her and holding her tight. "You're pregnant," he murmured softly into her hair. "I wish I would have known. I'd have been back sooner."

She nodded. "I am. I'm scared. She feels really important, Gabriel. I don't know why, but she does. Like she's bringing a change. A big one."

He took a sharp intake of breath and looked at her. "She? It's a little girl?"

She nodded quickly. "She is."

"Do you have a name for her?"

"Yes." Aubrey smiled tiredly. "Her name is Maxwell."

"Maxwell," he repeated softly. A small smile came to his lips as he set his hand on her belly. "I like it."

"Good, because you're stuck with it." Aubrey slid her hand back into his hair. "I can't believe you're here. I thought you were gone forever."

He nodded. "So did I. But I couldn't stop thinking about you. I thought I'd be able to get back into my normal activities and distract myself from missing you, but I couldn't. Nothing worked. And then I thought I heard a prayer. I could have been wrong…"

Aubrey's eyes lit up. "You did! I prayed to you. I felt so stupid, but I did. I wanted you to know about her. I thought about how disappointed you would feel if you ever found out you had a daughter and didn't know a thing about her. I knew you'd want to know. But I didn't know how the whole prayer thing worked and I've never been one to do it. It felt really strange so I only tried once. I wasn't sure if you would hear."

"I did. It wasn't very clear. But I thought it might have been you." He stroked a hand through her hair and pressed his lips to her temple. "I missed you so much."

"I missed you, too," she replied softly. "I was really angry with you when I found out I was pregnant, but it's probably my fault. For corrupting you."

He chuckled quietly and nosed her cheek gently. "You certainly did a lot of corrupting, but it takes two. We are equally responsible for the life inside of your belly." He set his hand on it again, and his jaw dropped when he felt Maxwell kick. He looked up at Aubrey. "Wow."

Aubrey smiled and nodded. "She's very active. Strong."

"That's good." He knelt down in front of her and pressed his cheek to her belly. "Hello, little one," he said softly. "I'm your father." He closed his eyes as Aubrey's fingers slid into his hair, massaging his scalp. He made a soft noise and leaned into her touch, sliding his arms around her middle.

They stayed like that for quite a while until Aubrey finally broke the silence. "Will Maxwell be like Chloe?"

"She could be," he responded. "I'm unsure if she will have wings or not. She'll have special abilities, of course. All nephilim do, which is why life is so dangerous for them. The angels become nervous. You'll have to keep her home until you realize what those abilities are and she is able to control them. We don't need any attention drawn to her."

"Okay. Will you be able to stay?"

Gabriel swallowed hard and looked up at her. He shook his head slowly. "No. At least not all the time. But I will make every effort to make it back as often as I can. It won't be nearly frequently enough, but I am willing to endure the punishment for visiting as often and as long as I can."

Aubrey's brows pulled together in the middle of her forehead as she frowned deeply. "They punished you?"

He nodded. "Yes, but it doesn't matter. It was worth it."

"What did they do?"

Gabriel shook his head. "It's not necessary to describe it," he replied quietly.

"Gabriel, what'd they do to you?"

He looked toward the ceiling and then sighed, defeated. He stood and turned so his back was to her. He let the blanket slide down his shoulders and back, exposing his branded skin. "Disobedient" would be inscribed between his shoulder blades forever.

He flinched when he heard her gasp.

"Gabriel, they're horrible!"

He turned to face her, pulling the blanket back around himself. "It was deserved. I forgot my duties for many months."

"Are you kidding me?" She stood, scowling at him. "They can't hurt you for taking a little break, Gabriel. That's disgusting. Angels should be above that kind of behavior!"

Gabriel took a deep breath and watched her, reaching out and setting his hands on her shoulders. "You know how corrupt your world is. Heaven is worse."

Aubrey stared at him. "No."

"Yes."

"It can't be, Gabriel. Don't tell me that."

"I won't lie to you, Aubrey."

"But God—"

"He's gone," Gabriel blurted. "He's disappeared. I think we've disappointed him. He's nowhere to be found. I'm not sure if he will come back or not."

Aubrey stared at him, obviously stunned. "He can't just *leave*!"

"He's God. He can do as he pleases," Gabriel replied sadly. "He could have created another universe entirely by now. Forgotten all about us. No matter how upsetting it is to you or me, it's His decision. If He is disappointed in how we have been acting, the only thing we can do to remedy the situation is to behave better—repair things. Which is what I plan to do."

"Even if it means going against your brothers?"

"Yes."

Aubrey nodded slowly and watched him. "Good. That's good. Maybe He'll see. Maybe He'll understand. We need help."

He nodded and pulled her closer, nuzzling his nose to the side of her face. "He is good. He will see. I am sure of it."

She nodded and closed her eyes.

Gabriel held her for a few moments more before stepping back to look down at her. "How has your pregnancy been?"

She shrugged and looked up at him. "Pretty standard, I guess. It won't be long now. I don't know how labor will be."

"It could be dangerous," he said softly, "because of the differences. And it will have to be a home birth."

She nodded. "I figured. Mom has been doing her research. She's going to deliver Max for me."

"Okay. I can help with the pain. I'm unsure of how these things work, but I'll be able to do something."

She smiled and nodded. "I'm glad you'll be here, Angel."

His eyes flitted over her face, and he smiled, sliding his hands up to caress her arms. "I am happy, too. I love you, Aubrey."

She smiled and slid her hands up his chest and around the back of his neck, pulling his head down to hers. "I love you, too, Gabriel. My angel."

2165

I FIDGET OUTSIDE BRIE'S ROOM, feeling stupid. I'm self-conscious of the gun that's strapped to my thigh. I'm not even very good at using the stupid thing. Besides that, I'm feeling this overwhelming, idiotic need to prove myself to him. Only a month ago, I didn't want anything to do with this rebellion, and now here I am, forced to become one of its *leaders*.

I bite my lip and finally knock on his door, figuring I may as well get it over with. We're supposed to begin going over my mother's journal. I'm nervous about it, but I hope everything will be explained.

"Come in!" he calls, sounding as though he's in a relatively pleasant mood. I step inside and look over at him as the door swings shut behind me.

He smiles. "Good morning. Did you sleep well?"

I nod. "Did you?"

"Yes. Are you ready to learn a little bit about your family history?"

No. "Yes."

"We'll go slowly. I don't want to overwhelm you. If you're feeling too anxious, ask me to stop. It could get dangerous if you lose control of your emotions. Are we clear?"

"Crystal." I fold my hands in front of me on the table, looking up at him expectantly. I hope my face doesn't give away how terrified I am to learn the truth.

Brie watches me for another long moment before passing my mother's journal over to me. "You can look through the first few pages while I explain to you what it says," he murmurs.

I open it up and instantly recognize my mom's slanted handwriting. The pages are yellowed and a pressed Aster flower sticks to the page. The date reads September 2, 2148. My fingers run slowly over the first few lines.

Dear Maxwell,

I'm writing to you in case I am someday unable to tell you this information when you're old enough to understand. I'm praying there won't come a day when you need me and I am not present, but your father thinks it would be a good idea for me to write everything down, just in case. You're going to be very confused when you read this, and you're probably going to be hurt, but I need you to know that you are loved and any deception you have suffered has been to keep you safe.

Brie's voice fills the room as he begins to tell the story of my mother and father's first meeting in the field beside my grandmother's house. I stare at the Aster flower as he speaks, and I imagine myself at home. I can see myself in my grandmother's garden, dirty hands full of flowers for my mother. I can imagine weaving flower crowns with Bear and dancing in the sun.

He gets as far as telling me about the days leading up to my birth, and then he stops, staring at a spot on the wall just past my shoulder. I look up at him. "There's something I don't understand."

He blinks and looks back at me, brown eyes sharp. "What's that?"

"Where's Matty? He's older than I am."

He chews his lip and then shakes his head. "Your brother, Matthew isn't your blood relative. Your mother fell in love with another man, a widower who had a son. You were six, he was seven. You bonded quickly and became as close as regular siblings would be. When your memories were taken as a child, you forgot that he came into your life later."

My brother is not my blood. "I think maybe that's enough for today."

He nods and reaches out, squeezing my hand. I pull away. "I know it's a lot to take in. We'll continue tomorrow, alright?"

"Sure."

I barely make it to the bathroom before I drop to my knees inside a stall and lose my breakfast into the porcelain seat. When I'm finished, I wipe at my forehead with a shaking hand, my hair sticking to the perspiration on my forehead. I can't believe Matty isn't my real brother. It makes me wonder about everything else I've been lied to about throughout my life, almost as though my life doesn't really belong to me. I'm not who I thought I was. My mother and father aren't who I thought they were. Even Matty. He's not my blood. My entire life has been a lie.

Leaning forward again, I collapse against the toilet as my stomach wrenches.

2148

"I AM AFRAID, URIEL," Gabriel admitted, looking up at his brother. "She's very close. I know nothing of childbirth, and what if something goes wrong? What if what happened to Michael's lover happens to her? She's confident in her mother's abilities to take care of both she and the child, but if something goes wrong, there's no guarantee we'll be able to fix it."

He'd been rambling his insecurities to his brother for the past hour or so. He'd gone to see him soon after he had met with Aubrey. When she'd gone back to sleep, he'd left to speak with his brother in hopes that he would gain a greater sense of confidence about the events to come.

Uriel watched him, eyes soft and sympathetic. It was a side to his brother that Gabriel was unaccustomed to seeing. Usually, Uriel was full of laughter and teasing. It was refreshing to be able to carry on a serious conversation and to share all of his secret fears—to let his guard down for once without constantly worrying about being a warrior.

"It will be okay," Uriel promised softly. "I can be there, if you'd like. And Lana. She will be able to help Mary with the delivery while I keep you calm."

Gabriel looked up at him and took a deep breath. "Really?"

Uriel nodded and smiled. "Of course. I wouldn't miss the birth of my niece for the world."

A whoosh of air left Gabriel's lungs, and he stepped forward and locked his arms around Uriel, closing his eyes.

Uriel smiled and hugged his brother back, squeezing tightly. "It will be okay," he repeated. "I promise you. Aubrey will be okay. Your daughter, Maxwell, will be fine. Better than fine. And you'll be there for it, and it'll be wonderful. Childbirth is a miracle, brother. Holding your small daughter in your arms will be the most amazing thing you have ever experienced."

He nodded and closed his eyes. "Thank you, Uriel."

His brother nodded and patted his cheek. "If you're truly worried about labor, I have an idea. I did it and it worked for Lana."

Gabriel looked up at him curiously. "What is it?"

He smiled. "There is a way to give her a piece of your grace. It calmed Lana a bit, and I believe it protected her throughout the hardest parts. It gave her the strength to carry on without the artificial drugs."

"My grace?"

He nodded. "Come with me and I'll show you."

Later when he would place the vial of his grace around Aubrey's neck as she lay sleeping, she would shift and murmur, a hand coming up to unconsciously hold the vial to her chest. She would let

out a sigh and then smile peacefully in a way that would help to ease Gabriel's anxieties about the remainder of her pregnancy.

2165

I SIT BESIDE BEAR after we've pushed our two cots together so we can sleep more comfortably. They're so tiny that they don't allow for much more room, but at least we can sleep close at night.

"How did your talk with Brie go?" he asks cautiously. I suppose I've been acting a little strange since I came back from Brie's room.

I take a deep breath and look up at him. "It was fine, I learned a lot about my family. Matty and I weren't related."

His eyes widen in surprise. "What?"

I chew my lip. "He and my dad sort of adopted mom and I, I guess. We haven't really gotten to that part yet. We've just established that my mother was in love with Gabriel way before she fell in love with Matty's dad."

He cautiously brushes a lock of hair from my face. "How are you feeling?"

I shrug. "I'm alright. Just homesick and missing Gran. I wish everything was back to normal, even if normal was shitty. I'm thankful you're here, though. I don't know what I'd do without you."

He pulls me into his lap. "Everything is going to be okay, Maxwell. And blood or not, your family will always be your family. They loved you with everything they had. There should be no doubt about that in your mind, and it should reassure you that blood really means nothing."

"Except for in this case, it actually means everything," I reply quietly, looking up at him. "This whole mess is partly because of me. This burden hanging over me is because of what I am. I'm not even human, Bear." I press my face into his shoulder. "And now I feel so fucking selfish for ever wishing I could have had things better."

He shakes his head and kisses the side of my face. "You're a strong girl. You've got Jamie, Brie, Vic, and I. Together we'll be just fine. We've got your back, no matter what."

I sigh shakily and lean my head on his shoulder. "What'd you do while I was with Brie?" I ask, changing the conversation so we won't linger on it.

He shrugs. "I hung out with Cami. She's pretty cool, you know? She lived at an orphan shelter for a while. Same one I was part of for a bit."

"Yeah, you seem to get along with her pretty well."

"I do. She's a sweet girl."

"That's nice." My stomach turns. I don't know where this jealousy is coming from. Bear and I have been together for years.

He frowns a little. "Yeah, it is."

"Hm."

"Is there a problem?"

I shake my head. "No. Definitely not."

"Yeah? Feels a little frigid in here."

I scowl up at him, suddenly angry. Who is he to get upset with me for being a little jealous? After all the stress I've been under lately, I have little control over how I feel. "Yeah? Maybe you should go get Cami to help warm you up."

"Yeah?"

"Yeah."

He scowls. "Guess you'd better get off my fucking lap then."

My eyes burn with anger. I stand quickly and leave, slamming the door behind me. Bear has *never* talked to me this way. I don't know if it's because of his resurrection or if he's just now showing his true colors. I don't understand what's going on.

I hang my head in my hands and slide down the wall, tugging at my hair.

The door opens after a few long minutes and Bear kneels in front of me. "Hey…"

I turn away from him. "Leave me alone."

He sighs and puts on his sorriest face. "Maxwell, look. I'm sorry. I need to work on being more sensitive. I know you've had a long, shitty day, and I shouldn't be trying to piss you off more."

I look up at him, completely exhausted. "I'm being jealous. I'm sorry." And I am. I need to work on letting go a little bit. It's not his fault I've had such a bad day. If he wants to be friends with Cami, I should be supportive of his decision. Sure she's pretty and smart. And he's obviously attracted to her, but I should believe in what he and I have before I get angry for something he isn't even doing.

He shakes his head and reaches for me. "Come here."

I swallow hard and slide my arms up around his neck. He picks me up easily and carries me back into our room. He lays down on the cot with me and strokes my hair until I am somehow able to fall asleep.

2148

URIEL SHOWED UP AS SOON AS GABRIEL CALLED HIM, distress fully present in his tone as he informed him that Aubrey was in labor, and that it was bad.

"What's wrong, Gabriel?" Was the first thing he said, eyes wide with concern as Lana slid behind them and into Aubrey's room.

"She can't do it, Uriel. She can't. The pain is too great," he moaned. His eyes were red-rimmed and filled with tears.

His brother took a deep breath and smiled. "Of course she feels pain. Childbirth is supposed to be the most painful experience a woman can go through. And with no drugs, it will be worse. You worry too much."

A particularly horrible scream came from the room, and Gabriel shrunk in on himself, hands going to his head. He moaned, shaking his head as he tugged at his messy hair. "It's all my fault!"

"She is going to be fine, brother. It's natural. Lana was the same way."

"It is *not* natural! The baby won't be human. There could be more complications!"

Uriel set his hands on his brother's shoulders and squeezed gently. "Let's go in. You'll see that it's okay."

"I can't," he muttered, looking down. He felt incredibly ill, like he might be sick. How could he have allowed Aubrey to get into this situation?

"Why is that?"

"Mary kicked me out." She'd gotten irritated with his panic, claiming it was no good for the baby or Aubrey.

"Angel!" The request came as a near scream from the next room.

Gabriel pushed past Uriel, white-faced. He burst into the room just in time to see Mary pull a tiny pink infant from Aubrey and wrap it in cloth. It wailed until it was placed in Aubrey's arms.

Mary glanced back at Gabriel and gave him a tired smile before looking back at her daughter and new grandchild. "Congratulations, you two. It's a girl."

Gabriel was hardly able to move. He stared at the bundle in Aubrey's arms, completely speechless.

Aubrey took a deep breath and looked up at him, eyes wide and warm, despite her exhaustion. They were wet with tears. "Well don't just stand there," she breathed, cracking a big smile. "Get over here and meet your daughter."

His knees felt weak, but he was somehow able to propel himself across the room and to her. He stared down at his little one and lowered slowly to his knees by the side of the bed.

Aubrey gave a tired giggle and looked down at the infant. "Say hello to our angel, Maxwell. I think we may have broken him."

Uriel barked a laugh from behind them, but it was unheard by Gabriel. He watched Maxwell, admiring her thick, blonde hair and her long lashes. He inhaled sharply when she yawned and stretched a beautiful pair of charcoal wings. Wetness trailed down his face and dripped from the end of his nose and he startled, reaching up to touch it and then looking down at his hand to examine the source of it.

Aubrey reached out and pushed her hand back through the front of his hair, making him look back up at her. "It's okay, Angel. You're crying, is all. It's normal."

"I'm not sad," he mumbled, throat thick.

She grinned. "I know. You're happy. You're really, really happy."

He nodded slowly and looked down at his daughter. "Would you like to hold her?"

"I might break her," he whispered, afraid to speak too loudly.

She smiled kindly. "You'll be just fine. You're her papa now. You'll be very careful with her."

He looked up at her, unsure for a moment, but willing to try. He reached for Maxwell and took her very carefully, cautiously holding her to his chest as he looked down at her. He gasped quietly, in awe of how tiny and beautiful she was. "Hello, Maxwell," he whispered. "I'm your father."

2165

I SIT ON MY BED, HOLDING MOM'S OLD JOURNAL IN MY HANDS. Brie let me take it to read on my own so I can process things alone with the promise that he'll be there to talk to and answer any questions I might have after reading. I stare at it unobtrusively, partly wishing I'd never seen the stupid thing before. I'm afraid to read more, but I'm even more afraid of not knowing what it says.

I finally open it slowly to the spot where I finished with Brie yesterday, and I read.

September 30, 2149

Dear Maxwell,

Your father just left. He came to stay for a couple of weeks in honor of your first birthday. You were very happy to see him. You babbled at him and held tight to his finger, and you seemed every bit in love with him as I am. He was only going to stay for a couple of days, but I think you changed his mind. He held you in his arms constantly, never tiring of your smile. He wouldn't lay you down at night until long after you'd fallen asleep nestled against his chest.

It made me smile.

But now I'm hurting again. Every time I see him, I am filled with so much hope and love that it hurts, and then he is taken from me so quickly and I am left with a broken heart. Your grandmother says I need to move on, I shouldn't wait for him. He can visit and see you and be my friend but I should find love elsewhere. It's impractical.

I know it's impractical, but that won't stop me from loving him. I wonder if I'll look back on these letters years from now and question my decisions. Right now, I don't think I will. But I do wonder.

You haven't done anything very spectacular yet, thankfully. And by that, I mean you haven't shown your powers too obviously. You have managed to keep yourself entertained at night by using some sort of telekinesis to move your mobile round and round and also to bring yourself small toys. It scared me a little at first, but your grandmother and I have both gotten used to it. Your father wiped your memory of your ability to do it, but he said it may happen again. He said it'll be hard to keep your powers under control until you're older because then, when he wipes it away, it will be more difficult for you to get it back.

He says maybe we should wait until you're a little older before we take you very many places. Just to be safe. I'm fine with that. I like having you to myself. Our world isn't the safest place. It's very corrupt and I'd like to shade you from that for as long as I possibly can.

I'll love you always, Maxwell.

Mommy

There's a picture of me tucked inside the pages. I'm wearing a birthday cone on top of my head. It doesn't feel real. I sigh and tuck it back into the pages, and then I read the next couple of letters. There isn't much that's new except for an accident involving a small fire I set in the bathroom. Gran caught it right away and put it out in time, but it scared my mom.

When I was two, I found a small bird dead on the ground and brought it back to life. Mom found me playing with it. There was blood stained on my new dress from a nosebleed. She panicked, but Gabriel visited and everything was fine.

I close the book and set it under my pillow. I rub at my eyes and then stand. I strap my gun to its holster and throw my hair up into a ponytail. Then I walk to the training room.

Upon initial examination, I see Jamie and Bear are in the room already with Cami and a few other people who I don't yet recognize. There are so many people down here that it's been difficult for me to remember names and faces.

Jamie and Cami are duking it out in one of the rings. Except it isn't really a fair fight. Jamie keeps knocking Cami down with little to no effort, and Cami isn't protecting herself at all. Jamie keeps shaking her head and pulling her back up.

Bear stands on the sidelines, watching with a smirk, arms folded in front of himself.

"Can you at least protect your face? Jesus, Cami." Jamie frowns, watching her. "It's like you're not even trying."

"I'm better with a gun."

Jamie shakes her head again and looks over at me. She smiles. "You're not skilled in fighting either, right?"

I shake my head. "I don't have any training, if that's what you mean." But I'm pretty sure I can hold my own, at least against Cami. She may act tough in her position as second in command of the raiders, but she's obviously not a threat in the ring.

Jamie smiles. "You take my place then. Keep your hands up near your head so that you can protect your face, alright? Don't be afraid to get physical. It's the only way either of you will learn."

I take a deep breath and nod. I take off my gun and boots and set them outside the ring and then let Jamie tape my knuckles before I step inside. I smile at Cami. "Go easy on me, okay?" I say softly. "I have no idea what I'm doing."

Cami laughs, twirling her long brown ponytail around her finger. "Yeah right. Have you seen my performance so far? I'm pathetic."

"We can get better together."

Jamie smiles and watches us. "No special powers, alright Max?"

I nod. "Of course," I promise, bringing my fists up protectively.

We circle each other. I take a nervous breath, watching Cami. I don't want to accidentally hurt her. It doesn't look hard to do. What if I don't know my own strength?

Cami's fist comes out of nowhere, catching me in the jaw. My head flies back, and I let out a surprised gasp, taking a quick step back and looking back at her with wide eyes. She grins and takes another quick shot, hitting me in the nose and bringing her knee up into my gut. Her fists begin to fly, pummeling into me until I'm on the ground, and then she kicks me hard in the ribs to add insult to injury.

I groan, curling in on myself. I get to my knees to pick myself up, but Cami is already on top of me again.

She sits on me and boxes my ears with both fists. I can't hear anymore, and my vision is swimming. I'm so disoriented that I'm pretty sure my fists are flying, but they're not making much contact. I gasp and shift, trying to buck her off. Cami leans down and sets her forearm over my throat, pressing down hard on my windpipe.

And now I'm legitimately afraid. I reach up, grabbing at Cami's arm. I kick her legs. I can't breathe, and everything hurts. It's getting harder and harder for me to think. I can maybe hear voices in the background yelling for Cami to get off, but they're getting fainter and fainter as the seconds tick by.

Cami leans down and sets her lip to my ear. "Guess I'm getting better at this, huh?" she breathes in a sugary sweet voice.

I can feel a warmth growing in my chest, getting hotter and hotter until it's almost burning. I grasp Cami's shoulders and then shove with every bit of strength I have left inside of me.

And then she's suddenly gone and Jamie is at my side, eyes wide. Her lips are moving but I can't hear a word she's saying. I gasp for air, an ugly rasping sound. I hold my throat, shaking and choking.

Jamie brushes my hair from my face. "Hey, you're okay. You're fine. That was a shitty trick."

Bear rips me up to my feet, furious. His face is red and scowling. "What the hell were you thinking, Maxwell? You could have *killed* her!" He shakes me with every furious word that spits from between his lips.

I frown and look over at where Cami lies, a good twenty feet away, in a heap against the wall, gasping out loud, ugly sobs as she holds her ribs.

Jamie scowls and sets her hand on Bear's arm. "What was *Maxwell* thinking? Are you joking? Cami was going to kill her!"

I look up at Bear, eyes wide with tears. I can't believe he's so angry with me for trying to protect myself. I jerk my arm back away from him. "Don't touch me that way. Don't you *ever* touch me that way."

Bear glares at me. "You're both crazy. You fight dirty." He shakes his head and then exits the ring, walking to Cami and picking her up carefully.

I stare after him in disbelief, a sick feeling pooling in my gut. I open my mouth to respond, but nothing comes out. I look up at Jamie instead, shaking my head. "I thought she was going to kill me."

Jamie nods and rubs my back. "You didn't do anything wrong. The objective was to fight, not to kill. You were supposed to be practicing. You were protecting yourself." She looks over at Cami. "What happened to being a hot mess in the ring, huh? You fucking liar."

Cami's lip quivers, and she curls into Bear, glaring at us both. "She's crazy! You both are! I'm going to—" she breaks off with a gasp, clutching her side and gritting her teeth. She glares at me, eyes murderous. "I'm going to tell everyone what you did. Nobody is going to follow a couple of psychopaths who unleash their weird angelic shit on unsuspecting people."

I pull away from Jamie, shaking my head. "I didn't mean to hurt you! But you should have stopped. You knew you'd already won. You knew I couldn't fight you anymore."

Cami lays her head on Bear's shoulder, face pale with effort and streaked with tears. "She's crazy. I think she broke my ribs. I need to see Ari."

Bear nods and carries her out, not even glancing back at me. It hurts.

My body quivers with effort to keep myself from crying. I swallow hard and lick a line of blood from my lower lip. Rub at my arm.

Jamie watches me, frowning. "That's enough for today, alright? Let's go relax a little."

I nod numbly and allow myself to be pulled from the ring, equal parts shaken and upset.

Bear doesn't come to bed.

2163

SOMETHING DIDN'T FEEL RIGHT. It was so quiet in the house that Maxwell was afraid to descend her ladder. She was so used to a bustling, busy house. Jamie and Uncle Vic had gone to the market earlier, and Matthew had been working in the garage, trying to finish repairs on a neighbor's hovercraft.

She climbed slowly down her ladder and looked around, ears straining for a noise.

And then she heard it: crashing in the garage.

She frowned deeply and hurried outside, not even bothering to close the door behind her. She ran into the garage and saw Matty standing over the Nova Dawn, smashing it into pieces with a sledgehammer as he yelled in an obvious fury.

Her eyes widened in shock, and she reached out, grabbing his arms as he swung back for another go at it. "Matty, what are you doing?! Stop!"

Matthew blinked and looked down at her, his entire body trembling. He looked down at the bike and his lower lip quivered. He dropped the hammer and took a step back, shaking his head.

"Matty, what's going on?" Maxwell's throat felt tight. She was afraid for him to answer. "Is Gran okay?"

His shoulders slumped, and he looked away. "Gran's fine," he muttered.

"Then what is it?"

He gestured toward the work table, and she wandered over to it, looking around. A letter lay crumpled at the edge. She picked it up and read.

```
The President of the United States,
        February 1, 2163


    To: Matthew D. Odyssey
    209 W. McKimmy St
    Davis, IL 61019

Greetings:
    You are hereby ordered for induction into the
Armed Forces of the United States, and to report at
Lobby of the U.S. Chicago Library, Chicago, IL. on
February 8, 2163 at 7:00 a.m. for forwarding to an
Armed Forces Induction Station.
    May God always be with you.
                        Franklin M. Shumaker
                        Member of Local Board
```

Maxwell felt as though she would be sick. She shook her head back and forth quickly, looking away from the paper. She looked to her brother. "No."

Matty laughed, high and hysterical. "Can't believe I'm even surprised. Of course I would be drafted. They've wanted to get rid of me since they offed mom and dad. They'll come after you next. You and Gran. Probably Vic and Jamie, too." He laughed again, turning his face up toward the ceiling. "Of course they will."

Maxwell dropped the letter and leaned forward, trying to catch her breath. Blood rushed in her ears and her vision swam. "Matty."

"It's over, Max."

She looked up at her brother and watched as a thousand different emotions passed over his features before he finally fell into sobs. She stepped forward and gathered him in her arms, holding him tight. His weight slumped against her, and she lowered him slowly to the

floor, clinging to him. Her hand slid into his hair, trying to give him as much comfort as she was able in her shocked state.

She looked up toward the grimy ceiling and whispered a prayer to a God she didn't believe in.

2165

"I STILL THINK YOU SHOULD WEAR CONTACTS," Jamie says, staring at me as I finish strapping my gun in its holster under my shirt and tying up my boots.

"I'm not going to wear them. They suck," I reply, scowling up at her. I look back down at my clothes, black from head to toe, and tug at them self-consciously.

Jamie frowns worriedly, obviously not pleased with my answer. "Your eyes are recognizable. If something goes wrong—"

"Nothing is going to go wrong, Jamie." I wish she would have more confidence. I'm not looking forward to going back topside. In fact, I'm nervous as all hell, but I'm not planning on screwing up. I want to go up, check out the scene, and get back as soon as possible.

"Your mother had the same eyes. They're already after your family. They're on the list. *You're* on the list. As soon as your Gran was listed as a rebel, your name was blackened. You're a goner if someone recognizes you."

"We won't get close enough for people to see them. I tried them on, and they're difficult to see out of." They were uncomfortable and clouded my vision. "I want to be as alert as possible, and they'll only be distracting."

Brie steps forward, watching us. "Just pull your hood up, Max. Keep as much of your face in shadow as possible. Same goes for you, Jamie. Please be careful."

I nod. "Of course."

"Bear won't be accompanying you?"

I shake my head, the corners of my mouth turning down. "Of course not. Bear doesn't want anything to do with me right now, and quite frankly, I could have done without the reminder. Thanks."

Jamie rolls her eyes and reaches around to pull my hood up. Her hands slide down the drawstrings of my hood, and she tugs lightly, a smile lighting up her face. Her forest green eyes shine with mischief. "Are you ready?" she asks, excitement bubbling up in her voice.

I shake my head at her. "You're ridiculous. I can't believe you're excited for this. You're... you're cra—"

Before I can finish my thought, Jamie grabs my face between her hands and presses her lips to mine. I can feel her soft skin and taste her cherry chapstick.

"—zy..." I breathe, staring at her dumbly as she pulls back, a satisfied smile upturning the corners of her pouty lips. She licks them and watches me expectantly.

I blink slowly and watch her, my mouth opening and closing like a stupid fish.

Brie snorts and shoves us both forward. "Okay. Enough. Go check out the upside. Make sure you're paying attention. I want to know everything you can find out about the angels and if there's been any news on nephilim. *Please* be careful."

"Aw, Brie, you're turning into a softie," Jamie teases, punching his shoulder gently.

He chuckles and watches her fondly, ruffling her hair and messing up her ponytail. She squeals in displeasure. "Yeah, well maybe I'm starting to get a little attached to the two of you. Only God knows why."

2153

HE WALKED SLOWLY UP TO THE HOUSE, staring as Aubrey worked in the front garden. She wore shorts and rubber boots that came nearly to her knees. A loose, white top blew around her midriff as she worked with the plants, arms and knees covered in dirt. She sang to herself, the sound sweet to his ears. He smiled and stopped walking when he got just behind her. He set his hands on his hips and watched her.

She turned around and looked up at him, and a huge smile broke out across her face. "Gabriel."

He grinned and knelt down into the dirt with her. He pulled her into his arms and pressed his mouth to hers.

Aubrey kissed him eagerly, dirty hands sliding up his neck and into his hair. She grinned against his mouth. "Missed you." She kissed him again.

He kissed her back, hands searching and feeling eagerly along the curves of her body.

"Daddy!"

They broke apart quickly, both gasping and smiling. Gabriel turned to his daughter and caught her as she jumped into his arms. She was five now. He'd only just missed her birthday. He held her close and closed his eyes, setting his face in her hair.

"Hello, my darling girl," he murmured, rubbing her back. "Did you miss me?"

"Yes! I always miss you," she replied, pulling back slightly to look at his face. She grinned and kissed his cheek. "Mommy said you would come soon."

"She's a very smart woman," he responded with a knowing nod. "She's right nearly all of the time."

Aubrey smiled and watched the exchange, setting her hands on her hips. "Guess we'll have to get something ready for daddy for supper, huh?" she asked Aubrey. "Something special."

Maxwell nodded, blonde curls bobbing. "Yes. Mommy and Gran are teachin' me how to cook. I'm gettin' pretty good, Gran says."

"Maxwell!"

They all turned to look as a little boy with dark hair and blue eyes came running into the yard. Gabriel thought he must be around Maxwell's age. Maybe a little older.

Max grinned. "Bear! Hey, come meet my daddy!"

The boy hurried over, smiling brightly. He had a light splattering of freckles over his nose. His shirt was on backward, and his jeans looked shabby. His shoes were tattered and worn. He took

Maxwell's hand when he was near enough and held it tightly, turning to look up at Gabriel.

Max smiled at him and then looked up at her dad. "This is my friend, Bear. He's a year older than me. He lives at the shelter down the street," she said knowledgeably. "His mommy and daddy are gone, so he comes over here to play a lot. Gran said we're gonna try to adopt him." She turned back to her friend. "This is my daddy. He's an angel, like me. Except more. And he's got wings. They're a lot bigger than mine."

The little boy called Bear looked up at Gabriel, eyes wide. "*Really?* That's so *cool!*"

Gabriel frowned and looked up at Aubrey, who shook her head quickly. "Maxwell, hush. Don't speak of such nonsense."

Bear frowned up at him. "She's telling the truth. I know because I've seen them."

Gabriel frowned deeply. "Who else have you shown, Maxwell?"

Max shook her head. "Nobody. Only Bear, on account of he's my best friend. He won't tell anyone, will you, Bear?"

The boy shook his head. "Cross my heart and hope to die."

Gabriel looked up at the sky, worry plain on his face. He knew what he would have to do now, and Aubrey wouldn't like it. He didn't like it, either. The idea of it caused his heart to seize in his chest and his blood to run cold.

2165

"SO, UM..." I CLEAR MY THROAT, looking over at Jamie. "What was that about?"

Jamie's cheeks flush, and she stares ahead, trudging on as we make our way into town. "What was what, Max?"

I take a deep breath, brushing my fingertips lightly over my bottom lip. "You kissed me."

"Oh, did I?" From the corner of my eye, I see her smirk.

I huff out a laugh, shaking my head. I look down at my feet and kick at some loose gravel. "You did."

"Hm."

"Yeah…" I look up at her. "So?"

"I guess I was just thinking we could die at any moment in time, and I wouldn't have had the opportunity. So I did it. Before the chance got away from me."

I rub the back of my neck and try not to smile. I can feel a ferocious heat in my cheeks. I shake my head.

"Was it okay?"

"I mean, yes, but—"

"Because if it wasn't, you should tell me. It felt like you liked it, but if it wasn't okay…" She shrugs. "I don't want to overstep my bounds."

"I'm still with Bear."

Jamie looks up at me, all traces of fun erasing from her face. "He's different now. He doesn't treat you with respect anymore, Maxwell. He's horrible to you. Sarcastic and unfaithful and cynical. He doesn't trust you to be able to take care of yourself. He doesn't treat our revolution with respect. If he can't stick beside you in this incredibly important moment of your life, he isn't worth it. You are more than he can handle."

"You know who he is."

"No. I know who he *was*."

"Something changed. When I brought him back, he just… He *is* different. Cami is a bad influence on him. She brings out the worst in him."

"Sometimes you have to learn to let people go, Max."

I laugh without humor, looking up at the sky. "Yeah. You say that like I haven't had to do that. I've lost everyone, Jamie."

Jamie stares at me. "And I haven't?"

I swallow hard, quieting.

Jamie shakes her head, stopping in her tracks. She turns to face me, halting me by stepping so close that we're breathing the same air. "Listen. I know the last few months, hell, the last few years, have been extremely hard on you. I know you've lost a lot of people you love. But you need to know you are *not* alone. You have Gabriel, Vic, the others. You have *me*, Maxwell. I'm standing right in front of you. I don't know how to make that any more obvious to you."

I stare up at her, filled with uncertainty. I know Jamie cares about me. She's done a lot for me through the years. She's always been more than a sister. But I'm scared.

I can see the warmth in her eyes. I swallow hard and watch her, eyes traveling over her ivory skin, her soft pink lips. I bite my own. I reach up and slide my hand over a loose strand of dark hair on Jamie's face and push it back behind her ear gently before I look down, clearing my throat again. I pull my hand away and then turn, walking quickly toward town.

Jamie sighs quietly behind me.

"What do you think we'll find?" I ask.

"I don't know. I haven't been here since Bear was shot."

"Yeah."

"We're just going to drop by the house and grab whatever's in the safe. Then you're going to wait outside while I go in to buy the medical supplies."

I wrinkle my nose "We're going to pay for them?"

"It causes less of a scene, you klepto."

"Yeah, because normal people go in and buy out the pharmacy. And anyway, I'm telling you, there's not much in that safe. We haven't had money in years."

"It'll be good to go back anyway. You'll get to grab your music, I won't have to listen to you whine about it anymore, and you can grab more clothes. I'm looking forward to having more than three outfits."

I look toward the sky. "I guess. I'm not looking forward to going back in there, though."

Jamie nods. "Yeah. I don't blame you. You could wait outside if you want."

"No. I just hope the bodies are gone."

We approached the house casually, trying not to draw any attention. There are soldiers everywhere, wandering up and down the streets with heavy guns in their hands and endless ammo attached to their persons.

"Keep your weapons hidden," Jamie murmurs softly from the corner of her mouth, glancing over at me.

"This is spooky." *Please don't let Gran be in that house.*

"I sure hope nobody recognizes you."

"You used to live here, too, you know."

"Yeah, but you kind of stand out."

"I don't."

"You do to angels. I'd bet anything. Your grace is kind of obvious. Maybe it's just because I'm around you often, but you're practically glowing."

"What are you talking about?"

"You are. You never learned to contain your grace because you had your memories taken young. Gabriel probably put a binding spell on it to be sure you would stay safe and hidden. You'll have to learn."

I exhale. "Okay."

"You can't see souls yet, can you?" Jamie asks, quiet so as not to be overheard.

I shake my head. "Souls? No. What do they look like?"

Jamie takes a deep breath and smiles, shaking her head. "It's hard to explain. It depends on the person. Yours is very bright. Could be confused with grace. Maybe that's part of the problem. It's nearly blinding. It's a shame Brie and Vic can't see them anymore. They'd be really impressed. But Cami's? It's dark and thick. And Bear. His was brighter, but it's dimmed. It's changing slowly. It was warm and whole, but now it's stringy, sticky. It's scary to watch. You won't like it."

My mouth feels dry. "That's my fault. For bringing him back. Putting him in danger in the first place."

"That's not true. You couldn't help it. I don't blame you for bringing him back."

I shake my head quietly and climb the stairs leading to the door. I open it up and peek inside. The bodies are gone but so is nearly everything else. Cupboards are hanging open, the table has been overturned. "Damn."

Jamie follows. "I guess I'm not very surprised, but this sucks. Think there'll be anything left?"

"I don't know. I suppose there could be." It's hard seeing my old home torn to pieces like this. A piece of broken china on the ground pulls at my heartstrings, and I close my eyes for a moment against the sting of tears. Another couple of deep breaths later, and I'm fine.

I look around again. The ladder to the attic has been pulled down. "The music will be gone. I bet the clothes, too. Hang on. I'll check." I hurry up the ladder and shake my head when I see the state of my room. Sure enough, my record player and all of my records are gone. My bed has been stripped, and so has my closet. The only things left are a few ripped up canvases, the art nearly unrecognizable.

I chew my lower lip as I walk back toward the hatch to climb back down but let out a gasp as my foot falls through the floorboards. I hit the ground hard without an ounce of grace. "Shit!"

"*Maxwell?*" Jamie's voice sounds worried from below.

"I'm fine! I tripped. I'm okay," I call from the opening. I pull my foot from the wreckage and look down at the mess. A sliver of color catches my eye, and I kneel beside the hole, pulling up a loose board. I slide my hand inside and feel around. My fingers close around a thickly bound book. I pull it up and cradle it in my hands carefully. It's black, bound in leather, and I wonder how much it had to have cost. I slide it into my backpack and then peek inside the hole. I pull out a sketchbook and bite my lip, trying to contain my eagerness. I push that into my bag as well. Anything that belonged to my mom is exciting. I'll have time to look through them later. I feel around beneath the floor, but there's nothing else. I zip up my bag and hurry back down the ladder.

Jamie looks hopeful. "Anything?"

I wrinkle my nose. "No. I mean, a couple of my mother's things under the floorboards, but nothing else. No clothes. Sorry."

"There was nothing left down here, either," Jamie sighs wistfully. "Oh well."

"I guess we'd better get back."

"Yeah, I guess."

"Wait!" I shoulder my bag and step back outside, looking toward the garage. The padlock hasn't been touched. My heart does a little leap in my chest and I drop to my knees besides the stairs, reaching under for the rock that hides the spare garage key. My left hand closes around the cool metal of the key and I stand quickly and hurry to the garage.

I unlock the padlock and toss it aside as I pull the door open with every ounce of strength I have. The door is normally heavy, but it's even worse without continuous use. It finally slides open and I hurry inside. My baby is sitting in her place of honor. She's a little beat up, but I know she'll run just fine. She always works when I need her to.

Jamie steps inside, smiling. She sighs. "I suppose we're bringing Nova back to the underground."

"We could use her, right? We can travel faster with her."

"She's not very inconspicuous."

"Sure she is." She's way smaller than the luxury crafts the big people are zooming around on. She won't make a big fuss. "Please? I don't even have to fly her. She can stay grounded."

Jamie laughs quietly. "You know I can't say no to you. It's so unfair."

I grin. "It's nice to know I have that effect on *somebody*."

"You're such a pain. Let's go before Brie starts to worry." Jamie pulls two helmets from a shelf on the garage and gestures for me to follow.

I wheel Nova out after Jamie and climb on. I take my helmet from her and pull it over my head. It smells like my garage, warm and familiar. It's comforting and warm and it makes me feel happy to be alive.

Jamie climbs on behind me. "Stay on the ground."

"Yes, ma'am."

She pulls her own helmet on and then wraps her arms around my middle. "Try not to get us killed."

"I'll do my best." I kick up the kickstand and flip the ignition. I start Nova up and then pick up my feet as we begin driving slowly down the road.

I survey my surroundings. The normally bustling streets are quieter, lonely. There are people scattered around, but everybody looks tired and miserable. Everything is dirty. Even the sky is gray.

"It's so different," I say. "I mean, it was shitty before, but—"

"Maxwell." Jamie's tone is urgent.

"What?"

Jamie points down the street.

An angel stands at the end of the street, surrounded by a group of people. His wings are folded neatly behind him and his arms are crossed over his chest. He looks familiar, but I can't make out his face from so far away. I stare, in awe of the grace that is pouring from him.

"We need to go!" Jamie's grip tightens on my shoulder.

I wet my lips, surveying the scene before me. The angel seems to be directing a group of soldiers. They have a line of people in front of them, all on their knees. "What are they doing?" I whisper.

A soldier steps forward, gun in hand. He points it at one of the people, an older man.

The angel is yelling, something about rebels and an inability to follow rules, the disrespect for God. And then the trigger is pulled, and the man slumps forward in a pool of his own blood.

Goosebumps rise along my arms. There's something familiar about a soldier who stands near the back of the line. The way he stands, slightly bowlegged with his head ducked. My eyes widen in shock. "Matthew... *Matty*!"

I'm speeding up before Jamie has a chance to scold me. It doesn't take long to get to the group. I cut Nova's engine just before we reach them and climb off, leaving Jamie. I throw my helmet to the ground as I hurtle the rest of the way to my brother.

"Matty!

Matthew's head raises, and he looks over at me, blue eyes wide in shock. I throw myself at him, nearly knocking him over.

"Oh my god. Maxwell?" He pulls me into a bear hug and squeezes tight.

"I thought you were gone! I thought you were dead!" My eyes filled with tears. "I was sure of it."

Matthew takes a deep breath, shaking his head. "I didn't think I would see you ever again, Maxwell. Jesus Christ, kid, you're here! You're okay! When I saw the house, I thought... Is Gran okay?"

"She's gone," I reply quietly, pulling back to look up at him. "I'm so sorry, Matty. I tried."

"Well, isn't this a heartwarming scene?"

The familiar voice sends shivers down my spine. I turn slowly, feeling the man's presence directly behind me. My eyes widen when I recognize Mr. Davis standing there, staring at me with something darker than mischief lighting up his hazel eyes. Except he isn't Mr. Davis. He has his face, but he's also an angel, wings folded in back of him. He towers over me now. I take a step back, bumping into Matthew.

"Oh my god," I murmur, staring up at him. I glance around in a wild panic. Jamie and my hoverbike are nowhere to be seen.

"It's Azazel, actually, but I'm flattered." He grins, showing a row of perfect white teeth. "And you, Maxwell. I've been looking all over for you. I thought maybe you were the one. But now I'm sure of it. Your grace is fighting against your vessel. It pulses brightly. I suppose now all the hours spent watching you and suffering through the drab vices of humanity have been worth it to find that you are, in fact, exactly who I thought you were. Oh, just wait until the big boss hears about this."

I shudder, staring up at him. "*You*. You're an angel? Really?" Panic makes me brave. "I didn't realize angels were so pervy."

Matty stiffens beside me, taking a step back and pulling me behind him.

Azazel's lips twist into a scowl. "Stand down, soldier."

Matthew shifts, standing tall in front of me.

Azazel's fist connects hard with Matthew's jaw, sending him to his knees.

I'm instantly furious. "Don't you *dare* hurt him!"

He laughs, throwing his head back. "I ought to smite him right here for disrespecting me. But I have other things in mind. Smiting is too quick. Some say it's supposed to be nearly painless. I'd rather not let things end so easily for your trashy family."

I step in front of Matthew as he spits blood into the dirt. The hair at the back of my neck stands on end, and I feel a warmth growing inside of me, threatening to spill.

Azazel laughs again, watching me. "You look so angry, little one. You'd better control yourself. Aren't you tired of losing people on account of your filthy genetic makeup?"

My hands clench into fists as my anger builds. It rises up into my throat. I tremble with it, trying hard to keep it all contained. I feel a sharp pain at my back for just a moment, and then a heaviness in my shoulders as my wings reveal themselves. "Keep talking, Azazel."

"You're an *angel*?" Matthew gasps from the ground, staring up at me.

"Hardly!" Azazel spits. "No. This abomination..." he says, looking around at the gathering of spectators, "is what we like to refer to as nephilim. Dangerous. Bent on destroying our world. Her kind is responsible for all the heartache, all the anger in the world. All the destruction and disease."

"You're a liar!" I yell, wings flaring out dangerously. A few soldiers are forced to duck to avoid being knocked over by the sudden movement. "It's the angels! The angels are responsible for the destruction! They've chosen to start the apocalypse. They're only pretending to weed out the so-called rebels and the sick. They're going to kill you all!" I look around at the crowd. *Where the hell is Jamie?*

"Ridiculous!" Azazel holds out a hand toward me in an effort to bring me down, but I'm too quick.

I grab his head in my hand, forcing as much energy into him as I can. He drops immediately to his knees, eyes squeezed tight in pain. "Ah!"

"Relatively painless, huh?" I growl, eyes narrowed in fury. "Were they right, Azazel?"

He gasps, trembling beneath my hand.

I focus more energy into him, feeling him burn hot beneath my fingertips. My eyes fill with heat, and then he bursts, covering me and the surrounding crowd in gore.

The silence following is broken a few short moments afterward when gunfire breaks out. I feel the impact as several bullets hit me at once, but they don't bring me to my knees. I stare at the soldiers who have guns on me, and I make a sweeping motion with my hand, knocking them all over. The crowd gasps and then breaks into a panic, running away.

I shake my head and grab Matty's hand, hauling him up to his feet. He's in a panic, staring at me in shock and shaking his head back and forth. His mouth opens and closes. Tears stain his bloody face. I look away, surveying my situation.

"Maxwell! Over here!" It's Jamie, face full of fear. She waves her arms wildly from where she's seated on Nova.

I hurry over, Matthew in tow. Nova sits two comfortably, but trying to force three people onto her is pushing it. I climb on behind Matthew anyway and close my eyes. "Jamie, drive!"

I hear Jamie let out a sob. She fumbles with the key, trying her damnedest to get it started. Her hands aren't working. I hear the gunfire and feel another peppering of bullets hit my back, knocking the air out of me.

"Jamie…"

"Fuck!" Finally, the engine roars to life. We begin speeding away, but not fast enough. The bullets just keep coming. I raise my wings and then wrap them around all of us. I close my eyes and dream of home.

A moment later, we're back in the tunnels. Jamie's still got her foot on the gas, so when we hit the ground, Nova bucks, spilling us all to the ground.

My wings flutter uselessly. I feel suddenly drained and my body burns with pain. I look down at the bullet wounds that pepper my body. Blood runs in rivulets down my torn clothing.

I look up, eyes connecting with a panicked Brie, who is running toward me.

"*Maxwell!*" I hear him yell before I collapse in a heap of blood and   feather

PART III

2153

"YOU'RE GOING TO DO *WHAT*?!" Aubrey yelled, backing quickly away.

Gabriel stared at her, his misery obvious. "I have no other choice, Aubrey."

"You *have* a choice! She won't tell anyone else. You heard her! Theodore won't say anything either!"

"You don't seem to understand the danger of our situation. Maxwell will be hunted down and slaughtered like an animal if word gets out that she even exists."

"No! No one will find out. You can't do it, Gabriel. You can't take away her memory!"

Gabriel squeezed his eyes shut tight, a lump in his throat. He slumped down onto the edge of the bed, holding the bridge of his nose. He let out a shaky breath. "I don't have a choice."

"There's always a choice!"

"I will not let my daughter be hunted. I will not let her die!" he yelled back at her, eyes wide with tears. "I will not! I will *not* let her be put in danger!"

"Who will you be to her if she doesn't even *know* who you are? How am I supposed to explain your visits?!"

His heart seized, and he set his hand over it, pulling at the fabric that covered it. Tears rolled down his face. "I will be an old acquaintance. A friend of the family," he responded almost inaudibly.

"No! She needs to know you! She needs to *know* you! *Please*, Gabriel! You'll be robbing her of half of who she is!"

He shook his head, a pressure building steadily in his chest. "I have no choice," he choked, putting his head down between his knees and pulling at his hair. "The boy...I'll need to wipe his memory, also."

Aubrey walked out, slamming the door with an angry sob. She left him alone to wallow in his misery.

He held his daughter longer than usual that night, long after she'd fallen asleep curled against his chest. He stroked her blonde hair and closed his eyes, laying his cheek against the top of her head. He kissed her hair and swallowed hard against tears.

She would never know him as her father again. He would be a stranger, a mere acquaintance of her family. She would never again look at him with the same wide smile and blue and brown eyes filled with warmth and excitement at seeing him for the first time in months. She would never again run impatiently to greet him, shouting his name with delight on her tongue. She would have no father.

He would be nothing to her.

But she would be safe, and that was the only thing keeping Gabriel from breaking down. He needed to keep her innocent. It was dangerous for her to share information, dangerous for her to know too much. It had to be done.

He set his fingers to her forehead and took her memory of him away. He took away memories of her first flight, a clumsy one, inside the house. He took away her first bike ride, which he had been present for. He took away memories of him holding her, kissing superficial wounds away with kindness, reading before bedtime, praying at the dinner table. He took away kisses and cuddles and laughter.

When he left her room later, tears drying on his cheeks, he saw Aubrey sitting quietly at the table. Her hands were folded in front of her, and her forehead rested against them. She couldn't even look at him.

"Is it done?" she asked quietly.

He took a shaky breath and nodded. "Yes."

"You should go."

Gabriel closed his eyes and swallowed hard past a lump in his throat. He nodded. He disappeared and didn't return for an entire year.

2165

"I'M SORRY! I'M *SORRY*! I PANICKED!"

"She could have *died*, Jamie!"

"I know. I know. I'm sorry. I failed! I—"

"Being sorry doesn't fix anything!"

I can hear Jamie and Brie fighting, but I'm unable to open my eyes. I hear Jamie begin to sob and leave the room. Now there's silence.

I think I can feel a hand on my head, stroking my hair back from my face. I feel lips brush against my forehead, but I know I must be dreaming again.

I'm dreaming.

It's a cloudy day, dreary. It matches the atmosphere perfectly. It's always gloomy on a hanging day.

But today is worse than usual.

Gran begs me to stay home, but I refuse. I want to be there for them, even though comfort will be impossible.

Today I'm going to lose my parents.

We trudge toward the gallows. Matty has his face turned down so I won't see his tears, but I know they're there. He holds my hand tightly. So does Gran. I squeeze both of their hands and walk with them.

I refuse to put my head down like Matty. I don't care if people see me crying. I'm going to lose Mom and Dad, and maybe if they see how much they've utterly destroyed my family, the people will feel sympathy and understand that the judge was wrong. The government is wrong. The whole system is fucked.

Bear stands on Matty's other side. He's staring forward in a daze. His face is pale, and his eyes are red-rimmed.

I can't even look at Gran.

When they bring my parents out, my mom looks like a queen. Her head is held high, and it makes me hold mine higher. She walks slowly, surely up to the noose. She looks around at the people, an eyebrow cocked. She understands that she's dying for a cause. She's okay with it. I am not.

My daddy isn't, either. He's sick over the edge of the platform, and he drags his feet. It makes the men angry as they try to shove him up beside mom. He's panicked. Matty makes a wounded noise beside me, and I squeeze his hand harder, enough to hurt.

The judge begins to read the sentencing. My stomach tightens.

They put the nooses around their necks, and I lose my cool entirely.

"*MOM*!" The scream rips loose from my lungs without thought.

Gran squeezes my hand, but I tear away from her, running toward the platform. "*MOMMY! DAD!*"

I need to hug them one more time. I need one more kiss from my mother. One last stroke of my hair. I need to tell them I love them.

The men surrounding my parents raise their guns toward me. I don't care. They won't kill me. At least, I don't think they will.

My mom is panicking, seeing the guns turned on me. She shakes her head and yells for me to go back to Gran, but I can't. She doesn't understand. I can't let them kill her without being able to hold her one last time. I haven't been able to touch her since she was arrested a month ago. I haven't been able to look on her face. She's been locked up with no visitors. I can't lose her. I can't. I can't.

A man steps in front of me, blocking me from the men with guns. He has cropped, reddish-brown hair and eyes the same color. He's got tears pouring down his cheeks. He looks scared to death. There's something familiar about him.

He catches me in his arms, and I scream, striking at his shoulders. I need to be let loose. I need to talk to them. I need to touch them. I need to hold them.

The man holds me tighter, setting his face against my hair. "I know, Maxwell. I know," he croaks, voice shaking. "I know."

"*NO!*" I scream. "*NO, PLEASE! MOM! MO—*" The platform disappears from beneath their feet, cutting off my shriek.

They don't die. At least not right away. Their feet jerk from underneath them, searching for ground that is no longer there. Their eyes bulge. Their faces turn purple. They die slowly. I scream, watching them. I scream and scream and scream until I no longer have a voice.

The man carries me away and sits with me in his lap, and I cling to him. We sob together, though I have no idea who he is. There is no comfort for either of us.

2154

WHEN HE FINALLY RETURNED, Gabriel was afraid. He wasn't looking forward to the coldness from Aubrey and the lack of recognition in his daughter's eyes. He stood in front of their door for a long time before he finally knocked.

The door opened a few moments later, and Aubrey stared out at him, eyes wide with shock. Her mouth opened and then closed. She held his gaze for a long time, and then she reached out and grabbed his shirt sleeve and pulled him into the house.

Gabriel stumbled along after her as she jerked him up to her room. She shut the hatch door when they were inside and pushed him against the wall, immediately attacking his lips with her own.

He stared at her, eyes wide for a moment before he melted against her, kissing her back with need. He tangled his hand in her hair and held her hip with his other, pressing close to her.

Aubrey pushed him to her bed and shoved him down to it, crawling over him. She tugged at his shirt. He pulled it off and tossed it away before he caught her face in his hands and kissed her again. She made love to him like she never had before, urgency in her every movement. He got the feeling she wanted to swallow him up, clip his wings, and keep him close. He wished she would.

He lay with her afterward and held her as she cried, her face pressed against his neck. She clung to him and tangled her fingers in the back of his hair. "Didn't think you'd come back, Angel," she mumbled after a long time, tears finally finished flowing. "Didn't think I'd see you again."

"I was afraid to return to you," he admitted quietly, looking at her. He pressed his forehead to hers and looked into her eyes. He stroked her cheek. "But I knew I would. You've got a hold of me, Aubrey. I belong to you. I'm supposed to belong to God, but it is to you that I will always return."

She nodded slowly and then pressed her mouth to his once, twice, and then rolled on top of him to rock him to his core once more.

It was she who consoled him later when Maxwell looked upon him with no recognition in her eyes and kept her distance, shy.

2165

I WAKE WITH A GASP, eyes flying open. I'm shivering but covered in sweat. I look around quickly, trying to figure out where I am.

I'm underground again. Brie is sitting beside me. He takes a deep breath and sets his hand over mine. "Maxwell?"

I stare up into his face. His russet eyes stare down at me, filled with concern.

My thoughts travel to the man who saved me at my parents' hanging. The same eyes stared at me then. I take a deep breath and sit up quickly, ignoring the pain that screams through my body. "I know you."

He frowns, watching me. "Maxwell."

"You were there. At the hanging."

"I was."

"Oh my god," I whisper, looking up toward the ceiling.

"I looked in your backpack," he murmurs, watching me cautiously. "Did you look through either of the books?"

I shake my head quietly, my mind spinning out of control.

"We should look together," he says quietly. "It will explain a lot."

I have a feeling I know what's going on, but I nod anyway.

"How do you feel?"

"I'm fine. I'm f—" I wince as I try to straighten. "I hurt. But I'm okay."

"You were shot many times. We counted eleven."

"Feels like twelve."

"Your body pushed the bullets out while you were unconscious. We stitched you up. It was a very close call, Maxwell. But your power decided to push through in your time of need, and—"

"Don't get me wrong, Brie, I want to know about all of this. But I want to look through the book now. Book first, talk later. Okay? Let's just get this over with."

He stares at me, long and hard, and nods. "I suppose it is for the best." He stands and grabs my backpack, and then he sits down on the bed beside me and pulls out the sketchbook and photo album.

He sets the album in my hands and takes a deep breath. "Open it up."

The first thing I see is Brie, staring up at me. His eyes are wide, startled, and his hair is longer and messy. He looks like a startled owl, but he's got the beginnings of a smile tugging at the corners of his mouth.

The next page is a photograph of my mother and Brie. She's kissing his cheek, and he's grinning, eyes closed. He looks like the happiest man alive. She looks on the verge of laughing, and I can almost hear it. She looks so free.

My eyes fill with tears and I shake my head, not looking up from the photograph.

I turn the page after a few minutes, my hand shaking. The pictures go on, my mother and Gabriel dancing, kissing. There are a few of Gabriel covered in paint. He's always staring at the camera with love in his eyes, as though the person behind it were the only one on Earth.

Then there's a picture of my mother, bright-eyed. Her belly is round, and I know it's me who she's carrying.

Brie makes a quiet noise beside me, and his hand goes to his mouth.

I swallow hard and turn the page.

Brie is holding me and looking down at me with wonder lighting up his face.

"How did I not see it before?" I whisper, staring down at the photograph. "How did I not know?"

Brie, or should I say, *Gabriel*, looks up at me, eyes red-rimmed. "I wanted to keep you safe. I didn't know how you would react if you knew who I was. I wanted to earn your trust first."

"Oh my god." My head spins. I set the book down and push my head between my knees, holding it in my clammy palms. "You said my father was dead. The angels killed him."

"It's a little more complicated than that," he replies quietly, watching me. "I fell from Heaven."

I open my eyes and raise my head, looking up at him. "Why?"

"To protect you."

"I don't understand."

"Uriel had a daughter. You know the story. Michael and the others wanted to punish us for spending so much time on Earth. Uriel gave up. He ripped out his grace. Fell to Earth. I did the same. I knew they were suspicious of me, especially after finding out he had a family and had been staying on Earth to specifically be with them. I couldn't let the same thing happen to you, Maxwell. I was terrified.

"And then I didn't come back. I was there at the hanging. I had to be. That was the last place I saw you. I wanted to take care of you, stay with you and your mother, even Stephen, but I couldn't because I didn't want them to track me to you. If they knew about you, you would have suffered the same, horrible fate. And after watching it happen to little Chloe, I—" Gabriel can't finish. He puts his hand to his mouth, eyes downcast. He shakes his head, trembling.

I reach out slowly, setting my hand on his arm.

Gabriel shakes, his normal posture unravelling as he falls apart. It's frightening. I've come to know this man as a soldier, strong and brave, but he's coming undone before my eyes. He lets out a sob, which is quickly followed by another, and then another. He slumps forward, hands reaching to tug at his hair, which has grown considerably in the past couple months.

I swallow hard and shake my head once before pulling him into my arms. I close my eyes as he sets his face in my shoulder and cries. I rub his back because I don't know what else to do.

"Gabriel…" I murmur softly.

"I'm so sorry," he moans quietly, shaking his head. "I wanted to take care of you and Aubrey. I wanted to stay. But I was too afraid to disobey. You learned too much. I had to take away your memories. I had to leave. I was a stranger. You didn't remember me. It was so hard, Maxwell. She was so angry. She told me to leave, but I was desperate.

"I should never have come to Earth in the first place. But you don't understand. For years, I lived in Heaven, never questioning, never disobeying. And then I came here. I came and I met her and everything changed. *Everything*. I didn't know what it was to love. I didn't understand my Father's obsession with humanity. I didn't understand what it *was* to be human, to love and to hate and to have free will. To question and to hope and dream and aspire. I was a soldier. A messenger.

"But she opened my eyes and she made me happy and she taught me about art and music and how to laugh. She scared the hell out of me, Maxwell. Your mother was light. She was fire. She burned me up. Made it impossible for me to breathe. Everything I had been missing before, she made possible. She was everything to me."

He looks up at me, eyes red-rimmed. "She made me want to stay. She made me want to be different. But I was so scared of disobeying that I went back to Heaven. I couldn't stand the distance for long, so I came back down. She was pregnant with you. I stayed to see you born. It was the most extraordinary thing I have ever witnessed. I held you in my arms, and I couldn't speak. I was overwhelmed. I was in *love*. I knew there could be nothing else in the world more perfect than you.

"You grew, and I visited, and you were always so happy to see me. Always thrilled. I knew it was stressful for your mother to have to wait around, raising you alone. She had Mary's help, of course, but Mary had other responsibilities, too. And she had so many dreams. She wanted to expose what was going on behind closed doors in the government. She wanted to return hope and justice to her people.

"One day you were with Theodore and you mentioned your wings and he said you'd shown him and I knew everything had been too good to last. I took your memory. If anyone had seen or found who you were, they'd have taken you from me. They'd have killed you and Aubrey, and probably Mary. After that, your mother wouldn't speak to me. We were no longer together. I came back once, but she grew tired of waiting. Tired of my inexplicable need to return to Heaven at Michael's beck and call.

"She met Stephen and fell in love. She gave you a family with him and his son. You were happy and oblivious to how different you were. She made you safe. I visited once more in secret so I could rework your memory. You were still young. I knew Stephen and Matty would never give any of our secrets away, so I left them alone. I never wanted to take your childhood away from you."

"You kept me safe."

He swallows and watches me, doubt in his eyes. "I attempted…"

"You succeeded. I'm still here, aren't I? Even after everything that's happened."

"There have been many other casualties, though. All because of me. Mary, for instance. Theodore. Aubrey is gone, too."

"That was not your fault," I reply, taking his hand. "As much as I hate to think about it, she made her decision. She knew the consequences, but she sacrificed herself willingly for change. That's who she was."

He wets his lips and looks down at the ground. "There have been many unfair trials and tribulations placed on your shoulders, Maxwell, because of what you are. Because of who you are. I'm so sorry. So many people rely on you, and it's not your fault. I have been very hard on you. I haven't made your journey any easier."

"I appreciate the pushing. I need it. I know. I forget about the bigger picture sometimes. I need to be reminded that I'm not the center of the universe, you know? All that stuff with Bear and Gran—" I take a deep breath and shake my head. "I know I've been really selfish. Everyone here has lost somebody they love. And I know Gran is in a better place. And Bear is a distraction. He isn't the same; it's true. There's something dark inside of him. And maybe it's something I won't be able to fix."

He looks up at me, solemn. "It's okay to grieve for those you've lost as long as you don't lose the fire in your heart to be able to rebuild and fight for redemption."

I nod quickly. "Oh, it's there." I set my free hand to my chest. "I'm not letting those bastards get away with what they've done to us."

"You get that from your mother." Gabriel nods. He takes a deep breath. "She was a firecracker, and you're the same as she was. Just make sure, *promise me,* you won't lose track of who you are while you fight toward your goals. Take advantage of the friendships you have. Jamie, for instance. She adores you, and she's an excellent influence. Although I'm not very pleased with what happened while you were out earlier. She abandoned you. She froze up in fear."

"Don't be angry with her. She's been very good to me. And it would have been even more dangerous had she exposed herself. He would have known she was nephilim, too."

"Yeah, and about him... Maxwell, how did you know Azazel?"

I smooth my hand over the photo album in my lap. "After mom and dad died, Gran had to take in boarders. Financially, we were pretty much screwed. We were fined just about everything we had. I'm surprised they didn't just kill all of us, to be honest. But he came as one of her boarders. He said his name was Mr. Davis. He asked for favors. Told me he'd go to the police about Gran allowing too many boarders, about harboring rebels. He knew about Jamie. That she was part of the rebellion. I didn't want her to get in trouble."

Gabriel's jaw clenches, and he looks down, cheeks flushing in anger. He holds my hand tighter. "I should have been there."

I chew my lip. "It happened and it's over and he's dead."

"He was an angel, though. You're sure? Jamie told me he was, but Azazel fell years ago. It was a punishment for teaching humans about deception and treachery. He encouraged warfare and disturbed the peace."

"He was definitely an angel."

"He must have regained his grace in exchange for looking for you." Gabriel shakes his head. "Michael must have passed judgment in his favor." He pauses, looking up at me. "You smote an angel."

"He hit Matty. He was going to kill him. And he hurt me."

"You misunderstand. I'm not scolding you; I'm actually impressed. I'm proud."

"It was really intense. It felt like I was burning up on the inside."

"Your grace is pushing through. Your wings have shown themselves."

I nod, pushing one of them forward so I can examine it. The black feathers are soft beneath my fingertips. I take a deep breath and look up at my father. "What color are your wings?"

Gabriel straightens and allows his wings to appear. They're black, just like mine. I smile a little, looking at them. "I'm glad they look like yours."

He ducks his head for a moment and then meets my eyes, a small smile on his face. He lets his wings disappear. "Me, too."

I watch him for a moment longer before reaching for him. He pulls me into a tight hug and sets his face in my hair, letting out a sigh.

"I wish I could protect you," he says quietly, holding me and stroking a hand through my hair. "I wish I had the power I once did. I fear for you every day."

I think we're going to be okay," I reply quietly. "I really do. I feel a change coming. I feel hope. For the first time in forever."

"They know who you are now. I'm sure Michael is aware of what happened. They know you're mine. All of those people saw."

"Yes, and all of them saw what he was doing. He had a line of rebels and he was making soldiers shoot them one by one. People aren't blind. They understand right from wrong."

"Michael is very persuasive," Gabriel murmurs. "I'm worried." He looks down at his lap and then over toward the door. "There are a couple of people who are really looking forward to talking to you, now that you're awake. Shall I let them in?"

"Yes, please."

He gives me a tiny smile and pats my knee before standing and heading for the door.

"Gabriel?"

He stops. "Yes, Maxwell?"

"I'm really happy you're my father," I say softly, sincere.

He swallows hard and nods, watching me. "Yeah, me, too. I love you, Maxwell." He smiles sadly before he opens the door, stepping out as Jamie and Matty rush in.

2154

"I'M SO EXCITED TO SEE LANA AND URIEL! Maxwell will have a great time with Chloe, too. She likes spending time with older kids," Aubrey said, looking up at Gabriel as they walked toward Lana and Uriel's home. "It's really great that he got to come down to visit the same time as you did."

"Yes," Gabriel nodded slowly. "Quite a coincidence." He hated himself for lying. He'd never told Aubrey that Uriel had defied their brother's orders and stayed on Earth for years to spend time with his wife and child. He didn't know exactly how she would take the news, but he expected she would be furious.

It was a source of constant guilt to him, but although his short trips to Earth were the best parts of his life, he was unable to refuse Michael for as long as Uriel was. He wished he could.

Lana and Uriel greeted them excitedly, arms wide for hugs. Uriel scooped Maxwell into a big hug and laughed when she squirmed away from a sloppy kiss on her cheek. She took off as soon as Chloe showed up, happy to be spending time with an older girl.

It was at the dinner table later that evening when everything unraveled.

Lana passed the mashed potatoes toward Aubrey, who took them gratefully. She shot her a smile and then looked toward Uriel. "It's great that you got to come down to visit at the same time as Gabriel."

Lana looked over at her, obviously taken aback. "What?"

Aubrey frowned. "Excuse me?"

"Uriel never left. He's been here for years." Lana smiled confusedly at her.

Aubrey stared at her and then looked over at Uriel, who was guiltily studying his mashed potatoes. Her attention turned to Gabriel. "I thought you said you'd been pulled up to Heaven."

"I was requested by Michael. I could not disobey."

"Okay. Was Uriel requested?"

"Yes."

"But he didn't return."

"No."

"Oh."

His stomach sank as he stared at her. She'd wiped her face free of emotion and was busy cutting the steak on her plate, careful to avoid his gaze. "Aubrey."

"You said you weren't given a choice."

"I wasn't—"

"But Uriel disobeyed. And he's fine. He stayed with his family. Watched his daughter grow up."

"Aubrey, you don't understand."

"You're right. I don't." She stood, pushing her plate away. She glanced over at Uriel and Lana and didn't even bother forcing a smile. "Thank you for dinner, but I think I'd better leave."

Lana stood. "We could keep Maxwell for the night?"

"Yes. That would be great. Thank you." Aubrey left, slamming the door behind her.

Gabriel stood and followed her quickly. "Aubrey, stop." A tickle of warm summer breeze met him as he reached for her shoulder. Crickets chirped peacefully in the grass and lightning bugs created their own universe of shooting stars in the night sky.

Aubrey jerked quickly away from him. "Don't touch me! Don't you ever touch me again, Gabriel!"

He swallowed hard, shaking his head. "I didn't have a choice."

"You *never* have a choice! You let everybody do the thinking for you! You don't give a damn about our family! You never have! You let everyone push you around, and you never make a decision for yourself because you're so fucking scared of making a mistake! Well guess what? I'm *done*!"

"Aubrey."

"No! You could have been here! Do you know how hard it's been for me to raise her on my own? She's growing up without a father, Gabriel!"

"She would have been growing up without knowing me anyway, Aubrey. It's dangerous for her to know my true identity, don't you remember?"

"Maybe if you'd been here like Uriel you would have been able to teach her how to keep it a secret. She could have known you! Oh God, she could have had a regular, unbroken family. She could have kept her memories, but you didn't care enough to stick around!"

"I *do* care, Aubrey!" Gabriel yelled, fury causing him to tremble. "I *wanted* to stay!"

"Not badly enough! We've never been enough for you!" Aubrey was paler than usual, shivering. Her eyes were bloodshot and filled with tears. "I have been waiting and waiting and *waiting* for you! I've become someone I never wanted to be! I never wanted to rely on another person. I'm so *stupid*! I had dreams—I *have* dreams! I'm supposed to be out there making a difference, not sitting around here waiting for you to come back!"

"I wanted to stay," Gabriel repeated, his voice shaking. His hands balled into fists. "I would have given anything to stay."

"You always say that. Always. '*I serve God, Aubrey... I'm supposed to belong to God, Aubrey, but it is to you that I will always return,*'" she mocked furiously, shaking her head. "You're a liar!"

"I am not a liar!" He yelled back at her. "I am many things! *Many* things, but *not* a liar! A coward, insensitive, a follower... Not a liar!"

"You *are*, Angel! You said you didn't have a choice!"

"My name is *Gabriel*!"

Aubrey flinched back at the volume of his voice. "I want you to leave, Angel. And this time, I don't want you to come back. I have things to be doing with my life. And you're right, you're not in Maxwell's life, so we won't be needing you around here anymore. I'm tired and I can't wait for you."

"Aubrey..." Gabriel's eyes stung with tears. He was unable to believe what he was hearing.

"I have dreams, and you aren't part of them anymore. I'm glad to have met you because I have an amazing little girl, but that's the extent of it. You need to leave," she muttered, looking away.

His shoulders slumped, and he wrapped his arms around himself, feeling his heart shattering in his chest. He could hardly breathe, frozen to the spot.

She walked away, leaving him in the warm summer air to fall apart alone.

2165

"I'M SO SORRY, MAX! I froze! I was so scared!" Jamie's dark eyes are wide with tears.

I shake my head, reaching for her. "Get over here."

She complies, hurrying over and launching herself at me. I catch her and hug her tight, closing my eyes. She hiccups on a sob and buries her face against my shoulder. "I was so afraid. I've been training for something like this for ages, but you could have died and it would have been all my fault!"

I stroke my fingers through her hair, holding her close. "No. It was better for you not to reveal yourself. It's dangerous enough that they know who I am now. And I'm the one who ran right into trouble, not you. It was my fault."

I take her face in my hand and set my forehead to hers, looking into her eyes. "Everything is okay. I promise."

She lets out a shaky breath, setting her hand to my face. She nods. "Okay. Okay. You were amazing, Max. And your wings are beautiful. They're perfect."

My face burns. I hold her as I look over at Matty. He's examining the album that I looked through with Gabriel, a frown on his face. He looks up at me, catching my gaze.

I'm a little stunned by how different Matty looks. It hasn't been long since he was drafted, but his face is so much older and tired than I've ever seen it before. His hair is buzzed short, his face clear of any stubble. His eyes look weary, but they're still the pretty indigo color that I remember.

"I'm sorry," he says softly.

"I understand why you couldn't say anything."

"You're still my bratty kid sister."

"I know."

He nods slowly, and then sets the book down, closing it. "I'm real glad you're okay. I was so afraid."

I nod. "I was afraid for *you*, too. I was sure I'd never see you again. When you left... I've never seen Gran so sad. She didn't think we'd see you again, either. She thought for sure they'd put you in a bad situation where you wouldn't be able to make it out. Because of who you are."

"Our family does have a reputation." Matty shakes his head, letting out a breathy laugh. "Turns out its grown even more after that little performance."

I scowl, not understanding how he can make a joke out of what just happened. "It was not a performance, Matty. You have no idea what he's done to me. And he wanted to kill you. Us."

"I know. I know." Matthew frowns, looking down. "I'm sorry. God, it's been so long since I've thought of you as an angel."

"*Nephilim*," I correct, watching him. "That's what I am." I nod toward Jamie. "Jamie, too. Daughter of Michael."

"I kind of figured."

"Gabriel is my father. That man who was just in here."

Matty nods. "We met years ago."

Jamie takes a deep breath and smiles. "You finally know."

"I don't know how I didn't before. It was obvious. I've been so blind."

Jamie smiles and pats my knee. "Just distracted. Are you happy about it?"

"I am. He's been difficult to be around, but I understand why now. We looked through photos together. The way he looked at me when I was young, the way he spoke to me about my mother today... I know he loves me. He wanted to be in my life, but he wanted to protect me more."

She nods, watching me. "That's very lucky. Most angels aren't so noble. Michael, for instance, would be happy to kill me."

"Does he know you exist?"

She shrugs. "I don't know. I can't imagine I would have lived for this long if he suspected I actually survived."

I take her hand and squeeze it, frowning.

Matty glances down at our hands. "So, where is Ted?"

Jamie glances over at Matty and gives him a tiny shake of her head in an attempt to ward off the conversation, but I shrug. "He doesn't want anything to do with me lately. He died. I brought him back. He hasn't been the—"

"I'm sorry, you *what*?" Matthew sits up straighter in his chair, leaning toward me like he's just seen a ghost.

"Well, I'm a necromancer, too. I'll have to fill you in on the details. Besides being a messenger, Gabriel is also an angel of death, so I've been passed on some of his power."

"Jesus Christ," Matthew murmurs, shaking his head. "But Ted... that asshole been giving you problems? I'll take care of him, Maxwell, I swear to God."

"Don't worry about it, okay? Please. It is what it is. I'm beginning to accept that."

He sighs. "I suppose you can take care of yourself better than I can, anyway. You did kind of save both of our lives. Killed an angel right in front of everyone."

"Can we maybe not talk about it anymore?"

"Yeah. Yeah, sorry."

Jamie presses her lips to the side of my face. "Are you hungry? You must be. You were drained of most of your energy. You need to build it back up."

"I'm not really—"

"Maxwell."

"Okay, okay."

2163

"MAXWELL?"

She didn't respond, curled up on her side to face the wall. It was covered in paint splatters and blood. Afternoon light trickled in through the window and highlighted the dust floating around the room.

Jamie stared at her friend, biting her lip. She knew just how hard Maxwell was taking Matty's draft. He'd left the day before, and Maxwell hadn't spoken to anyone since. She'd refused to allow anyone to sleep with her, to help ease the pain. It was like she wanted to soak in it. She was punishing herself.

Jamie swallowed hard, looking toward the blood on the walls. There were a few fist-sized holes in the plaster. She took a deep breath and looked around, grabbing a bottle of water and an old sheet. She sat beside Maxwell on the bed and reached out, brushing a lock of tangled hair from her face.

Max didn't flinch. She stared forward, eyes wide and empty.

Jamie ripped the sheet into strips and wet a few. She took Max's right hand and began carefully cleaning the area around her wounded fist. When she finished, she wrapped it in a clean cloth and moved on to her next hand.

"It's okay to grieve," she finally said, looking down at her friend. "Don't let anyone tell you it's not. But don't hurt yourself anymore. Please."

Maxwell curled in on herself more, turning her face into her pillow. "Jamie...?"

"Yeah?"

"What happened to you?"

Jamie swallowed hard and watched her friend, pulling one of her injured fists to her mouth to press a healing kiss to it. "I don't understand."

"When Uncle Vic brought you here, you were hurt. What happened?" Maxwell's voice sounded strangely hollow.

"It's not a story you want to hear, Max."

"I do."

"It's not a story I want to tell."

Maxwell sighed and looked up at her.

Jamie held her gaze for a moment and then let out a big sigh, shaking her head. "It's not going to make either of us feel any better, but okay." She set the remaining cloths on the ground with the water bottle and watched Maxwell, reaching out and stroking her hair.

"I guess it would help if you knew what happened to my family. My mom died when I was born. I was adopted by a woman named Ana. She raised me as her own and taught me about the unfairness of the world and told me that someday I was going to help change it all. She was wonderful…

"Ana was a nurse. She worked at a local hospital. It was the perfect job for her. She was always bringing home animals that were injured and nursing them back to health. She would stop on the street when we were out if she saw someone who looked like they were in pain, and she would give them advice or take them home and give them a check-up. We were poor, but we were happy. I was doing well in school and things were pretty good.

"One night, we were watching a movie. She had the night off. We fell asleep on the couch. But then these two people broke in. She told me to hide." Jamie shook her head, eyes glazing over as she remembered the night that changed everything.

2160

JAMIE LAY NESTLED AGAINST HER ADOPTIVE MOTHER. The two had fallen asleep on the couch during a movie on one of Ana's rare nights off. They were extraordinarily close.

When Ana had originally taken Jamie in, she hadn't expected to fall quite as in love with her as she had. But the little girl with the enormous green eyes had captured her heart and allowed her to experience motherhood, something she never could have imagined taking part in. Now, thirteen years after she'd taken her in as a newborn, Ana couldn't fathom a life without her.

She'd been there for her during her first steps, her first word, her first instance of magical use. Every "first" was special, and Ana found herself documenting every single moment of it.

Around midnight, a crash, like a window breaking, reverberated around the tiny apartment they shared. Both girls woke, looking around quickly. Ana was instantly on edge, aware of the danger that her adopted daughter was always in.

She turned her eyes to Jamie. "*Hide,*" she whispered, brown eyes flashing in panic.

Jamie ran to the closet and closed herself inside obediently, instantly terrified. She knew the danger that she could be in. Ana had never hidden it from her. It would have been a disservice.

A man and a woman came crashing into the living room, instantly yelling at Ana. She recognized them as her siblings, Kushiel and Adriel.

Kushiel shoved her back against the wall. "Where is the girl?" he spat, pinning by her throat.

Ana stared up at him, eyes wide. "I don't know what you're talking about, brother. But this seems a rather rude greeting after so many years of no contact."

Kushiel sneered and shoved her to her knees while Adriel stepped forward and placed her hand on Ana's forehead, forcing a surge of pain through her body.

Ana shuddered, mouth opening in a scream. Her head snapped back and her back arched. Her body nearly left the floor.

Adriel smirked and removed her hand from her sister's forehead. "I suggest you cooperate. Michael has made his orders clear. You know what it means to disobey. Now where is the girl?"

Ana shook her head, tears rolling down her cheeks. "I have no idea what you're talking about, Adriel. I'm sorry."

Her sister scowled and set her hand back to Ana's forehead, sending another surge of pain through her sister's body.

Ana's screaming picked up, louder and more agonizing than before.

Kushiel shook his head and set his hand on Adriel's shoulder. "Step back, sister. It's clear we won't receive her cooperation. We don't need to wake the entire city with her shrieking."

Adriel scowled but stepped back obediently.

Kushiel stared down at Ana. "We will find her. Your death is in vain."

Ana tipped her chin up in defiance, glaring up at him. "There will be consequences for your actions. Perhaps Lucifer would like some company in hell."

He raised a machete in the air and brought it down across his sister's neck. Her blood splattered her siblings and the surrounding area as her head slid away from her body and landed to the ground with a grotesque thud.

For a moment, there was complete silence.

Kushiel sighed and tilted his head to the side, staring at his sister's body. "What a waste."

Adriel snorted and rolled her eyes. "Find the girl."

Kushiel turned, surveying the surrounding apartment. His gaze landed on a closet in the hallway, and he walked to it with a smirk. He stood in front of it silently for a moment before he gripped the knob and pulled it open quickly.

Jamie had been ready. She'd heard Kushiel coming and had scrambled for something to defend herself. She'd found Ana's toolbox in the bottom of the closet and grabbed a hammer. When the closet door opened and he stared down at her, she flew at him, panicking and putting the hammer right through his skull.

Kushiel blinked slowly, and then he dropped to the ground. He pulled the hammer from his head and glared at it for a moment before tossing it aside. He growled and reached for Jamie again.

She stared up at him, eyes filling with light, and then she bounced forward, pressing her hands to his chest.

He gasped and tipped his head up toward the ceiling. He blinked stupidly, and then he exploded.

2163

MAXWELL SHUDDERED AND SAT UP, taking Jamie's hand in her own. She squeezed it tightly. "Jamie—"

Jamie didn't respond to her touch. She stared at her knees, eyes clouded by tears. "He died when I hit him with the hammer... He had a machete; it was covered in Ana's blood. I took it. The woman came when she heard me kill her friend. I swung, but I missed. She hit me pretty hard. I hit the ground, and she stepped on my stomach. I thought I was going to die. She grabbed my hair and pulled me part way off the floor and reached for her knife. I could barely reach the machete, but I got it. I swung again. And this time I didn't miss."

She turned her gaze toward Maxwell. "I don't remember very much after that. I went to the phone. Called Vic. He was good friends with Ana. They worked together. I think there might have been something going on between them. He was over for dinner at least once a week. I didn't know who else to call."

"He came right away. I guess when he found me, I was sitting in a pool of Ana's blood, holding her head. I wouldn't let him take me away at first. But I was getting sleepy. I hit my head pretty hard, and I'd lost a lot of blood. I passed out some time after he picked me up. And then when I opened my eyes again, you were the first person I saw." Jamie squeezed Maxwell's hand and allowed her to take her into her arms. She lay her face against the other girl's neck and breathed her in. "And that's it, I guess. I never got to go back and get any of mine or Ana's things. I never got to see her again."

Jamie slid her arms around Maxwell and set her face in her hair instead, kissing the top of her head. She rubbed her back in slow circles. "I know you're sad about Matty. I've felt that kind of loss. But I'm here for you. Gran and Bear and Vic are here for you. We're gonna get through it together, okay?"

A nod against her shoulder told Jamie that her friend understood, and she sighed, closing her eyes. "Now let's try to get some rest. It's been a long day and I'm tired."

Maxwell nodded and allowed Jamie's heartbeat to slowly lull her to sleep.

2165

"I JUST DON'T UNDERSTAND," I murmur, staring at the wall as Jamie brushes through my tangled hair and begins to braid.

"I know."

I look down at my knees and sigh. I can tell the difference in Bear is growing. He's barely looked at me over the past week. He hasn't asked about my wings or commented on my near death experience. He spends most of his time with Cami, doesn't share a room with me anymore, and I have a sneaking suspicion he's been keeping her warm at night, but I don't dare voice my thoughts aloud.

"Gabriel is right, though, you know?" Jamie says softly. "He's not the person you knew before. It's not your fault. The man you knew died loving you. You can't help what happens now."

"I try so hard to let him go."

"I know."

Jamie abandons the braid, leaning down and wrapping her arms around me from behind instead. She nuzzles the side of her face to mine and plants a long line of kisses down my jaw. "Maxwell," she whispers.

I turn from where I was sitting on the floor and get on my knees, turning to face her. I shove my face against her lap and make an exasperated noise.

Jamie closes her eyes and slides an arm around me, rubbing my back with one hand and stroking my hair with her other. She holds me close and presses her lips to the top of my head, trying to pacify me.

A knock comes at the door and I look up. "Who is it?"

"It's Bear," comes the reply, soft and a little unsure.

My head shoots up, and I look toward the door, wiping my face quickly. "Come in!" I call, before Jamie has the chance to answer.

The door opens slowly, and Bear steps in, arms hanging at his sides. He watches the two of us for a minute before clearing his throat. "Do you think maybe we could talk?" he asks softly, nodding toward me.

I sit up quickly and nod. "Yeah, sure."

"Alone?"

I nod again and look back up at Jamie pointedly. "I'll see you in a little while, okay?"

Jamie chews her lip and then nods. "Call if you need anything, alright?"

I kiss her cheek. "I will. Thanks."

She nods and watches me for another long moment before standing. She brushes a lock of hair behind my right ear and then walks past Bear and out of the room.

I look up at Bear and take a deep breath. It's been so long since we actually talked, so long since he's even looked at me. It's a relief that he wants to spend time with me.

"Can I sit by you?"

I nod quickly. "Of course."

He nods and walks to me and sits slowly, the cot squeaking as it moves to accommodate his weight. "I owe you an apology."

I take a deep breath and shake my head. "It's okay."

"No. I do. I don't know what's happening to me…" he admits quietly. "Sometimes I'm in control but sometimes it's like I don't know who I am anymore. I forget who I used to be. And it's scaring the hell out of me."

I frown, watching him. Hearing him say it is both a relief and also very scary. If it's something he can't help, it has the potential to get worse.

He swallows hard. "I'm afraid I'm going to be a danger to you. And I don't want to be. I think the only way to fix it will be for me to leave."

"Bear, no. You know you can't leave."

He shakes his head. "I think it's the only way. It makes sense. I won't be near you, so I won't need to worry about controlling myself as much if I slip up. It'll be a protection to you."

My eyes narrow. "Bear, you can't leave. Let me fix it. Let me be here with you to keep you grounded. Please."

He watches me sadly and reaches out, setting his hand over mine. "I think it's a little more serious than that. I don't remember much of what's happened through the last few weeks. I woke up this morning in Cami's bed, and I was disoriented and confused, and I don't want to hurt you."

I look down at the grungy floor and swallow hard past a lump in my throat. My eyes are burning. "Bear—"

"I know you're trying to hold onto your old life, Maxwell. I know how hard you're struggling right now. How much you wish things could be different. But they can't, and it's time to realize that. It's time to understand that this is so much bigger than you or I. You have a huge job to do, and it's not fair that it's all been pushed onto you. But you can do it. I know you can. And Jamie has been a good friend to you. She loves you; I can tell. She's going to take care of you. You can lean on each other."

I shake my head quickly, a thousand panicked thoughts flying through my head. I climb into his lap and take his face in my hand, setting my forehead to his. "Stop."

"Maxw—"

I set my fingers to his lips. He needs to just shut the fuck up and let me convince him that everything will be okay. "Stop trying to push me away. Stop trying to make things better. They won't be better. Just, please." I stroke his cheeks with my thumbs. "Please let me try. Let me help you be better. Let me help you stay."

He lets out a wounded noise, his eyes shining with tears. He closes them and lets out a shaky breath.

"Let me help you be better. Let me help," I repeat. "Please let me help you stay." I press my lips to his.

He kisses me back, tears finally starting down his cheeks. He slides a hand up into the back of my hair and holds me there, his other arm sliding around me to hold me tight against him.

I kiss him fervently, having missed this, the closeness and the feeling. I can taste salt from his tears. This emotion, this pain, it's a relief. The fact that Bear wants to be with me but is afraid of who he's becoming is scary, but it makes me feel loads better in a screwed up kind of way. Everything makes sense now.

Bear kisses me eagerly and suddenly turns us over, pushing me further up on the cot and pressing against me. He pulls back for only a moment to relieve me of my shirt, the extra fabric getting in the way. He presses kisses down my neck and chest, hands sliding down to pull off my jeans.

I arch up into him, my breath catching in my throat. I bite my lower lip and tangle my hand into his hair. I sit up a little to pull off his clothing and then pull him back over me, sliding my legs around his hips and pulling him into a deep kiss. We make love, and afterward, I'm sure I'll be enough to ground him. Hold him together. I have plenty of love in my heart to swallow him whole and keep him safe.

But when I wake in the morning, he's gone.

2157

IT TOOK THREE YEARS FOR GABRIEL TO RETURN TO EARTH. Maxwell was nine years old. He saw her playing in the yard with her friend, Theodore, when he approached, shoulders stiff and back straight. He didn't know if he should have come, but he had to see Aubrey, to know she was doing okay. It was all that mattered. He'd been going insane thinking about her and their unresolved differences.

Another little boy played with them in the front yard. He was probably eleven or twelve, and he was teaching them how to play catch.

"Are you ready, Maxwell?" the boy asked, getting ready to throw the ball.

"Yeah! Not too hard, though, okay, Matty?"

The boy nodded and smiled before he tossed the ball toward Maxwell. She caught it easily and then jumped excitedly. "I got it!"

He grinned. "Good job, Max! We should ask mom if she can sign you up for the team with me."

She nodded excitedly. "Yeah! Bear, too."

Gabriel watched them quietly for a few moments longer before he stepped up the stairs toward the door.

Maxwell stopped playing and looked over at Gabriel. She walked to him. "Who're you?"

He stopped and looked down at her. He took a deep breath. "My name is Gabriel. I'm a friend of your mother's."

"Oh…" She dropped her glove and the ball and looked back at the two boys. "I'll be right back. I'm gonna go find mom." She walked around Gabriel and opened the door, stepping inside. "Mooooom?!"

A man came to the door. He was tall with red hair and freckles. His eyes were warm and brown. He smiled. "Can I help you?"

Gabriel took a deep breath. "I'm looking for Aubrey. Aubrey Addams?"

The man smiled. "It's Odyssey, now."

"Excuse me?"

"Aubrey Odyssey. She's married. Hang on, I'll go get her. What's your name?"

He swallowed hard past a lump in his throat. "I'm Gabriel," he said quietly.

The man's eyes widened. "*Gabriel.* Okay. I'll go let her know." He gave him a small nod and then turned away.

It was Aubrey who returned to the door. She smiled when she saw him, but it didn't look quite right on her face because it was nervous, unsure. "Hello, Angel," she said softly.

He stared at her, taking her in. She looked different. Still beautiful, but less free. She was wearing clothes that were more restricting than her usual flowing apparel, and her hair was wound into a bun at the base of her neck. Her eyes were tired, the beginnings of wrinkles at their corners. He opened his mouth to speak but was unable to find words.

"Would you like to come in?" she asked softly. "I'm just finishing dinner."

He nodded. "Please," he replied quietly.

She smiled and nodded, opening the door further to allow him passage inside.

He stepped in and looked around, taking in the changes in the house. There had been definite upgrades. The cabinetry looked new, the carpet plush. Everything had been updated. "It looks really great in here," he murmured.

"Thank you. Stephen and I have a couple of really great government jobs. Knowledge keepers. Just like I always wanted. So we aren't hurting for money anymore. Life has been easier in that respect. The job takes a toll on our mental health, though."

He frowned, watching her quietly. "That's quite important."

She smiled and shook her head, waving away his concern. "We're doing just fine."

He nodded slowly. "That's good. I'm very pleased to hear that you are well. And Maxwell seems happy."

"She is. And healthy. Strong little thing. And so stubborn."

"Like you, then."

Aubrey laughed, setting her hand to her mouth. "Yes, I suppose so."

"Have there been any *incidents*?"

She shook her head. "No. She remembers nothing. She's safe."

"Good. That's great."

"Are you going to introduce me or what?" The man who had opened the door stepped toward them, smiling kindly.

Aubrey looked back at him and grinned and then looked at Gabriel. "This is my husband, Stephen. We met during class. We have the same ideas, the same dreams. He was a widower, a single dad. We're a good match."

The dryness in his mouth made it difficult to speak, so Gabriel merely nodded, looking over at Stephen.

"Stephen, this is Gabriel, Maxwell's biological father. You know about him already."

Gabriel looked at her questioningly, brows raised.

Stephen took a deep breath. "You don't need to worry. I promise. I won't say a word. I care for Maxwell as if she were my own. I would never put her safety in jeopardy."

"Okay," Gabriel replied cautiously, turning his attention to him.

Aubrey smoothed her hands over her apron. "Stephen's son is named Matthew. Max loves having an older brother. She adores him, and he takes care of her. They're sweet together."

The tightness in his chest refused to cease. "I'm happy for her. For all of you," he finally said, watching her.

She smiled, soft and sweet. "How have you been?"

He shrugged. "Very busy. It's been chaotic upstairs. Michael is still very angry with me. He's been searching for Uriel. Growing more and more irate at his inability to find him."

She nodded and watched him. "You won't tell."

"Absolutely not. It would bring death to his family. He's happy here. I think he will decide to fall soon. Last time I visited, Chloe was turning 15. He has adjusted very well to this lifestyle. He won't be leaving. I miss him, but this is where he belongs."

"Does falling hurt?"

Gabriel took a deep breath and shrugged again. "I'm sure it isn't a pleasant experience. There are two ways to fall: willingly and not. If an angel falls willingly, he retains his memories and his form. He begins to age again and will die after a normal lifespan. His grace is left in Heaven. Angels who fall unwillingly, who are forced out as punishment, are separated from their forms. Their grace is ripped out. If they survive the fall, they will land somewhere as an infant and be born again on Earth. They will retain a small amount of grace as they grow, but will most likely never remember their true identities. To forget is a punishment."

Aubrey nodded slowly. "That sounds awful."

"It is. There have been angels who have fallen as punishment who forget about Heaven and lose their faith entirely. I cannot imagine what it would be like to be skeptical. I guess that's what it means to be human, though. Always questioning. Always searching for answers they will never find."

Aubrey stared at him quietly before looking back up at Stephen. "Babe, would you mind finishing dinner? I'm going to go on a short walk with Gabriel. Catch up a little."

Stephen smiled warmly and nodded, leaning down and giving her a soft kiss. He looked back at Gabriel, no trace of insecurity or animosity in his expression. He was all warmth and kindness. "It was great to meet you, Gabriel. I'd hoped I would."

Gabriel nodded. "Thank you for taking care of Maxwell," he responded, before turning back with Aubrey and heading down the steps. He walked slowly down the street with her.

They were silent for a few moments, the gravel crunching beneath their feet the only sound besides their breathing.

"Are you happy?" Gabriel finally asked, staring at his feet as they walked.

"I am. I'm very happy. I'm not the same person I was. I'm more disciplined, more down-to-earth. But I'm very content with where my life is. I guess that's what happens with growing up."

"Do you still paint?"

"Oh, no. I don't really have time. I'd like to, but I've got bigger things to worry about, you know?"

He nodded. "I suppose so."

"Maxwell paints, though. Beautiful things. She's a little prodigy. She loves music and painting. Her friend Teddy does, too. They do everything together. They're inseparable. I'm sure they'll marry someday, provided he isn't drafted before they're able to. We've officially adopted him into our little family since he has none of his own."

"Is she happy?"

"She's thrilled. She loves her life. She's such a free-spirit. And she's full of questions. She never stops talking. She's creative, and loving and most importantly, she's kind. We've taught her to keep an open mind."

He smiled. "Good. I am very happy to hear that. I wish things were different and I could be a part of her life, but I am pleased that she is leading an enjoyable one. That she's being taken care of. I knew you would do just fine on your own."

Aubrey laughed. "I'm hardly on my own. I need help every day. Help from Stephen, from Mom, even from Matthew. But we're doing pretty alright."

Gabriel watched her, noticing the way the light caught her eyes. A light smattering of freckles rested across her nose, probably from too much sunlight. He noticed the way her pink lips turned up in a smile when she talked about her life, her family, and he felt a strange sort of contentedness, even though she was happy without him. It was only important that she was happy. His sadness was lessened by it.

A sudden ringing in his ears brought him to his knees, hands clasped over his ears.

"Gabriel!" Aubrey dropped to her knees beside him, setting her hand on his back. "What's wrong?"

He gasped and gritted his teeth, closing his eyes tightly. He made a pained noise. "My brother is in pain."

He felt Uriel's pain singing through his veins. He saw red. Thick, horrible red so dark it was almost black. So much red that he felt as though he was drowning in it. He heard his brother screaming his name, agony and horror filling his connection with urgency.

"I must go."

2165

JAMIE FINDS ME IN OUR ROOM. She walks to my cot and sits on the edge, reaching out and sliding her hand slowly over my back.

I close my eyes, wetting my lips. "He's gone."

"Yeah, I know."

"I thought I'd gotten through to him. I wanted to help him."

"Not everybody can be fixed," Jamie replies quietly.

When I don't respond, Jamie sighs and climbs into bed behind me, sliding her arms around me and pulling me tight to her chest. She nuzzles her face into the back of my neck and kisses it gently.

I shift, hugging Jamie's arms and snuggling against her. "Thank you," I whisper.

"I want to go back up."

"Absolutely not."

I stare at my father, eyes narrowed reproachfully. "You've said yourself that this is my war. Correct?"

"Yes, but—"

"But nothing. Gabriel… *Dad*… Please."

His features soften as he stares at me. He takes a deep breath. "We will talk about it another time. Alright? I want you to get in a little better shape with your training. You're strong, but you need to learn how to focus your energies into productivity."

I shake my head. "Jamie gets to go."

"Jamie didn't reveal herself in front of an enormous crowd of people. She didn't smite an angel in their presence."

I scowl. "Technicalities."

He huffs out a laugh and squeezes my shoulder. "Soon, little one. Okay?"

I sigh but then look up at him seriously. "Watch her. Keep her safe?"

He nods. "Of course, Maxwell. I will keep your girlfriend safe."

I can feel the heat rise in my cheeks, and I frown deeply. "She's not my *girlfriend*."

He laughs, throwing his head back. "Technicalities," he replies, wiggling his brows at me. He kisses my forehead and then heads to the weaponry room to stock up for their trip.

I sigh and wander over to Jamie, where she is finishing tying up her boots. I cross my arms over my chest. "Be careful, okay?"

She smiles warmly and nods. "Of course. We'll be back in no time. Just have a few newbies to pick up across town. We'll grab them and their supplies and then we'll be back and it'll be like we never left."

"I wish I could go."

"I'm glad you aren't, to be honest. I hate to think of what would happen if someone recognized you. There's a reward on your head. Your face flashes all over the afternoon announcements."

"Yeah, yeah." I roll my eyes. "So I'll dye my hair. Wear the stupid contacts."

Jamie smiles and sighs, looking wistful. "I'll miss the blonde."

I snort and shake my head. "Go. Be safe."

Jamie pulls me into a tight hug and nods. "Always," she replies softly. "Maybe this time I'll be able to redeem myself."

"There's nothing to redeem."

"Yeah, of course not. I almost got you killed, is all," Jamie replies sarcastically, bumping her forehead to mine.

"You did not. How many times are we going to fight over this, huh?" I ask, watching her. "I'm the one who ran right into trouble. You were the smart one."

"No, I was the one who was busy wetting myself like an infant."

Matthew steps in, decked out in all black gear. "We ready to do this or what?"

Jamie looks at him and laughs, flipping her long brown braid over her shoulder. "You're dreaming if you think you're coming along for the ride."

He looks injured, glancing between the two of us. "There's no way you're leaving me behind. I've got military training."

"That's precisely why we're leaving you behind," Gabriel speaks up, stepping out. "That and I don't think Maxwell would forgive any of us if your sorry ass got shot while we were out."

Matthew scowls, shaking his head. "Seriously?"

"Seriously," Jamie replies, smirking. "You stay here and spend a little quality time with your sister. She can give you a little practice in the ring. She's getting quite good."

I smile proudly and stand a little taller. "I am. I'll whoop your ass."

Matty rolls his eyes. "Dream on, little sister." He looks over at Jamie. "You be careful, alright, sweetheart?"

Jamie snorts. "Yeah, alright, Casanova."

"Seriously. Don't know what we'd do without you here."

"You really like that word, don't you?"

Matthew scowls. I laugh, entertained by her obvious lack of interest and his wounded ego.

Jamie laughs. "We'll really be okay. Promise. You two have fun."

2157

WHEN HE ARRIVED AT URIEL'S HOME, he ran inside. The first thing he saw was blood. It was everywhere. The second thing he saw was his brother, Michael, standing over Uriel, who was on his knees in the middle of the gore, bloody hands covering his face as he rocked and sobbed, a horrible, ugly, choking noise ripping from deep inside his chest.

Gabriel stared in horror, panic spiking his insides. "Uriel," he choked, running toward him.

Michael held out his hand, stopping Gabriel in his tracks. "Stop!" he hissed, not looking away from Uriel's face. "He is to handle this pain on his own. It is his fault. He brought it on himself."

"Lana... My Lana..." Uriel moaned, his face twisted in pain. He tugged at his blonde hair, dying it red with the blood from his hands.

"Gabe. Gabe, they took her! My Chloe! They murdered my Lana and took my daughter!"

Gabriel put his hand to his mouth, staring at his brother in pain. He looked to Michael, anger coursing through his veins. "You had no right!"

With a flick of his wrist, Michael had Gabriel on the ground, face pressed to the blood-soaked carpet. "This is very disappointing behavior coming from two angels. *Archangels*, especially. What will the rest of our brothers say? However, it will give good example to the rest of our brothers on what behaviors to avoid. The monster's execution will show them not to do as you have done. Earth is best to be avoided if this is the kind of behavior that is going to come from it. There is a reason why we were created to avoid free will. It is dangerous," he spat, glaring down at his brothers.

Uriel moaned, in total agony. "My daughter... My baby..."

Michael threw his head back, laughing sadistically. "She's a monster. You know she is. All nephilim must be disposed of."

Gabriel felt another pulse of terror flow through is veins. "Chloe has done nothing wrong. She's a sweet girl, a kind girl. She's never hurt a soul in her life. She knows to behave. She's far from a monster."

Michael glared at him and stepped to him, setting a heavily booted foot on his neck and pressing down hard. "You'll be punished very severely for helping him keep this secret. You'll both wish you were dead by the end."

"Michael, you can't harm the girl. Please. Uriel is your brother. He wouldn't allow Chloe to cause any harm. Look at him. He has been punished enough," Gabriel pleaded, unable to take his eyes from Uriel's agony. "Please. *Please*, Michael."

His brother only scoffed a laugh, shaking his head. "This is only the beginning of his punishment." He rolled his eyes. "It's been nice having this little heart-to-heart, but we have an execution to get to."

Uriel's yell of despair was cut off as Michael zapped them back to the heavens.

A rush of color flowed past Gabriel, burning his eyes. He quickly closed them. When he dared to open them again, he was in the middle of a wide circle, Uriel beside him. Michael was a few feet away, the picture of grace, standing tall in front of their brothers and sisters. He reeked of authority. Angels were everywhere around the circle, staring in at them. Some of them looked confused, others horrified. Worse, some were smiling, pleased with the fact that their disobedient siblings were about to be dealt with.

Uriel was barely functioning beside Gabriel, face pressed to the ground and body shivering violently. He was muttering to himself, shaking his head quickly back and forth. Gabriel wrapped his arm around him and pressed his lips to his hair, trying to bring what little comfort he could to his brother.

"*Daddy!*" Chloe's shriek echoed throughout Heaven as she was brought to the middle of the circle.

Angels backed away from her instinctively, doubtless already knowing what she was. They were afraid of her, Gabriel realized. It was a ridiculous thought, but it was true. They'd been brainwashed into thinking that all nephilim were dangerous, horrifying monstrosities that needed to be taken care of immediately to ensure they did no damage.

Chloe's ivory wings spread and beat at the air, trying to lift her from the ground. She was terrified, twisting in the arms of the angels that were holding her down.

Uriel stumbled to his feet and ran toward his daughter, but Michael held out his hand, stopping him.

Michael turned back to the angels who were standing around them. He smiled, wide and shark-like, looking every bit the politician he was. "We are gathered here today as an example," he began, gesturing toward Uriel, who was struggling in place, unable to move by the binding spell he had been placed under.

"You have all been warned continuously about the dangers of fraternizing with humans. During the beginning of time when we copulated with humans, we created monsters that were capable of exterminating us. We lost many powerful angels trying to bring them down. You have all been warned numerous times of the dangers of it. Yet here we are today, standing here with your brother, Uriel, and the monstrosity he has created."

Uriel's face was wet with snot and tears as he stared at his daughter. "Please! Please, Michael! Let her go! Let my baby go!"

Michael rolled his eyes, shaking his head slowly back and forth. "Your brother, Gabriel, has been helping Uriel keep this horrible secret. Rest assured that he is to be punished, as well.

"Today is about setting an example. This girl, though she may appear relatively harmless, is very dangerous. She has powers that could allow her to kill any one of us. Do not look upon your brother with pity. He has been brainwashed by his time spent on Earth. He has been tainted. He is incapable of understanding the error of his ways."

"She has done nothing wrong!" Uriel yelled, looking around wildly. "My Chloe has done *nothing*! I have sinned! I have stayed on Earth for far longer than I was allowed. I have laid with a human. I have produced a daughter, but she is good! She is kind and sweet and loving! What about *your* daughter, Michael! The one you had with your human lover! You're just upset that they perished and now you're forcing your pain onto everyone else!"

"Lies!" Michael hissed furiously, glaring over at him.

"Uriel speaks the truth," Gabriel spoke up, looking around. He was terrified, but he couldn't watch his brother suffer as a traitor when he had done nothing wrong.

Michael shook his head and looked toward the angels who held Chloe. "Take her wings."

"NO!" Uriel screamed, eyes wide in panic. He struggled where he stood. "NO! NO! NO!"

Chloe began to sob, thrashing against the angels who were holding her. "No! Please! Don't let them!"

Gabriel felt physically ill. He felt bile rise in his throat. He shook his head quickly. "Michael, no," he breathed. He tried to move forward but was held in place by the same binding spell as Uriel.

Uriel twisted, eyes wide in horror. "FATHER!" he screamed. "FATHER, *PLEASE*!"

There was no response to his prayer.

Chloe was shoved to her knees, bound where she stood. A tall angel stood behind her, saw in hand. She shook her head quickly. "Please don't! Please!" Her pleading turned into screaming as he began to saw her wing from her shoulder.

Uriel screamed beside Gabriel. His shrieking combined with the sounds of agony coming from his daughter, turning the atmosphere hellish. Everyone else was silent. Gabriel fell into tears. He lost the contents of his stomach, keeling over.

Gradually, Chloe's screaming died down. She fell silent as her second wing was taken, and Gabriel knew it was because she had perished. He braved a look and was horrified to see her once flawless, ivory wings lying in a pool of blood, hacked away carelessly like a carcass at the butcher. The girl lay beside her wings, eyes staring wide and blank, mouth open in a silenced scream.

Uriel's screaming and sobbing had ceased, as well. When Gabriel looked at him, he saw his brother was standing quietly, shoulders slumped. There were tears on his face, but he showed no more sign of fight. He was frighteningly blank, void of emotion.

Michael turned to Uriel. "If you think that was the end of your punishment, you're wrong," he said quietly, voice low. "It has only just begun. But I hope you take this as a lesson for your wrongdoings, and I hope you pray for forgiveness."

Uriel stared blankly back at him.

"It is *you* who needs to pay for forgiveness, brother," Gabriel spat, fury blackening his vision. "You have committed an act of murder against an innocent child. Her blood is on your hands."

Michael seemed less annoyed with Gabriel's fury than the lack of reaction from Uriel. He stepped toward him. "Don't you have anything to say?"

Uriel set his hand over his heart, gripping his shirt. He closed his eyes and then plunged his hand into his own chest, gasping. The atmosphere filled with a light so bright it was painful to look upon as he pulled his grace from his body. A moment later, he was gone.

Gabriel stared, wide eyed, at the spot where his brother had been. Tears poured down his face. He had never expected for Uriel to decide to fall now that his family was gone. There was no reason to. He shook his head quickly and glared at Michael. "Look at what you have done!"

Michael grinned. "I think Uriel has decided your punishment for you, Gabriel. It's time for you to lose your grace, too. It will bother you more than him. You have a harder time staying away from home."

Gabriel shook his head quickly, horrified. He didn't want to be cast from Heaven. It was the entire reason he'd decided to stay rather than to live on Earth with Aubrey and Maxwell. He didn't think he could handle the distance from his home or the closeness to his father. "You can't."

"I can. And it'll be worse for you. You never wanted to fall. You'll grow up on Earth, doubting, sinning. You'll be just like one of those filthy apes you so often disobey us for."

Panic spread through Gabriel's body. He didn't want to be forced to fall, to forget who he was, or to lose his memory of Heaven. He swallowed hard and reached into his chest, feeling the hotness of his grace burning inside of him. He gasped at the overwhelming heat and power. He pulled it from his chest, hearing an angry yell from Michael before he disappeared.

And then he was falling, falling through the heavens and the atmosphere. Free falling from one prison to another.

2165

I GATHER AROUND THE HOLOGRAM PLATFORM WITH VIC, Gabriel, Jamie, Matthew, and the others who are in charge of running our underground commune. Our tech people have hacked into the network and allowed us to stay connected through daily announcements. It's a helpful way to stay in tune with the outside world.

Leighton, Darren's incredibly talented son, flips a switch and we sit, staring as the hologram flickersand Michael comes to life in front of us. Goosebumps rise on my arms, as they always do when I see his horrible, perfect face.

I'm not prepared for what comes next.

Michael introduces two new people to his audience. Cameron and Bear. I gasp, staring at the screen. I shake my head, wide-eyed and horrified. "What?!"

"Hush, Maxwell," Uncle Vic scolds, setting a firm hand on my shoulder as he leans toward the platform.

Michael grins, gesturing to his two guests. "As you know, rewards come with information. I would like to introduce you to a couple of old friends. Gadreel and Remiel. They both ran into trouble many years back. Gadreel fell willingly, Remiel did not. Either way, all of us are worthy of second chances if we give reason. The two of them have given us valuable information about a couple of nephilim who are responsible for a rising death toll in this area. As a reward, these two will be obtaining their grace and allowed back within the gates of Heaven. They have also agreed to be of future help in our fight against these revolting creatures."

I take a step backward, bumping into Vic, who tightens his hold on me. He's trembling. I shake my head quickly, unable to believe what I'm seeing.

Bear looks up into the camera, and then down, shame-faced. He's pale and perspiring. He wets his lips. Cami stands beside him, smiling proudly. Her stance is straight and strong, like a soldier.

"Remiel, would you care to let the audience know the information you have already delivered to me?" Michael asks, staring at Bear.

Bear takes a deep breath. "Uh... I..."

"Go on," Michael encourages, smiling widely. His teeth are too white. His mouth too big.

Bear rubs at the back of his neck. "Maxwell is in the care of the fallen angel Gabriel. He's been hiding her for a while now. He's very protective. Highly dangerous. He's working with another fallen angel, Uriel, who is also protecting a nephilim. Her name is Jamie. She's got long, brown hair and dark green eyes. She's tall and thin. Usually dressed all in black. Her skin is pale. She's got freckles across her nose. Max is blonde. Average height, athletic build. She's got heterochromia iridium. One eye is brown and one is blue. She's got black wings. She can bring people back from the dead."

Cameron grins. "Gabriel is a Caucasian male, he has brown hair, and a beard and eyes the same color. He's tall and muscular. Sometimes goes under the pseudonym Brie. Uriel is Caucasian as well. He has long, brown hair, a reddish-brown beard, and amber colored eyes. He's average height and slim. He has freckles across his nose. Sometimes goes under the pseudonym Vic. He runs a commune of rebels. Neither have any powers to speak of, but they are highly armed and good with weaponry. Caution should be practiced around them both.

"Maxwell Odyssey is a name you may remember from nearly five years ago, when her parents, Aubrey and Stephen Odyssey made headlines for acts of treason. They were hanged publicly. She has a very rebellious streak and is extremely dangerous. Besides being able to raise the dead, she has killed one of our own, Azazel. She smote him in broad daylight, in front of an audience. Jamie is also very dangerous, but her skills lie mostly in hand-to-hand combat and weaponry. Both girls are pathological liars and cannot be trusted."

Michael grins at them both and then looks back at the camera. It feels like he's staring into my soul, icy eyes piercing through me almost violently. "So now you know what to look for, citizens of Chicago. The sooner these two are caught, the better." He looks to Bear and Cameron and sets his hands on each of their shoulders. They both throw their heads back, mouths and eyes open wide as what looks like lightning bolts strike straight through them. It lasts only a few moments, and then Michael lets his hands fall away, and they stare down at themselves in wonder.

Bear looks down at his hands, a knowing expression settling on his face. He grins broadly and looks to Michael. "Thank you, brother," he murmurs, back straightening. "It feels great to be back."

Michael grins at him and then stares back into the camera. "For those of you who have fallen for any reason, be it a past punishment or poorly made decision, you will be gifted your grace if you come forward with information. If you help us, we will save you. We will allow you to come home. Those of you who are human and striving to secure your place in Heaven after death, you should come forward and we will grant you that wish."

I don't *think* I'm going to be sick. I know it. I pull away from Uncle Vic and stride out of the room, slamming the door behind me. I get to my room before I lose my breakfast into a trash can, heaving until I have nothing left inside.

It seems that emptying my stomach has only allowed a thick, fiery rage to fill it back up. I'm shaking with an effort to contain myself. I drop to the ground, my wings flying out and wrapping around me protectively. I shove my face into my knees and let loose a scream, nails digging into my bare legs as light bulbs around me explode.

2157

WHEN HE CAME TO, Gabriel found himself lying miraculously in the field beside Aubrey's home. He must have wished for it to be so as he fell, and with his last bit of grace, been returned safely to a place he had once cherished as his own home. He looked down at himself. He was filthy, covered in dirt and blood with rags for clothing. He got to his feet quickly and limped as fast as he could to Aubrey's house. He barged in, not bothering to knock.

"Aubrey!" he shouted, voice coming out shaky and panicked.

"Gabriel?" It was Stephen, and he looked horrified at Gabriel's state. He reached for his arm, trying to lead him to a chair to sit in, but Gabriel shook his head quickly, pulling away.

"No! I need to speak with Aubrey! Now!"

Stephen chewed his lip and then nodded quickly. "Okay. Okay, I'll get her. But you should sit, Gabriel. You look awful."

"I *cannot* sit! I would not be here if it were not important, Stephen. Please! Go get Aubrey."

Stephen nodded quickly and turned to go find his wife, but she was already there, summoned by the noise. She frowned deeply as she took in the sight of him.

"What's happened, Angel?" she asked worriedly, eyes wide with fright.

Gabriel snorted at the nickname, shaking his head back and forth. He gave an almost maniacal laugh. "Angel? I am no longer an angel."

Aubrey's eyes filled with tears. "You fell."

"Obviously."

"What happened?"

"They found Uriel. His family." He felt a horrible pain twist inside his chest, crippling him. He gripped the edge of the counter to keep from falling, and instead sunk slowly to the ground, putting his head in his hands. He had felt pain before, felt emotion, but never to this level. Never as a human. He had no control. No ability to keep the pain from consuming him.

Aubrey looked over at her husband. "Take the children up to the attic. Play some music. Have them paint. Something. Keep them busy, okay?"

Gabriel didn't hear the exchange. He was too preoccupied with his misery.

Aubrey knelt in front of him, taking his shoulders in his hands. "Can you tell me what happened?" she whispered, as though she were afraid to hear his answer.

Gabriel let out a quiet moan, shaking his head. "Uriel called to me. He was in pain. Michael killed Lana. He destroyed her." He was trembling so hard that it was difficult to speak, difficult to do anything.

"Oh, Gabriel," Aubrey whispered, a tear rolling down her cheek as she brushed her fingers back through his dirty hair.

"We were taken to Heaven," he continued, staring at the ground through blurred eyes. "We were surrounded by my brothers and sisters. Michael announced the punishment. Execution for the nephilim. He took Chloe's wings. He sawed them from her back. She died in front of Uriel, screaming for him. He could do nothing. We couldn't help her. Couldn't save her. I tried. I—" he broke off as heavy sobs erupted from his chest, overtaking him completely.

He let himself be gathered against Aubrey's chest and rocked like a small child, tears pouring down his cheeks as he gasped and hiccupped and whimpered against her.

Aubrey held him for a long time, her own face wet with tears. She set her face in his hair and pressed her lips to the top of his head, trying to comfort him as best as she could. "They're sick, Gabriel. It's wrong. It's so wrong." She rubbed his back and held him close.

He closed his eyes, having been reduced to sniffles and the occasional hiccup. "They were going to punish us further, but Uriel ripped out his grace. He fell. They were going to do the same to me. Take my grace. Force me to grow from an infant, unaware, not remembering who I am. So I ripped mine out, as well. I'm human now. I will grow. Age. Die. But I came to tell you that you must take extra precautions now."

She nodded. "Anything you need me to do, I'll do. I want to keep our baby safe."

"Do not let anyone take interest in Maxwell. Let her grow, but keep her from any oddities. Do not allow her near anyone who feels unsafe. Don't draw attention to her. Don't mention her. She is special, but she shouldn't be allowed to know it. Any special talents should be discouraged. Any supernatural dreams, forgotten. Keep her home. Keep her safe. Do not ever mention my name. Let her believe Stephen is her real father."

"But if you're human now, you could stay," Aubrey said softly, looking up at him. "Be a part of her life. Help Stephen and I raise her."

He shook his head. "Aubrey, I'm telling you right now that I can never be a part of her life ever again. Not as a family friend, not as an acquaintance. I do not want her to ever lay eyes on me again. I cannot watch her suffer the same fate as Chloe. I cannot watch her die."

Aubrey took a shaky breath and nodded slowly, wiping at her eyes. "I understand."

"That vial of my grace… you keep a tight hold of it, okay? Lock it away. Never let her see. Never let her know it's there. It should serve as a form of protection for the vicinity of the house, keep the others off of your trail. But you need to be very careful. Do you understand?"

She nodded again, eyes wide. "Yes."

"I need to leave now."

"You could stay the night. Get cleaned up. Fed."

"No. I need to go. Get as far away as I dare. Maybe I will find Uriel."

Another tear dripped down Aubrey's cheek. "You're right, of course." She swallowed audibly, shaking her head. "But, Gabriel?"

"Yes?"

She took a deep breath and took his face in her hands, leaning forward and kissing him. He could taste her salty tears on her lips. He kissed her back, eyes closing.

Aubrey whimpered when she pulled away, and then she stood quietly, taking his hand and pulling him up. She enveloped him in a hug. "You be careful, you hear, Angel?"

He closed his eyes, tucking his face in her hair. "I am no longer an angel," he reminded her miserably.

She shook her head. "You'll always be my angel. Always," she murmured, pulling away.

The corner of Gabriel's mouth turned up in a sad smile. "Always," he replied quietly, before walking out of her life forever.

2165

"MAX!" THE URGENCY IN JAMIE'S TONE has me up off of the floor quickly. I allow my wings to disappear before I open the door, staring up at her with wide eyes.

Her eyes are bloodshot and wide with terror. She takes my hand. "We need to go. Emergency meeting."

"I can't believe it." I close my eyes briefly against the memory of Theodore's face as he described me and the dangers I pose.

"People are so angry, Maxwell," Jamie whispers. "You need to talk to them or there's going to be an uprising. Against *us*."

I feel my blood run cold. "*What*? Why?"

"They're upset because they're afraid of Michael. And besides that, they're unsure about us again. Oh, Gabriel and Uriel are furious. I've never seen them so angry before. I'm afraid they're going to put people off even more. We can't look like the bad guys, Max. We'll all die if they sell us out."

"We've already been sold out!" I exclaim, pulling at my hair.

"At least no one has come knocking yet. Now come on!" She pulls me from my room, down the corridor, and to the main hall, where we usually have our meals.

Everyone is there. It's loud. People are shouting, cursing, causing an insane uproar. Gabriel and Uriel are standing before the crowd, trying to calm them to no avail.

As soon as we step into the room, it gets louder. Marlene, a woman I recognize from the kitchen crew, steps forward. "You have *destroyed* us!" She shouts, visibly shaking. "You have ruined our community. We are all going to die because of you!"

Another man steps up beside her. I remember him from combat training. His wife was killed a few weeks earlier on a raid gone wrong. His face is gray, eyes narrowed. Sweat dribbles over a bulging vein in his forehead. "How do we know you're the ones we should have put our faith in? How do we know Michael is the one who's wrong?"

Marlene shakes her head. "We put our faith in a couple of children. Our lives. Everything. We trusted you."

I stare between the two of them, trying to calm my trembling. I take a deep breath. "I know you're worried. You would be stupid not to be."

"And necromancy?" Marlene continues, eyes narrowing. "That is *devil's* work! You brought that boy back from the dead, and look what's happened!"

I look up toward the ceiling in an attempt to gather my wits, and then I look to her. The woman I see in front of me is desperate, broken. She has given me everything, as she says. She's put all of her faith in me, and what have I done for her? Absolutely nothing, except for put her in danger by bringing back a boy who was not what he seemed to be and who has potentially killed us all. What can I say to her to make it better? I can make promises I'm unsure I can keep. I can try to be positive about the situation, brush it to the side. But it will come out inauthentic. I know we're in danger. I just need time.

"I did bring Theodore back from the dead," I admit, looking around at the crowd. It's too difficult to look her in the eye.

The entire commune erupts in angry shouting.

My father steps up beside me, furious. "Enough!" He yells, voice vibrating throughout the crowded room. He has a gun in his hands, and it makes me nervous. I glance up at him, and then back at my people, who still look frantic.

"I was unaware of what I was doing when I did it," I continue, looking out at everyone. "And I am so sorry that it happened. I had no idea he was Remiel. I am just as shocked and horrified as the rest of you. I could never have imagined he would do something as horrible as this."

Jamie stands tall beside me. "Neither did I. Uriel and Gabriel are just as shocked as the rest of us. They told me Remiel fell many years ago. He used to be very faithful, but around nineteen years ago, when God seemed to disappear and Michael began ruling Heaven, Michael decided that Remiel had spent too much time fraternizing with human women on Earth. He cast Remiel's grace from his body and sent him to Earth. We have no idea if he was truly guilty or not. He would have been reborn as a human child with absolutely no memory or concept of Heaven.

"We also don't know how Gadreel could have known who Remiel was. But she must have figured it out somehow. Gadreel got into a lot of trouble. She fell before she could be cast out and lose her memory. She is very rebellious. She got into a lot of trouble before the flood. She created many nephilim. Taught them warfare. Mischief. God was forced to step in. It was a dark time."

"So God doesn't like your kind!" a faceless spectator shouts from the back of the crowd. They all jeer.

I wince and look to my father for help.

"Not those particular nephilim," he breaks in, staring out toward the source of the comment. "You have to understand that Gadreel was particularly fond of chaos and not at all fond of humanity. So she created monsters. She made them angry, made them lust for blood. She created an army. Your bible recalls them as fierce giants. They weren't exactly giant, but certainly created a hellish mess. What probably happened is when Maxwell accidentally brought Theodore back from the dead, his memory was sparked by his descent toward Heaven and then his path back from the dead. As soon as Gadreel got wind of who Remiel was, she would do everything she could to use it to her advantage. Remiel was in much better standing with Michael than Gadreel was."

"So it *is* your fault," Marlene spits, staring at me.

"Maxwell has already stated that she had no idea what she was doing when she brought Theodore back from the dead. She didn't even know what she was. Now that she knows, she has refrained from bringing anyone else back, even though she holds the power to do so. Her gift was given to her by God. She has been chosen to carry this burden for a reason."

Jeremy has been standing quietly in the back, but he steps forward, dark eyes filled with tears. He turns to face the rest of the commune. "You all know that Cami has been part of our team of raiders for years. She has been your friend and ally. She has brought you food and clothing and provided protection for your community. Nobody could have known her true identity. If we didn't recognize it, how could we expect these newcomers to know she was actually a snake?"

I look toward Jeremy, feeling pity for him. He and Cami had been close, and her betrayal toward him must feel a lot like what I'm feeling about Theodore. I appreciate his courage in the face of so many angry rebels, but he is widely ignored by his people.

The man standing beside Marlene shakes his head, heading for the door. "I'm leaving. If any of you are smart, you'll follow!"

Marlene stares at me for a moment, long and hard, and then she follows him and is trailed by more and more people.

Jamie shakes her head beside me, looking out at the crowd in shock.

Gabriel raises his gun. "Who wants to leave?!" he yells, fury plain on his face. "You're as good as dead if you leave, and I won't have anyone giving away our position. Line up, and I'll shoot you to make it go quicker!"

My eyes widen in shock and I shake my head, grabbing the end of his gun and pointing it at myself. "No!"

"Maxwell, if they leave, we will be destroyed! They'll go to Michael! They'll give away all of our secrets!"

"We are *not* like them!" I yell, my voice cracking. "We will not kill those who disagree with us!"

Marlene has stopped walking. She stares back at us, eyes wide.

Gabriel scowls, still holding the gun. "Be reasonable, Max. If all of these people leave…"

"They will have made a decision for themselves. We will not hold prisoners here. Our people are free to leave as they see fit. I will not allow them to be punished for being afraid. Their fate will be left in their own hands. We do not get to choose for them."

I stare Gabriel down until he finally lower his gun, looking incredibly distraught.

"We've already knocked down the main tunnels. They'll know the only other way in," he says quietly.

"Then they'll just have to know," I shrug, not knowing what else to do. "There's no way I'm going to let anybody else die in this stupid war, especially people who are only angry because they don't understand, because they're afraid."

Gabriel looks to Jamie, questioning her with his eyes.

I feel her hand squeeze mine, holding it tightly. She stares back at him. "Maxwell is right," she replies softly.

Uriel steps forward, face pale. He sets his hand on my father's shoulder and squeezes it gently. "I agree with you, brother, but perhaps we should listen to our girls. We can't expect them to lead if we don't allow them the opportunity to make decisions for the group."

Gabriel looks up at him, eyes narrowing in disbelief. He shrugs Uriel's hand from his shoulder and gives me a long stare. "Sometimes you are far too much like your mother for your own good," he says quietly, looking pained. "You will be the death of me."

I shake my head and reach out, taking his free hand in my own. I squeeze it tightly as I look out at the crowd. "Those of you who wish to leave are free to do so. We will even provide you with food and weapons."

Gabriel makes an exasperated noise beside me, but I choose to ignore it.

"I *will* let you know that what I've seen so far of the world above us has been very ugly. There are angels and soldiers keeping guard over civilians. They're everywhere. Every day, more people are being killed. When we went up last, I not only ran into a sadistic angel who wanted me dead, but I also saw a group of civilians who were labeled as rebels and who were being made example of by being shot in the street in front of everyone. If anyone finds out where you've been or what you've been doing here, you will be killed without question. It's very dangerous.

"I'm not telling you what to do, but you need to know what it's like up there. A lot of you have been down here since you first came. It's not the same. Not at all. And it won't be until Michael is dead and order has been restored in Heaven."

I look around at the men and women in front of me and take a deep breath. "Those of you who still wish to leave should all gather your belongings and then meet us at the east hall so we can show you the way out. Could you please raise your hands so I can take a headcount?"

Surprisingly, there aren't many hands in the air. Obviously, Marlene and her group of friends are still eager to leave, but aside from a few scattered hands throughout the room, there aren't many people who are angry enough to risk their lives topside.

I nod, trying to smile. "Alright, then. We'll meet you in the east hall in about an hour. I ask that you please not give our position away."

Something twists in my gut, and I look away, down toward the ground, trying to keep breathing normally. I'm worried about my choices. I know I am tired of death, but I also know there is a chance of angels trying to bribe information out of those who are leaving. Hopefully I have made the right decision.

I stand in the communications room with Leighton, Darren, Jamie, Vic, and my father.

Leighton is sweet and reminds me very much of a golden retriever, warm and happy and eager to please. I also realize he reminds me a bit of Matty, when he was younger. It must be that same warm smile. He can't be a day over fifteen.

"I've been wanting to get the chance to talk with you for a while. I've got some pretty good ideas," he begins excitedly.

"Now, Leighton," Vic begins reproachfully, but Darren interrupts him, eyes shining proudly.

"Just hear him out. Please. He's come up with something wonderful."

I grin, turning my full attention to him. "What are your ideas?"

Leighton grins and licks his lips. "Well, I'm a hacker. I've been keeping tabs on the tower's activity for ages, and I've figured out how to cut into their broadcasts without being traced. We'll be able to relay audio or holo messages to everybody topside without being caught or letting our location be known."

"Really?" I glance over at Gabriel, who looks as impressed as I feel. "That would be great."

Leighton blushes, smiling bashfully. "I can block them from cutting us out prematurely, and as long as they keep the broadcasting system up, which they *will* because it's how they communicate to the public, we'll be able to reach everyone. The only real danger is exposing our faces on camera."

I watch him thoughtfully. "Maybe that's exactly what I need to do."

Gabriel frowns and opens his mouth to speak, but I silence him with a shake of my head.

"I want them to know exactly who they're dealing with. That I am not a coward, and my intentions are very clearly to end them."

Gabriel huffs out a small laugh and runs a hand back through his short hair, shaking his head. "You'll be the death of me." It's the second time he's said it in the past few days.

"You think it's a bad idea?"

"I think it's brilliant. Stupid and gutsy and dangerous but necessary and brilliant."

Leighton grins and watches me. "Do you want me to set it up?"

I smile brightly and nod. "How soon can you get it ready?"

"Twenty minutes."

I will *definitely* not be ready in twenty minutes. "How about you program it for tomorrow morning?"

"During the morning announcements?"

"That'll be perfect."

I stand in front of the holocam, trying to control my breathing. I'm terrified, even if it doesn't show. The others stand behind the camera, watching me. Gabriel has his arms crossed over his chest, and he's chewing his lip so hard that I'm worried it might come off. Jamie stands beside him, smiling at me encouragingly. It's sweet and endearing and sets butterflies aflutter in my stomach.

I look toward the television screen that's beside the holocam, waiting to see Michael for the morning announcements. It doesn't take long. Not even a minute later, the hologram flickers to life and Michael stands in his usual spot, smiling his big, creepy smile.

"Good morning, citizens," Michael says.

"Ready, Max?" Leighton murmurs, tapping a couple of buttons.

I stare forward, momentarily stunned as I see a hologram of myself appear in Michael's place. I take a deep breath and then I smile. "Hello, citizens. You may remember me as Maxwell Odyssey, daughter of traitors to the government. I've been flashing all over the news lately." I brush a lock of hair behind my ear and smile sweetly.

"Thank you for that, *Remiel*. I won't forget it. Remind me to return the favor, huh?

"Anyway, I just wanted to say hello and let you all know that the man you've been watching every morning is not who he says he is. Michael has been trying and failing to run Heaven since his father's disappearance years ago. The working theory is that God left us because his children have been rebelling against him, sinning and doing wrong.

"Michael's main goal is the apocalypse. Why else would he be encouraging the slaughter of hundreds on our streets every day? His goal is to first obliterate all nephilim, offspring of angels and humans, like me. My mother was Aubrey Odyssey. My father is the former Archangel Gabriel."

I allow my wings to fly out, stretching high above me. They look ethereal in the glow of the hologram. Gasps echo from around the room, and it makes my smile grow.

"My father fell to keep me safe. He knew I was important in leading this revolution. I am working with another nephilim, Jamie. You've heard about her, too. She is the daughter of Michael, much as he may not like to admit it.

"Michael is afraid of us because we have the power to fight back. Humans are nothing to angels. Defenseless. But Jamie and I want to help you. We want to take our city back. We want our home back. We want to stop the endless, pointless slaughter. We want to give life back to our city. We want our people to thrive. We want to protect you. First it was our corrupt government, and now it's a band of angels who want to destroy our entire planet. We need to take our home back. We need to stand together and—

I'm silenced as my image is replaced by Michael, face twisted into a furious scowl. "Who has allowed this to happen?!" he screams at someone off camera, before becoming suddenly silent as he realizes that their connection is back. He shakes his head and tries to smile, but it's obviously forced.

"I apologize for that disgusting display of rebellion," he says, his voice strangely calm. "As we have previously informed you, Maxwell Odyssey is a pathological liar and highly dangerous. All nephilim need to be executed immediately. If you have any information on her whereabouts, you will be greatly rewarded for it.

Heaven's will is all that matters. There is no higher power. I will pray for you all to recognize the truth of this situation and for forgiveness for those who doubt. Thank you all."

The hologram cuts out, and I look up at Gabriel. "I didn't get to finish."

He's smiling, russet eyes wide and bright. "It doesn't matter, Maxwell. It was enough." He shakes his head, giving a quiet laugh. "It was enough."

"No powers!" Jamie reminds, grinning at me as she gets into position across from me. We're practicing hand-to-hand today.

My nose scrunches up. "You'll kick my ass."

"No way! You're getting much better! I promise." Jamie smiles kindly.

Bullshit. I know she won't hurt me on purpose, but I'm going to be covered in bruises tomorrow.

"No wings, either. Unfair advantage." Jamie sticks her tongue out.

I laugh and shake my head. "Okay, okay." I take a step forward and swing at Jamie, who ducks and immediately grabs my leg, pulling it out from under me. I slam into the mat with a groan, turning my head to the side. "Shit."

She looks down at me innocently, smiling. "You just need to warm up."

"Ugh." I squirm out from under her and get to my feet.

Again and again, I hit the floor, knees slamming into the mat with a thud. I continue to stand, growing more and more determined with each loss.

I'm finally able to catch Jamie's ankle on a kick, and I twist her around, slamming her down on the mat and sitting on her hips to pin her there. I grip her wrists, pinning them on either side of her head and grin down at her victoriously. "Gotcha."

Jamie laughs breathlessly, tipping her head back. "I'm just getting a little tired, is all."

"Uh huh." I stare down at her. Her porcelain skin is flushed from effort, pink lips never chapped, despite the fact that she's constantly licking and biting at them. She stares up at me, eyes filled with something that looks suspiciously like wonder.

Jamie takes a deep breath. "Maxwell...?"

I watch her for a moment longer before I finally allow all of my annoying little inhibitions to slip away. I lean down and kiss her.

Jamie lets out a surprised sound and then melts into me, kissing me back.

She has beautiful lips. So much different than Bear's. So soft and gentle. She tastes like cherry chapstick. I can't get enough of it.

Jamie pulls back first, looking up at me with a dazed expression on her face that quickly turns into a delirious smile. "Max..."

I blush to my roots, lips turning up into a smile. "Was that okay?" I breathe, reaching up to run a thumb over her swollen bottom lip.

She laughs breathlessly and pulls me back down, attacking my mouth with her own.

My eyes close as I revel in the feeling. It's as though a thousand flying insects are beating against the inner walls of my chest. My grace grows burning hot. I gasp against her mouth as her fingers rake through my hair and against my scalp, chasing a shudder throughout my body.

"You were supposed to be practicing!" A familiar voice accuses from the other side of the room.

I groan and my wings fly out, sheltering the two of us from sight. I shake my head and set my forehead to Jamie's.

Jamie giggles and slides her arms around me, pulling me close. She nuzzles her nose to mine. "Don't worry about him."

Matty huffs a sigh, clearly annoyed. "I'm supposed to get the two of you for dinner. Maybe calm down before you get in or everyone'll know something's up."

"Oh, good," I murmur distractedly against Jamie's cheek, closing my eyes.

Jamie laughs again. "Go on, Matthew!" she calls. "We'll be in in a moment."

"Yeah, yeah."

...And that concludes our daily announcements for Wednesday, August 07, 2165. Thank you and God Bless...

Newscasts have never been particularly reliable. We're only shown what those in power want us to see, nothing more. It's why we have no idea what's going on outside our city, much less our entire country. When the walls went up after the war, we lost all information we *had* been allowed to see. Now, with Michael ruling over our city and supposedly in the works of cleansing our entire country, I've been thinking more and more about what could be going on everywhere else. Are the angels attacking other countries? Are nephilim coming forward to challenge them? How can we get in touch with them? Getting rid of the angels will extend past ridding them from our city or country. It'll require global cooperation.

Gabriel never mentions the rest of the world. Probably because he feels just as hopeless as the rest of us. We know we have to start somewhere, but figuring out where has been a real problem.

I finish wiping Nova down as the daily announcements finish playing through the radio. She definitely took a beating when I teleported her underground, but she's made of material that was designed to take a hit. The Nova Dawn was created to be a race craft. Racing has been banned for years, so now the only hovercrafts on the market are big luxury crafts for rich government employees and their families, or military crafts, which are bigger versions of the Nova with built-in artillery. Their increased size means that Nova is still faster than them. She's still more efficient.

Cleaning her up makes me wish I could be outside again, riding her around.

The daily announcements usually finish around early afternoon. I still have at least two hours before curfew. I'm pretty sure I won't be missed if I leave for just a little while.

I sit down on the Nova and close my eyes, visualizing the field beside my childhood home.

A moment later, I'm there. Miraculously, the field has remained unscathed in the recent chaos. Wildflowers grow wild and unrestricted all over the field. They're beautiful.

Jamie loves wildflowers. She used to wear them every day in the spring and summer. She'd tuck them into the buttons of her dress or behind her ears or even in her hair. I set to work picking a huge bouquet for her. They'll make her smile.

I pull my hair down from its band and use it to hold the flowers together. I open Nova's back storage compartment and lay them inside carefully. They should be okay for now.

I climb back onto Nova and start her up. She purrs as she springs to life. She sounds like a dream. I take off through the field, heading for the main road.

I'm about to take flight when I hear a horrible, screaming cry. I swerve to my left, following the noise. A group of people stand in a circle, a woman in their center. She's been severely beaten. Blood pours from her nose, and her teeth have gone through her lip. Her bright blue eyes are nearly swollen shut. She's barely capable of movement anymore. I stop my bike and approach quietly from behind, needing to evaluate the situation.

The horrible crying isn't coming from the woman, but from a small child who lays beneath her. She's trying to protect him, but her hands are bound and by this point she's so broken that she's lucky to even be alive.

A woman glares down at her. But she's not just a normal woman; she's an angel. Her bronze-colored wings are folded neatly behind her as she surveys the scene in front of her. They flicker in and out of existence. Her glamour isn't holding. "You thought you could hide? You thought you could keep this monster a secret?"

I'm horrified to see the small child is bruised and bleeding. He's obviously nephilim. His ivory wings are bound so tightly to his small frame that there's little hope of circulation. Crusted blood covers the twine that binds him. He has dark, curly hair and light brown skin.

His wide eyes are a brilliant, blazing blue, but bloodshot and filled with tears. He howls in pain as his mother shifts to cover him.

I need to do something, but I can't let myself be known before I have the upper hand. I step closer, holding my breath.

The angel glares down at the woman and kicks her side. "Do you know how we dispose of nephilim?"

The woman lets out a choked sob, tipping her head back. Tears streak her pale, dirty face.

"We burn them with fire. It's a little preview for what they'll be answering to in *Hell*."

The little boy can't be more than two. It's impossible that the people watching this happen could think he is capable of causing harm. I'm disgusted by their complete lack of compassion and inability to tell right from wrong. I step up behind the angel and look over her shoulder at the woman.

I can tell the moment she recognizes me because her eyes meet mine and hope flickers over her pained face. "Please," she mouths, fresh tears leaking down the sides of her nose.

Before the angel has a chance to turn around, I close my hand around her neck as I focus my energy toward creating a burning heat. She drops to her knees with a hiss and looks back at me.

I glare down at her, hatred filling me to my core. "What's your name?"

"You're disgusting!" she hisses through clenched teeth. "You deserve to burn with the rest of them!"

I squeeze tighter, searing a brand of my handprint into the back of her neck. "I asked you a question."

Her eyes fill with light and she gasps for breath. She chokes. "A-Abaddon," she splutters, grabbing at my hand.

I scowl at her and throw her away from me. The crowd parts, staring between the two of us with wide eyes.

She makes to stand, but I shake my head, holding my hand out toward her. I focus my energy on building the heat I've created. She writhes as her body begins to smoke. Her fingertips catch fire first. It doesn't take long before the rest of her follows suit.

She's dead soon after.

The crowd stares, wide-eyed and horrified. I stand in front of them, still furious, but also wondering when it became so easy for me to kill. I step forward to the woman in the middle of the circle and dissolve her binds. She's too weak to stand, so I take her son in my arms and hold him carefully, trying not to shuffle his wings too much for fear of causing more pain. He's grown quiet, clearly exhausted. He lays his wet face against my chest and snuffles. I get slowly to my feet.

My face is wet. There's snot and tears on my face, but I don't remember when I began to cry. I look down at the miserable little boy in my arms and then back at the crowd. They're all so damned quiet. "You let this happen," I accuse. "This is on you. And we can't save you if you allow things like this to happen."

I kneel back down beside the woman and touch her cheek. "What's your name?" I whisper.

She lets out a long sigh, closing her eyes. "Emily."

I nod and slide my free arm around her. "I'm going to take you home now, okay, Emily?"

Emily's head rolls to my shoulder, but she nods against it. Her eyes close and her breathing slows dangerously.

I close my eyes and picture us back home, in the hospital ward of the bunker. We're there in less than a second.

"Ari!"

Ari's head snaps up quickly and she runs to us. "Max, what happened?!"

"She needs help! Emily needs help!"

Beth, Ari's assistant, helps lay Emily on a clean table. They work over her quickly, connecting her to IVs and ventilators. I don't know how to help, so I step back, cradling the boy protectively. He's crying again, his face stuffed into my neck as his tiny fists grip and twist my shirt.

There's a pressure building inside my ribcage that can't be held down. I stumble back against the wall and gasp for breath, clinging to the child.

"Maxwell?!" Jamie slides to a stop in front of me, hands reaching to clutch my shoulders. "What happened?!"

I tip my head back, gasping for breath. "Emily... Emily needs help!" I repeat, feeling dizzy. "She can't die. Her son..."

Jamie surveys the little boy and gasps. "Oh my God. Max. We'll help him, alright? They'll both be okay."

"I killed her. I killed her! It was so easy!" I can recognize that I'm hysterical, but I can't seem to figure out how to breathe again.

Gabriel moves forward, reaching for the child. I shake my head, holding him closer. "No!"

"Maxwell, who did you kill?" He asks, voice calm despite the pull of his brows.

"Abaddon! I set her on f-fire!"

He lets out a breath of air. "Maxwell, hand the child to Jamie. She will unbind his wings. He needs medical attention immediately."

"No!" They can't take him away. I need to make sure he's protected. He's got no one to look after him. If his mother dies, he'll be all alone. I can't let that happen to him. My breathing hitches and my vision swims. I slide toward the floor.

Gabriel grunts as he catches me. "Jamie, the child…"

She takes him obediently, and my arms suddenly feel very empty. I gasp and clutch at my hollow chest. My hand is smeared with blood that is not my own.

Gabriel carries me to a different room and sits down on the floor with me as I break and begin to sob. He doesn't seem to care when I cover his shirt in tears and snot and mumble hysterically. He takes my hand and wraps it around the vial of his grace that lays against my chest. It pulses a warm, steady rhythm that works to gradually calm me down.

"She was going to burn him," I mutter later, face pressed against his shoulder.

He nods and strokes my hair. "You did what you had to."

"They were all just standing there. They let it happen. Nobody tried to help."

"They were afraid…"

"Maybe they don't deserve to be saved." I know I'm wrong, even as I say the words.

"Maxwell," Gabriel replies, cupping my face in his hand. "Everybody deserves to be saved."

Jamie comes to our room, a sleeping toddler in her arms. I sit up immediately and reach for him as she offers him to me. His wings are heavily wrapped in gauze and he's got stitches above his left eye. I hold him carefully and press my lips to the top of his curly head.

He snuffles in his sleep and presses his cheek to my breast, drool leaking from the corner of his mouth.

I rub his lower back gently. "His mother...?"

She shakes her head, face grim. "Too early to tell. She woke for a couple of minutes. Long enough to ask about Zachary." She nods toward the sleeping boy. "She's in pretty bad shape."

"God, I hope she makes it," I mumble, looking down at Zachary. "He needs her."

She nods. "Ari and Beth have done their best. It's kind of up to her now. This little guy... He's not in great shape, but he'll be just fine. Gabriel doesn't think he'll fly again, though," she says sadly.

She perches on the edge of the bed beside me and allows me to lay my head against her shoulder. "You did well today."

"I don't want to talk about it," I mumble, closing my eyes. "Trying to forget..."

"Okay," she agrees. She's silent for a while before speaking again. "I love you."

I take a deep breath as my cheeks turn pink. "I picked flowers for you. But I forgot them."

Jamie presses her lips to my forehead and I feel them turn up into a small smile. "Thank you, Max," she whispers.

Emily is still very ill. She hasn't woken since she asked about her son, and we're all beginning to lose hope. Ari has been working around the clock to keep her alive, but it seems like the internal damage might be too much.

I've been keeping an eye on Zachary. I sing him the same songs my mother used to sing to me. He's still in pain, but it doesn't keep him from smiling now and then. He's very clingy, and though I've never been particularly fond of children, I feel an attachment to him. I allow him to stick close to me, and I make sure I'm the one who feeds him and changes his diapers. I want him to feel safe and loved until his mother is well again.

I'm sitting with him on the floor, watching him drink juice from a makeshift sippy cup when Gabriel approaches. He looks down at us and smiles wearily. "Afternoon announcements. Thought maybe you'd want to watch with us."

Not really, but I suppose I'd better.

It's been less than a day since I murdered Abaddon, and since it hasn't been mentioned in the announcements yet, I'm pretty sure it'll happen now.

I scoop Zachary up and walk with Gabriel to the communications room where we have all our meetings. I stand with the others in front of the holo platform and wait.

It's not long before Michael's hologram appears. He doesn't look very happy.

"Greetings, citizens," he begins, folding his hands in front of him. "It is with great regret that I inform you of a tragic death within our community." His voice is mournful and full of remorse.

I wonder how much of it is real.

"Yesterday afternoon, my sister Abaddon was attacked by Maxwell Odyssey. Be advised, the footage you are about to see is graphic and not for the weak of heart."

An image appears beside Michael. I can see myself standing in front of Abaddon, arms outstretched toward her. My loose hair blows back from my face and my eyes glow white.

Abaddon writhes, making a horrible pleading noise. Her body begins to smoke.

Zachary and his mother are nowhere in this picture. I have no idea who was filming us, but I feel nauseous at the lack of privacy. It's bad enough that a group of people watched me lose my shit and end a life, now everyone else is going to think I'm a psycho. They're also taking the footage out of context. Nobody can see that this angel was ready to burn a helpless child alive.

Abaddon catches fire with a scream. The image turns back to me as I watch her burn. I look pretty fucking scary. My eyes are still glowing, but tears are pouring down my face.

The video footage skips forward. My face fills the screen, dirty and smeared with blood. I'm glaring right at the camera. "We can't save you," I say.

The footage cuts out, and Michael shakes his head, looking straight toward his viewers. "This act of murder can't be forgiven. You've heard the words straight from Miss Odyssey's mouth. She wants nothing to do with helping you. She intends for the world to burn."

Gabriel promptly shuts down the holoprojector and the room is filled with a sickening silence.

I don't even know what to say to defend myself.

"Maxwell..." Jeremy looks over me, frowning deeply.

"They made it look worse than it was," I blurt, shaking my head.

"Yeah, it sure looks bad to me."

I close my eyes for a moment. "I said we couldn't save them if they allowed people like Zachary and Emily to be hurt. I was freaking out."

"A panic attack doesn't constitute setting someone on fire."

"She was going to *kill* them!"

"This is bad. People are going to be really upset." Jeremy shakes his head.

My eyes fill with angry tears. "What was I supposed to *do*? Let them die?"

Suddenly, the room is filled with a horrible piercing noise. It has me to my knees in no time, gasping for breath. Zachary presses his tiny fists to his ears and howls. I look up. Jamie seems to be the only other person affected. The others are staring at us incredulously.

Gabriel looks around quickly and shakes his head. "Close your eyes! Everybody!"

A loud crack like thunder causes the ground to quake and the room fills with a supernatural light.

I open my eyes when the ringing stops and I'm met with the most beautiful angel I've ever seen.

She's tall and statuesque, dark skin glowing transcendentally. Her ghostly wings rise high above her head predatorily. She's wearing a long, strapless, sheer dress, and her long black hair tumbles in perfect braids down her sides. Her eyes are dark and filled with fury. "Where is my son?!" she yells.

My eyes widen in shock and I cling to Zachary, trying to keep him safe. He sniffles and then wriggles from my arms and toddles quickly to the woman.

Her face breaks its cold expression and crumbles into something that resembles a terrified relief. She bends down and scoops him up in her arms, pulling him close and covering his face in delicate kisses. The gesture looks impossibly soft for someone who looks so exquisitely carved from basalt.

Zachary coos and smiles widely at her. "Mama," he says happily.

I stare in disbelief.

Gabriel curses quietly under his breath.

The angel looks toward him and arches a perfectly shaped brow. "Gabriel, is that any way to greet your sister?"

Uriel moves forward to stand beside my father. "Hael, you'll excuse us if we aren't very thrilled to have an angel in our place of safety. We are at war, you know."

Hael stands taller, shifting her son to rest on her hip. "I think you'll find we are on the same side." She pulls her long hair over her shoulder and turns around. Between her wings, a word has been branded into her skin in thick, dark scar tissue: Disobedient.

"I don't like that they're alone in there with her," I grumble to Jamie. We were kicked out of the room with everybody else to let Uriel and my father speak with their long-lost sibling. She has Zachary there with her, and although he seems to recognize and love her, I'm still feeling protective.

Jamie shifts and brushes her long hair behind her shoulder. "I don't like it either, but their judgement is good. They would know if she was here to cause trouble."

"I guess."

She squeezes my shoulder. "This could be really good. The angels are powerful, and if she knows any others who are willing to disobey Michael, we could really benefit from the extra help. She probably knows loads of inside information."

"I think they've been in there with her long enough."

"Max, it's only been twenty minutes."

"Like I said, it's been long enough." I get to my feet and walk back through the door before she can stop me.

The three angels stare at me as I enter. Hael raises an eyebrow. "Hello, Maxwell. I believe I have you to thank for my son's life."

I take a deep breath and look from her to my father and uncle who both look rather unhappy at being interrupted. I move toward them quickly. "You shouldn't be here alone."

Zachary breaks free from his mother and runs over to me. He hugs my leg, and I scoop him up. "Hey buddy," I coo, pressing a kiss to the side of his face.

Hael observes me skeptically, eyes trailing over my entire body. "This is the girl who's going to save the world?"

Jamie steps into the room and walks over to me. "Is everything going alright in here?"

"Yes," Gabriel says, exasperated. "We are quite able to handle ourselves without the help of our teenage daughters."

Jamie shrugs and looks toward Hael. "I'm Jamie."

"I know."

"Are you going to help us?"

"I am."

"How?"

Hael looks away from her and back at me. She stares at me for a long time before looking over at my father accusatorily. "You said nothing about an elioud."

Gabriel straightens and frowns deeply. "I don't know what you're talking about."

"She's practically glowing, Brother. Have you not been the least bit suspicious?"

She makes me uncomfortable as she talks about me like I'm not even there. "What's an elioud?"

Uriel is pale. He clears his throat. "We haven't had an elioud born in a thousand years."

"What is an elioud?" I repeat, running out of patience. I look toward Jamie but she only shrugs, clearly just as confused as I am.

"An elioud is born from two special parents. An angel and a nephilim mixed. She will have the status of a demigod. She will be extraordinarily powerful," Hael says.

Woah. She can't mean what I think she's saying. "I'm sorry, but I think you must be mistaken."

"You were in a relationship with my brother, Remiel, correct?"

"Yes, but…"

"Then I'm unsure why you're so shocked."

I feel dizzy. I set Zachary down on the ground and slump to a chair, putting my head in my hands. "Oh my God…" I moan.

Jamie kneels in front of me, looking a little green. She sets her hands on my knees. "Hey, it's okay."

"Are you fucking kidding me? Of course it's not okay! That asshole got me *pregnant*?"

Jamie blows out a breath of air. "You just need to keep calm. You have options."

"We've never had an elioud grow to adulthood," Gabriel murmurs, sounding quiet.

I look up between my fingers, grimacing. "Why?" There's a sinking feeling in my stomach. I lay my hand over my flat belly.

He shrugs. "Angels have always stepped in. Elioud are often very difficult to care for. They're temperamental. They cause scenes. They get into trouble. They're fond of causing natural disasters."

"What am I going to *do*?"

"I don't know, Maxwell. Nobody can make that decision for you."

My head is spinning. I stand with Jamie's help and make my way over to Hael. "Is there a chance that it could be good?"

Hael nods. "Of course. If you raise her with love and compassion, there is no reason she should become restless and angry. Teach her right from wrong, and I'm sure she will be fine."

"She?"

"Yes, she's a girl."

"Oh my god." It would be a lie to say I haven't thought about what it would be like to have children, but I made a solid decision long ago that I would never bring children into a world like this one. And I'm young. A year younger than my mom had been when she had me, and that was too young. I'm afraid of what Gabriel and Jamie think of me. Afraid of the situation. With everything that's going on, especially now, with all of the danger and the stress I'm under, I can't imagine giving birth.

But I have a daughter. She's growing inside of me and she has no idea what she's going to be getting herself into if I go through with this pregnancy.

Hael smiles a little, and I can see kindness seeping in through her tough façade. "Don't look so frightened. You were doing fine with my Zachary. Children are a wonderful gift."

Jamie takes my hand tightly and squeezes it. When I look at her, she's watching me thoughtfully, a shy smile tugging at the corners of her mouth. "It's your decision," she murmurs. "I'm not going anywhere either way."

It's just what I need to hear. Warmth seeps into my cheeks and I nod. "I know."

Hael clears her throat and looks toward my father and Uriel. "Where is Emily? I'd like to see her."

I chew my lip. "I can take you to her."

Hael nods. "Please."

When Hael catches sight of Emily, she makes a heartbroken noise, eyes filling immediately with tears. She hurries over to her and takes her pale hand, rubbing her thumb over her bruised skin. I can't bear to watch them together. It's too sad.

"Em," Hael breathes, leaning down and pressing her forehead to Emily's. "My Emily…"

Emily's swollen eyes flutter open miraculously and she stares up at her angel. "Hael?" she croaks. She shudders with effort.

"Hush, sweet one. Yes, I'm here," Hael murmurs softly, stroking her hand over her lover's hair. "God, what did they do to you?"

Emily moans quietly. "Knew you'd come," she breathes, closing her eyes.

"Of course. Of course, my love," the angel responds.

"Maxwell?" I look away from the scene toward my father's whisper. He takes me by the arm and pulls me carefully from the room. He shuts the door quietly behind him. "She's dying," he murmurs. "They need time."

My nose stings with the threat of oncoming tears and I nod once. "Yeah. Um…" I take a shaky breath and put my face in my hands. It's too much. Too much for one day.

He pulls me into a hug and I shove my face in his shoulder, barely containing myself for a moment before I begin to cry.

When my parents died, I didn't think I would ever be able to cry again. I thought I'd cried every tear my body could possibly ever make. Lately, that's changed. It's like I can't stop. Maybe it's hormones. Or maybe it's just my body catching up on every shitty thing that's happened since then.

"I'm sorry," I mumble when I've mostly contained myself. My voice is muffled by the fabric of his shirt. "I didn't know about the baby."

He takes a deep breath and sits down with me in the far corner of the room. "I would be lying if I said I wasn't shocked. But it's nothing you can't handle. You're an adult now; you'll be eighteen in a few weeks. You're more than capable of raising a baby if it's what you choose to do. You have plenty of people willing to help you."

I nod and sniffle, wiping my eyes on the back of my shirtsleeve. "Thanks, dad."

He pats my knee and says nothing more.

Emily dies later that night. Jamie says it's sweet that she was able to hold on until she could say goodbye to Hael. But when I can't escape the sound of Hael's heartbroken sobs through the wall, I just think it makes it all the more depressing.

"You have work to do."

I'm surprised by Hael's straightforwardness, especially since it's only been hours since she said goodbye to her human lover. I nod anyway, looking up at her. "What do we do first?"

"I have two other children. Farahnush in Egypt, and Nicole in Wales. They're part of a network of nephilim who can help you. I will put you in contact with them."

I blink, momentarily stunned.

Jamie shifts beside me. "A network?"

Hael nods. "They've come in contact with nephilim from all over the world. The walls and communications blockers in the United States have made contact nearly impossible, but my daughters are very gifted. They have found a way. They just need to exchange information with you."

"How many nephilim have they connected with?" I ask.

"Hundreds." Hael smiles a little. "There are more of you than you think."

"Wow."

"I have a code for you. You'll need to type it in when you've completed the set of instructions." Hael hands me a slip of paper. It's got a bunch of random letters and symbols on it. I have no idea what it means.

"You'll figure it out." Hael shifts Zachary to her other hip. "I must go. My girls need me and my son is in danger here."

"Wait, you're leaving? Just like that?"

She nods. "It was nice meeting you, Maxwell. Jamie. I have faith in you."

I stare at her, mouth gaping open. "But…"

"And Maxwell?"

"Yeah?"

"You'll do just fine with your daughter. I'll visit when the hysteria has died down. Thank you for saving my son. I am indebted to you forever."

I don't know what to say, so I only nod, watching after her as she swoops away, just as suddenly as she'd come.

I look over at Jamie, my mouth hanging open.

She frowns, brows pulling together. "I'll go get Leighton. He'll know what to do."

It turns out that having Leighton on our side has proven invaluable once more. He's eagerly tapping away at the holoscreen of his processor, working through one problem after another as though there's nothing to it.

"Where did you learn all of this stuff?" I ask.

He shrugs, smiling brightly. "My dad used to build this kind of stuff. He taught me everything he knows. I taught myself the rest. Once you've hacked into a few databases, everything else is pretty easy."

"You're sure this is going to work?"

"It should. I just need a couple more minutes. This thing is hidden really well. It'd have to be, of course. And breaking through the communications blockers was kind of a pain in the ass, but we're almost there."

"Huh."

I look at Jamie but she only shrugs, looking about as impressed as I feel. She sighs and wiggles her brows at me. "So, momma… How are you feeling?"

Leighton stops typing and looks over at me. "Holy shit, you're pregnant?"

I point to his screen. "Keep working, please."

He flushes and nods. "Yeah, yeah. Sorry." He scrambles to finish.

I glare pointedly at Jamie. "I'm tired, and I don't even want to begin to discuss the status of my womb."

She smiles apologetically. "Sorry."

"Got it!" Leighton crows suddenly, pumping his fist into the air victoriously.

The projection screen in front of us widens to fit the entire opposite wall and flickers to life. A young woman with wide blue eyes and long, curly brown hair stares at us from where she's seated in front of a light blue wall. She grins. "Hello!" She waves enthusiastically. "You must be Maxwell and Jamie."

I take a deep breath and smile. "We are. And you're Nicole?" I guess, using her accent as a hint.

She nods. "I am. Welcome to the network! I'm glad you were able to figure out how to reach us. My mother can be cryptic at times." She grins. "Sorry about that."

I laugh and shake my head. "No, this is great. We're so happy to meet you! We've been out of the loop, but this makes everything so much easier."

"Life is a little simpler over here. As far as I know, the States are taking the brunt of the angel action right now, which is why we're actually planning on coming for a visit. If we can get rid of them while they're with you, they won't be able to invade everywhere else."

Jamie nods. "That makes sense. But how will you get here?"

She shrugs. "Teleportation seems easiest. It's the only way we're going to get through the walls. Everyone has been training for days. We're going to use boats to get as close as we can, and then we're going to come inside. We'll travel by hovercraft for the rest of the journey. Since you're the only contact we've had in the States, you'll be the ones we come to. Michael seems to have made Chicago his home."

"Yes, unfortunately, he has. I think that's a great idea," I reply, watching her.

"Mam says you've already taken care of some of the angels on your own. That's amazing," Nicole says, eyes wide. "I can't imagine! She's so powerful! You must be very strong."

I shift uncomfortably. "Just desperate, actually."

She laughs. "I suppose. Alright, I need you to send me your location information. We can't stay connected for long because it makes it easier for us to be found. We'll give you another call in a month, after we've gotten closer to being ready. Same time?"

I nod. "Alright."

She grins. "Excellent. See you then." She cuts out and the projection screen glows a dull blue color.

Jamie takes my face in her hands and kisses me sloppily before pulling back, absolutely beaming. "This is really happening!"

I wish I could share in her enthusiasm. I really wish I could. Instead, I nod blankly, allowing my hand to travel to my stomach, where it rests hesitantly. I'm ready for this war to be over, but I'm scared of the sacrifices we'll be making in the near future.

It only takes two days for me to come to my decision. When I do, I announce it to both Gabriel and Jamie.

"I'm keeping her," I say softly, looking up at them. "For entirely selfish reasons."

Gabriel looks up at me and nods. He gives me a small, tired smile. "We will be around to help you. It will be difficult, but you will learn how worth it she is."

I touch my stomach, taking a deep breath. "She'll be a good girl."

Gabriel laughs and shakes his head. "Coming from a line of such strong-willed women, I believe we may have a problem on our hands," he teases.

Jamie sets her hand over mine, protective of my belly. "We'll make sure she knows right from wrong. She'll grow up surrounded by people who love her. I hope the war is over before she comes, though."

"She feels special," I blurt, looking up. "She feels like a change is coming."

Gabriel takes a deep breath, sobering suddenly. "That's exactly what your mother said about you. She could feel a revolution coming."

I look up at him quietly and then back down at my belly. "I'll need to be careful now. That's annoying," I say softly, after a long moment.

Jamie smiles and presses her lips to my shoulder. "That makes me happy. I'm glad you'll have cause to be more cautious."

Gabriel grins over at Jamie, and they share a look while I roll my eyes, irritated by their dramatics.

"I'm always cautious."

"More like never."

I sigh and curl into Jamie, closing my eyes. "Whatever. You're both annoying," I huff, smiling anyway as I breathe in her scent. She smells like evergreen trees and peppermint, and it feels familiar, sweet.

"Jesus, get a room."

I don't need to open my eyes to know that Matthew has just walked in. I fight to hide a smirk.

"You're so jealous, it's pathetic," I mutter, eyeing him suspiciously.

"I am *not* jealous." He rolls his eyes, crossing his arms.

I laugh and kiss the top of Jamie's head, feeling a sort of delirious happiness. Despite everything that's happened in the last few months, my life has finally begun to take a turn for the better. We've found allies overseas who are coming to help us, I have my father in my life, my brother is home safe and sound, and I've got Jamie to lean on. I'm not sure exactly what that means, and what all it will entail, but right now I don't have the energy to ask questions about it. I just want to bask in all of its glory and focus on the light that I have found in all of this darkness. I'm nervous about the child I carry inside of me, but I want to make it my mission to make sure she is cared for and loved. She will have her grandfather, her uncle, her mom, and Jamie, who could, in complete honesty, possibly become another parental figure for her.

While I sit here, surrounded by the people who I love, I know they can feel it, too. Gabriel is watching Jamie and I, a wide smile on his face. Matthew has abandoned his wounded, jealous expression, to smile sheepishly, shaking his head, and Jamie is holding me close, protective. She knows we have dark days ahead but is still able to smile and be happy, to enjoy this moment. This is precious, a gift, and I want to hold onto it for as long as I can.

Our happiness cannot last.

It is a Sunday when Michael takes his war a step further.

"Greetings, citizens," he smiles his charming smile.

I lean back against Jamie as I watch the hologram, trying to keep calm. Jamie slides her arms around me and I hug them, closing my eyes briefly. Yesterday marks the estimated fourth month of my pregnancy. My belly is barely a bump, but I've noticed that Jamie likes to smooth her hand slowly over it. Now is no exception. Her hand rubs slow circles over it.

"Today is the day things change for you all. Today is the day we begin our mass cleansing. You see, we believe that all people, all beings, deserve a second chance. However, sometimes these second chances at life stem from sacrifice."

I can already tell I don't like where this is going. I look up at the screen.

"Gabriel. Brother. We really need you to come back to us," Michael says, staring into the camera. "We know you will most likely fight us on this matter, so we have a great incentive for you."

A small video appears on Michael's left side.

When we all realize what we're watching, we gasp. A couple of people swear. I reach for my father, my hand clutching his arm. I watch a terrified version of myself follow the movement onscreen.

We have been betrayed.

The camera view changes, revealing different sections of the underground and giving away all of our secrets and the identities of everyone who lives here. The camera switches back to focus in on me, Gabriel, Jamie, and those who are with us. Michael's grin grows.

"Surprise!" he exclaims, throwing his arms out dramatically. His wings flutter with excitement. "We know exactly where you are. We know everyone who you are with. We know your secrets."

I shake my head, staring at the screen. The blood leaves my face.

"We've got you all figured out, Brother. It appears your followers are not quite as loyal as you thought."

I look over at my father, and then I glance around the room at the others.

Leighton ducks his head, shoulders hunched. He looks as though he wants to run, and I realize instantly who has given us away. No one else is as technologically inclined as Leighton. No one else would have been able to pull this off.

I shake my head, unable to believe it. "Leighton, no," I whisper. "You wouldn't."

He shrinks up, tears already rolling down his cheeks. He lets out a wounded noise.

Jamie turns a pair of defeated green eyes to him, shaking her head slowly. "But why?"

"Michael was going to take my dad," he responds quietly, through trembling lips. He looks back up at me. "I'm so sorry. I had no choice."

Darren stares at his son, disbelief plain on his face.

Vic turns on Leighton furiously. "You have killed us all, you idiot child! Destroyed your world."

"Uriel, brother. Stop," Gabriel murmurs, touching Uncle Vic's arm in a surprisingly tender gesture. Gabriel is exuding an almost eerie calm.

"Let us finish listening to our brother's speech. He always did like to be the center of attention."

Michael grins excitedly, observing our behavior second by second. His glass-colored eyes crinkle in amusement. "Thank you, Gabriel. I appreciate your cooperation. You should know we have you surrounded. We are prepared to come in at any moment. *However*, if you are willing to cooperate, no further action will be necessary."

Gabriel stares at the screen. He takes a deep breath and stands taller. "What do you want?"

"All of your followers are about to die. Keep that in mind, okay? And Heaven has no room for traitors. No room for rebels."

Vic makes a disgusted noise beside Gabriel.

Michael shakes his head. "You look sick, dear brother. Let me assure you that there is a way for all of those poor souls to live. And it all rests on your shoulders."

"Spit it out!" Gabriel growls, glaring at the screen.

"Sacrifice yourself, and the rest of your people will live. I will very generously grant each and every one of them a second chance. Even the two monsters that you seem to have such an attachment to."

Fuck this. I grab my father's hand tightly, worry pulsing through me. "Don't listen to him," I murmur urgently.

"Listen to me, Gabriel. If you don't surrender, everyone will die. You will die, our brother Uriel will die. All of your followers will be reduced to nothing but flame and then ashes."

Gabriel swallows audibly and shakes his head, staring at the screen. He looks back down at me. "Max…"

"Dad, *no*." My eyes widen in panic as I shake my head. "You can't. I swear to God…"

Vic frowns deeply at him. "Brother, you know he's lying."

"I will also grant our brother, Uriel, a second chance. He can have his wings back. All I need is for you to open that door and walk out to us," Michael continues, watching us intently.

"Everyone will die, Maxwell," Gabriel murmurs, watching me. "I cannot allow that to happen."

"Stop! What are you *saying*?! He's a liar! He'll kill you! And then we'll all die anyway!" I can't breathe anymore. My insides twist hard, and I shake my head, lips trembling.

Gabriel swallows hard and looks up at his brother. "Maxwell and Jamie will be spared? And the others?"

"Yes." Michael nods.

"What's the catch?"

"There is none. We've just decided that you will be sufficient to punish everyone. You'll be another Christ-like figure. You'll die for everyone's sins and then everyone gets to go to Heaven. Even the abominations. God is forgiving."

"This has nothing to do with our Father. Don't you dare pull him into your blasphemous decision making," Gabriel mutters angrily. "Our Father would never condone such despicable behavior!"

"Our Father left me in charge because he respects my judgment. But that matters not. The clock is ticking, Gabriel, and you have a decision to make. Die with the rebels in smoke and fire, or sacrifice yourself and save them all. It's up to you."

I pull from Jamie to move in front of my dad, staring up at him and blocking his view of Michael. I raise my wings in front of the screen to block him out purposely and keep his attention on me. "Dad, you can't."

He takes a deep breath and sets his hands on my shoulders. "Maxwell, you are a strong, beautiful woman. You remind me more and more of your mother every day. I'm proud to be your father. I'm so happy to have gotten the time we've had. But you cannot ask me to allow all of these deaths to occur."

"I just got you back. Please. Dad, listen. I just got you back. I can't watch you die. I can't let him take you away from me." My breath catches in my throat.

He stares at me, his eyes reflecting pain and desperation.

"Brother, you can't possibly be thinking about giving yourself up," Vic says, staring at him. "You know he's a liar. You can't leave."

"How are we to know if he's lying? If he's not, the world will see. They will understand. If I stay and everyone dies, we will never know if it could have ended differently."

I choke on a sob, shaking my head back and forth in disbelief. "I just got you back..." I repeat.

His eyes fill with tears, and he looks toward the ceiling for a moment before looking back down at me. "Your family is here, Maxwell. They will take care of you. You cannot lose your fight. You cannot lose your drive or your passion. They are what make you who you are. I am confident that you will be successful. That you will win."

He pulls me into his arms and closes his eyes, tucking his face into the top of my hair.

I slump against him, panicked sobs building in my chest. My fists grip the back of his shirt with surprising strength.

"I know you will be a wonderful mother. Be the parent who I couldn't be."

I'm unable to form words to respond. I shake my head instead.

He holds me close and glances over at Vic. Uncle Vic stares back, eyes wide with tears. He gives him a small nod. It makes me want to throw up.

"I love you, Maxwell," Gabriel murmurs softly. He presses his lips to the top of my head and then looks back up at the screen.

Michael grins. "Excellent. My men are waiting at the exit. Go to them. They will bring you to the square, and the celebration will commence."

He nods and then pulls away from me and walks toward the door.

He can't do this to me. I won't let him. I hurry after him, grabbing his arm.

He doesn't turn to look back at me. "Brother."

Vic steps forward and puts his arms around me, pulling me away from my father.

I shake my head quickly, letting out a cry of despair. "No!" I slam my fists into Uncle Vic, trying my damnedest to twist away from him, but he holds me too tightly, pulling me away just long enough for Gabriel to leave.

2160

GABRIEL STOOD IN THE STREET NEAR THE GALLOWS, trying to look anywhere but the offensive structure in front of him. In moments, the love of his life would be standing there, and then she would die in the public eye as a warning.

When Aubrey and Stephen had leaked private information to the public, it had caused an outrage. Government files were sent to every device connected to the internet.

They had been charged with counts of mutiny and sentenced to death. The day Uriel had told Gabriel of Aubrey's fate had been indescribably painful. He hadn't been able to sleep since, the day of the hanging pressing down on him with a crippling weight.

The people standing around the gallows all looked solemn. It was nothing like a normal hanging where everyone was excited to be a part of the festivities. They knew Aubrey and Stephen had scarificed their lives to give them some insight into how botched things were in higher places—how manipulated and used the people had been. They were tired of it. They wanted to know more truths, and they knew that now their only ways of learning those truths were about to be disposed of.

Gabriel was afraid to look at the gallows, but he was also afraid to look around to see if Maxwell and Mary would be there. He didn't want his daughter to witness such horrors, but he was almost positive she would. He finally chanced a glance and found her right away, standing beside Mary, Matthew, and Bear. There were tears streaked down her face already, and she looked awful.

Maxwell was thirteen years old. Her hair was falling out of a braid and her oversized sweatshirt looked dirty. Gabriel recognized it as one of Aubrey's old favorites, a relic from her father. It was covered in old paint stains. Maxwell was being held in one hand by Mary and by Matty in the other. She looked as though she was having difficulty standing. Her face was pale, and she kept swaying.

Aubrey was led up the stairs to the gallows on a chain. She didn't fight. She looked very calm. Stephen, on the other hand, was fighting his chains and dragging his feet. He had vomit down the front of his shirt and was sweating profusely. The soldier pushing him along gave him a swift kick, hustling him along.

Gabriel made his way to the front, staring up at Aubrey with wide eyes. He swallowed hard and wetted his lips.

Aubrey must have felt his eyes on her because she looked down immediately and caught eyes with him. She took a deep breath and gave him a small smile. "Hello, Angel," she mouthed, lips turned up at the corners.

His eyes filled with tears, and he shook his head quickly. "Aubrey…" he whispered.

"It's okay," she mouthed, tipping her head in a tiny nod. She watched him until they put the rope around her neck as the sentencing was read.

"MOM!"

The scream came from the back, so loud and shrill that it cut Gabriel to his bones. He gasped and turned back, watching as Maxwell broke free from her family.

"MOMMY! DAD!" she shrieked, running toward the stage.

Armed soldiers stepped in front of the structure, turning their guns on Maxwell.

"Max, don't!" Aubrey's calm façade melted as she watched the men turn on her daughter. "Baby, you're okay! Go to Grandma!"

The citizens standing around the structure began shifting uncomfortably, ducking their heads and rubbing their necks.

"NO! NO, *PLEASE*!" Maxwell fought her way toward the front.

Gabriel panicked as he heard the cocking of a gun. He jerked back to look at Maxwell, getting ever closer.

"Gabriel, grab her! Save her!" Aubrey pleaded, desperate.

Gabriel looked up at her, face full of fear, and he gave a nod. He turned and caught Maxwell as she slammed into him, trying to get closer to the front. She screamed when he caught her, hitting his shoulders and kicking at him, but he held tight to her, carrying her further away, toward safety.

"I know, Maxwell. I know," he murmured into her hair, tears pouring down his cheeks. "I know."

"NO!" she screamed. "NO, PLEASE! MOM! MO—" Her pleading cut off as the ground beneath her parents' feet disappeared and they were executed. She screamed in horror, suddenly clinging to Gabriel and shaking violently. She put her face in his shoulder and howled, eyes closing tightly. Gabriel refused to look back at the bodies. He had seen death over a million times and had never feared it, but today that had changed.

Gabriel began to sob, shaking as he carried her away. He carried her until the gallows were no longer visible, and then he sat with her in the grass and held her. She let him, though he was a stranger to her. She put her face in his shoulder and sobbed until her grandmother came to collect her and take her home.

For Gabriel, the day would come to be known as the darkest in his existence, and he swore to himself that his daughter would never be subjected to that kind of pain again.

2165

THE MOMENT HE STEPS OUTSIDE, Gabriel is surrounded by his brothers. Some of them look angry, but some of them just look as though they pity him, eyes sad, but faces carefully composed as they cuff him and tug him roughly toward the public square. A camera follows his every move.

He's led through a crowd that throws rotten fruit at him. He tries to ignore the smell of decay and the sticky matter that clings to his flesh, but it adds insult to injury. He had once been a figure of such power and grace, and now he's been reduced to this. A broken, filthy shell of what he once was.

But he thinks Aubrey would probably have loved this version of him the very best. Human through and through. She died as a human, and now by some sort of sick twist of fate, he will, too. He thinks she would be happy that he has gotten the opportunity to spend time with his daughter and teach her about her true self. That he has gotten to bond with her and know her.

Gabriel stumbles at a quick jerk to his chains and falls to his knees in front of Michael without a sound, gritting his teeth. He looks up into his face, eyes narrowed in hatred.

Michael grins down at him. He's dressed all in white, but it should be red, for all of the blood he's spilled in such a short time. "Hello, Brother. I have to say, I was shocked that you agreed to come. You're normally so selfish, so stuck on self-preservation. I thought you would allow them all to burn in Hell."

"Then you don't know me very well at all," Gabriel replies, lifting his chin in defiance.

A fist connects to Gabriel's jaw, and his head spins. He slumps to the side, off-balance with his hands cuffed behind his back. He blinks, spots clouding his vision. A trickle of blood rolls down his neck.

Michael grabs him by his hair and turns his face to the monitor up in the sky.

Gabriel sees his daughter there. Her hands are over her mouth, and she's shaking, staring at him. He wets his lips and takes a deep breath. She's going to watch him die.

He shakes his head, feeling a sense of urgency as his time grows short. He looks around, observing the large crowd that has gathered, some of it soldiers, some of it his brothers. The rest are citizens, just like his daughter, just like Aubrey. He stares at them, and then he begins to speak.

"Citizens. Brothers. I am brought here before you because I care too much about humanity. Because I wanted to raise my daughter and be a part of her life. Because I fell in love with her mother and created a life and fell in love with being human. Because I chose free will."

A boot in his side causes him to cry out, swaying to the side. Gravel digs into his knees.

"Shut up, Gabriel," Michael hisses near his ear, before cuffing the side of his face.

Even as his body reverberates with pain, Gabriel thinks about Aubrey and the voice she was able to give to her people. He's going to die; he knows it. The least he can do is to give one last fuck-you to Michael and the rest of his corrupt brothers.

"Michael will tell you that the nephilim are dangerous. They are powerful; it's true. But they are uninterested in hurting you. Instead, they want to save you.

"And what Michael *doesn't* want you to know, is that he too has a nephilim daughter. Her name is Jamie, and I am confident that she will be his downfall *because* of his plan to exterminate humanity. She wants to save you. All of you. She cares about *all* of you."

Michael's fingers claw into his back, and Gabriel tips his head back, letting out a cry as Michael forces his wings into view.

Gabriel squeezes his eyes shut, breath hissing from between his clenched teeth. "They will destroy you, Michael. Your reign will end soon enough, and God help you when he finds what you've done. You will burn in Hell for your crimes to the innocent people of this world. For your crimes against your own brethren!"

Michael presses a serrated hunting knife against Gabriel's right wing and gives a quick sawing motion. Warm blood immediately soaks into the back of Gabriel's shirt as a scream rips from inside of his chest. His head falls forward against his chest and he pants, tears rolling down his cheeks.

Michael grips his hair with his free hand and forces his face up toward the monitor.

Gabriel stares up at the monitor through blurry eyes. His daughter is sobbing, hands clamped over her ears. All of the hands that try to reach out to her are rejected as she refuses to allow anyone to touch her. Her mouth opens and closes soundlessly as she pleads without a voice.

Michael leans down and presses his lips to Gabriel's ear. "You shouldn't have done that," he whispers. He plants a wet kiss to Gabriel's jaw and then stands straight, grabbing Gabriel's wing in his hand. He sets the blade to it again and looks to his men. "Set them on fire. There will be no salvation today."

Gabriel's eyes widen in horror and his mouth opens to protest, but all that comes out is a scream as his brother hacks away what is left of his wing.

PART IV

2165

THE FIRE HAPPENS QUICKLY. Too quickly. I barely have time to notice as I watch my father die, his life pouring from his body in a waterfall of crimson. I slap the hands that reach for me.

And then the world around me blows apart, and I land somewhere far from myself, floating into the sky through clouds of smoke and billowing flames of orange.

"Maxwell!" The deep voice is something I could have recognized in a different life, but I'm too far gone now to cling to the memory.

I glance down from where I'm floating along the ceiling. There's a familiar brunette with wide, terrified blue eyes. He reaches for me, eyes bloodshot from either smoke or terror. It doesn't matter either way. I am forever out of his reach.

I wake from a terror of smoke and fire, gasping for breath I thought I'd felt the last of. My eyes fly open, wide and afraid. I bolt upright, looking around in terror.

I am nowhere familiar.

I let out a shriek as my eyes focus on the figure seated beside me. I scramble backward, nearly falling off of the bed.

"Stay away from me, Remiel!" I hiss, shrinking away from him.

He stares at me quietly, face full of pain. He shakes his head quietly. "You're safe here, Maxwell."

"What have you done with the others, you murderer?" I demand, clutching my blanket to my chest. I'm completely vulnerable right now.

"I don't know what has become of the others. I only had time to get you out."

I narrow my eyes at him. "Excuse me?"

"There was no time. I tried. I wanted to go back in, but it collapsed. It's a miracle that I was able to get you out alive."

"Why me?"

He flinches back from me, shoulders slumping. He gazes down at the sheets. "I am very sorry, Max. I understand my mistakes now, and I'm filled with the deepest regret."

"Like hell," I spit, an arm encircling my belly protectively. I stand, reaching with my free hand to my necklace. It's thankfully still around my neck. As I hold it, it pulses a warmth into my hand, promising life and strength.

Remiel looks up at me with all-too-familiar indigo eyes. "I was being manipulated, Max. By Gadreel. Cameron, whatever. She promised me Heaven. Things I had long forgotten about. She promised me my grace, and I was blind enough to follow. But I was wrong.

"This is wrong. Michael is sick. He sees no wrong in his actions, but he seeks to obliterate an entire race, a people who I spent my entire life so far with, interacting and loving and being a part of. When you brought me back, I was sick. Being pulled back through the veil was hard on my soul. It damaged me. I was pulled toward darkness, death. I thought that receiving my grace would heal me, but I have since been pulled into a situation even worse. And this time, I cannot die. At least not by my own hand."

I stare at him, frowning deeply. I'm still afraid of him, but the familiarity of him, of having someone I had once valued so much near, is nearly overpowering.

T.W.R. SHELTON

"You sold me out," I murmur. "Me, Jamie, my father. Everyone."

His face falls, tears filling his eyes quickly. He nods, looking away. "I did."

"My father is dead because of you."

He nods wordlessly, throat too thick with tears to respond.

"I hate you."

A sad noise escapes him, and he shrinks up more, hands reaching to grab at his hair. "I'm so sorry. It will never be enough."

"You're damn right, it'll never be enough. You're a snake, Remiel."

"Please. Please call me Bear. Theodore. Anything but that."

"You are not Bear."

"I am. I promise I am. Maxwell."

"Your promises mean nothing to me," I reply quietly, too disgusted to even look at him any longer. I smooth a hand over the fabric covering my belly. "And now the rest of my family is probably dead because of you. Congratulations, Remiel. You've single-handedly destroyed any hope we had of saving humanity."

Remiel curls in on himself, a sob escaping from between his lips. He shakes his head miserably. "I'm sorry. I'm so sorry."

"Why am I here? You planning to deliver me to Michael yourself, like a good little soldier?"

"Never. I would *never*, Maxwell."

"You already have."

His jaw trembles, tears spilling down his cheeks as he curls in on himself, arms folding across his chest in an attempt to keep himself together.

I can't look at him. Instead, I stand, clutching the blanket to my chest, and I walk to the opposite end of the room before sitting down against the wall, uncomfortable with the closeness.

Remiel lets out a wounded noise, head hanging in his hands. His shoulders shake with his sobs, and it's making me nauseous.

I can't feel this kind of sorrow for someone who I hate.

I no longer know who he is.

He is not Theodore.

So why is it so difficult for me to see him in pain?

I put my face in my knees and slide my hands over my ears, clamping down so as to avoid hearing him at all.

I can still hear him, his pain singing a muffled tune that twists my heart like a pretzel.

I'm trembling. How dare he share his pain so openly when everyone I love is dead by his hand?

"Shut up."

It continues.

"Shut up! SHUT UP!" I scream, keeling over and shoving my face into the floor. "SHUT UP SHUT UP SHUT UP!"

And still the torture continues.

"Please eat."

"Fuck you."

"Maxwell."

I don't even glance at him.

It has been three days since I woke up with Remiel, naked and alone. It has been three days since I lost the rest of my family. And I feel like I will be in mourning forever.

"If not for you, for the baby," Remiel pleads, kneeling in front of me.

"Don't pretend to care about my baby," I mutter, staring down at my lap. I pick at a loose thread in the sweatpants I'm wearing, pulling it so the fabric begins to unravel in one spot.

I am hungry.

I'm fucking *starving*.

But how can I eat when the others are dead? How can I bring a life into this world when I know how horrible it is? When I have nothing left to fight for?

"Of course I care about our baby," Remiel says quietly, voice hushed with hurt.

I roll my eyes and continue to unravel the fabric.

"Please. I made your favorite. Tomato soup and grilled cheese. Just like Gran's."

Tears fill my eyes and I lean my cheek against my knee. It's always difficult when he brings up things from home. From our childhood. It's a reminder that he wasn't always the monster he is now, in front of me.

He stands and disappears for a moment before he returns with a platter. There's grilled cheese and some lumpy looking tomato soup, as promised. But it's nothing like Gran's.

I stare at it critically, wrinkling my nose.

Oh, but I'm so hungry.

I reach for the soup first and take a bite, immediately wincing. The texture is wrong and it tastes smoky, like it was burnt on the bottom.

"Never could cook," I chastise, staring at the mess. "Even as an angel, you're fucking horrible."

His cheeks flush, and he shakes his head, rubbing the back of his neck self-consciously. It's a very human behavior, a very *Bear* behavior. "I know. I know, I'm sorry. I tried."

I push the soup away quietly and pick up the sandwich instead, taking a bite. This is better. A little soggy, but my insane hunger makes it easier to eat, and I am worried for my child. My stomach growls loudly as if to accentuate my hunger.

Bear sits slowly in front of me. I can feel his eyes on me, boring holes into my soul. I stare pointedly away.

"How are you feeling?" he asks softly.

"Don't talk to me," I snap, before tearing into the sandwich with more fervor than before.

"Maxwell."

"I need to leave this place," I say, staring down at the soggy crust in my hand.

"If they find out you're still alive—"

"I know."

"Okay. What can I do?"

"Just shut up and let me think."

2161

MAXWELL LAY BESIDE HER GRANDMOTHER'S GARDEN, head tilted back as she allowed the sun to kiss her golden skin. She popped a raspberry into her mouth and smiled at the burst of flavor on her tongue. She looked over at her friend Bear, who was busy weaving flowers into a crown. She smiled fondly and poked his side.

He jumped and smiled down at her, shaking his head. "Jerk."

Maxwell grinned. "Whiner." Her fingers traveled up his side and along his arm. "Are you almost done with that thing?"

He nodded. "Yeah. Almost." He weaved a couple more daisies into the chain and then closed it and set it atop Maxwell's head. "There. You're a princess now."

Max laughed and reached up, touching her makeshift crown. "Princess of the slums. It's an honor, let me tell you."

Bear smiled and lay down beside her, rolling on his side to face her and propping his head up with his arm. "You're only here because the King and Queen wanted you to grow up humble and caring of the people around you. You can't rule without empathy, you know."

"Oh, I don't know about that. The president doesn't know the meaning of the word, and he's still in power." Maxwell wiggled her brows at him and then sighed, reaching up and tweaking his nose gently. She smiled kindly at him. "You're so freckly."

Bear flushed, shaking his head. "Don't make fun of them. I can't help it."

"I'm not. They're cute. I love them."

Bear flushed more, turning his face into the soft grass.

Max laughed and shoved his shoulder gently. She sighed and then looked back up toward the sky. "Hey, Bear?"

"Hm?" Bear muttered, face still turned toward the ground.

"You remember when you kissed Melissa McEwin?"

"Yeah?"

She took a deep breath, worrying at her lower lip. "What did it feel like?"

Bear sighed and looked over at her with a shrug. "Wet. Kinda gross. She used full on tongue."

Max wrinkled her nose and looked at him, appalled. "Gross!"

He nodded. "Yeah."

"Maybe next time it'll be better."

He nodded again. "Yeah."

"Maybe you just need to practice."

Bear looked over at his friend, brow cocked. A light blush covered his cheeks. "Are you volunteering?"

Maxwell flushed deeply and looked away, up toward the sky. "I…I mean…I wasn't…I…"

Bear laughed, basking in how flustered he'd ended up making her. It was something that rarely happened with Maxwell. He inched closer, looking down at her.

She caught his gaze, cheeks pink and eyes wide.

Bear admired her eyes, expressive and rare. He leaned down and touched his lips to hers softly. Once. Twice.

She let out a little sigh and her eyes closed for a long moment. When she opened them, he was still there, hovering above her. Her hand traveled shyly up to his cheek as she pulled him down for another kiss.

He bumped his nose to hers when their kiss ended, and he opened his eyes, watching her.

She watched him, chewing her lower lip. "Well?"

He wrinkled his nose. "Well, what?"

"Any better?"

He laughed, tipping his head back for a moment and shaking his head before he looked back down at her, blue eyes wide with fondness and love. "Much better."

2165

I HEAR THE SCREAMING A FEW WEEKS LATER. It's horrible. Gut-wrenching. I run out of bed and to the bathroom, where the source of the pain is coming from. I pound on the door. Ice fills my veins.

"Remiel? What are you doing?!"

The screaming comes to a halt, but I can hear his panting, and the big, breathless sobs that follow. I pound harder. "Open the door!"

He doesn't.

I take a deep breath and then take the knob in my hand, wrenching it hard. It snaps off in my hand, and the door swings open.

He's lying in the bathtub. The shower is still on, water raining down on his trembling form. Something is different.

He's flat. Not his body, but his aura. Where it had glowed with grace earlier in the day, now it's just static.

I can't believe it.

I step closer to the tub and kneel in front of it. "What have you done?"

He curls up more, turning his face into the dirty porcelain. His body shakes. "F-fell," he murmurs.

I reach out slowly, touching his bare shoulder. "Remiel..."

He flinches and covers his ears with his hands, letting out another sob. "That's not my name. Max, please," he moans, sounding every bit as heartbroken as he looks.

I can feel my own eyes fill with tears. I look up toward the grimy ceiling and take a deep breath. "Bear..." I whisper, lips trembling.

His nails dig into his neck, and he drags them slowly across his flesh, opening himself up.

I shake my head quickly and pull his hands away. "Bear, don't."

"I'm sorry," he whispers, before he begins to sob even harder.

I don't know what to do. I stare down at him for a moment and then slide out of my shoes and climb into the tub. He shoves his

face against my stomach and lets out a stream of apologies as he cries, his entire body shuddering.

I hate myself for not being able to hate him.

It takes a long time to coax him out of the bathtub, but I'm eventually able to get him up and dry. I help him dress in some clean clothes, and I make him lie down on his bed. He snuffles and turns his face into his lumpy pillow, eyes closed.

My hand hovers over his back, wanting to touch him, soothe him with a gentle pat, but I don't let myself. Instead, I pull a blanket over him and turn out the light. "Goodnight, Bear," I murmur quietly, and then I leave, closing the door behind me.

"Max?"

I wake to the sound of my name, eyes opening immediately. I've never really been much of a light sleeper, but living with Remiel has changed that.

"Hm?" I mumble, looking up.

Remiel stands at the foot of my bed. It's dark, but my eyes adjust to his outline. His cupped hands are glowing, and it makes me sit up straighter.

"What is that?" I ask, staring at him.

He steps toward me. "My grace," he replies quietly.

"What are you doing with it?"

He lowers himself down on the edge of my bed and looks up at me. He opens his hands and lets me see it. He's holding what looks like a small light bulb. It's glowing brightly, his grace dancing around inside of it. It's attached to a plain black cord.

I look away from it and back up at his face, which glows, despite the darkness, as his grace illuminates the space around us. He chews his lower lip, still watching me. He holds it out to me.

"What are you doing?" I repeat in a whisper, staring at him.

"I want you to have it," he whispers in return, eyes wide and childlike.

A tightness gathers in my chest. "Why?"

He takes a deep breath. "It's my life..." he murmurs. "If it's let out and it touches you, you'll absorb it. You can use it to defeat Michael. He won't be expecting it."

"Bear..."

"No. I know Gabriel gave you a part of his grace. That's just a piece. It'll be powerful because you're his blood, but it doesn't guarantee you'll survive. If you take mine, you will. I know it."

"How do you know about Gabriel's grace?" I ask, my hand going protectively to my chest, where the vial hangs beneath my shirt.

He shrugs and looks down. "I saw it when you were sleeping. It didn't take long for me to realize what it was."

I take a deep breath and stare at him. "Bear. If I absorb your grace..."

He nods. "I'll die. I know. But this is bigger than you or I. Michael is going to destroy the world. He's turning us all against each other. Playing God when he has no right to."

"Gabriel thought his grace would be enough. He didn't say anything about absorbing it."

"He wouldn't have. He would have assumed you would fight him on it, Maxwell. I don't think he ever planned on living through this whole thing." Bear frowns deeply.

My chest tightens, and I clutch at it, letting out a big breath of air. I will my eyes not to well up, and for once, they obey. "More secrets." My daughter gives a swift kick to my ribs in response to my emotional upset. I swear she can always tell when something is wrong. I look down at my stomach and smooth a hand over it. "It's okay," I whisper to her.

Bear watches me, eyes wide. "She can tell when you hurt."

I nod.

He takes another deep breath and holds his grace out to me again. "Please."

"Bear," I frown. "I'm not going to kill you."

"I'm not asking you to. Gabriel's might be enough." He shrugs. "But if it's not..."

I stare into his face, and then I look down at the bulb. I know that by offering it to me, Bear is communicating to me that he is truly sorry, and that he trusts me enough to literally hold his life in my hands. I look back up at him and nod slowly.

He watches me as he slides the cord around my neck and then drops his hands into his lap.

I look down at it. Its warmth fills my chest. I bite my lip and set my hand over it. My gaze travels back to Bear. "How do you feel?"

He chews his lip and shakes his head, looking away.

"You should get some sleep."

"I can't."

"You should at least try."

He swallows hard and looks down at his lap.

I watch him quietly for a moment before heaving a sigh and handing him a pillow. "You can sleep on the floor if you'd like." I can tell he's afraid of being alone. And, truth be told, now that he's human again and closer to the person who I knew him to be, I'm not fond of leaving him alone.

He nods and slides down onto the floor with the pillow, curling up.

I lay a blanket over him before I climb back into bed and lay on my side. It takes a while, but I finally fall asleep with both vials of grace pulsing a calming rhythm against my chest.

My days are running together. I spend them missing my friends and family and thinking about my missed appointment with Nicole and the others. I have no idea if they'll still decide to come here, and I have no way of communicating with them. I don't know how long it's been since the rebellion was destroyed, and I haven't gone outside. Bear is too afraid to leave this broken down apartment.

Ripping out his grace did a real number on him. He was in pain for months, but now I think it's become more internal than physical. He refuses to talk about it if I mention it, but sometimes I catch him staring at the place where it rests around my neck. I know he's afraid of losing his place in Heaven. I know he's scared of Michael finding out what he's done. But more than that, I know he's changing.

I'm sitting on an old, dilapidated couch, staring at the faded diamond pattern that covers the blue material. I'm bored out of my fucking skull.

Bear jogs in, looking more excited than I've seen him since I arrived here. "Max!"

I look up quickly, a flicker of fear pulsing through me. "What?"

"They found the rest of the survivors. They were on trial today. I saw it in the announcements when I went out for food."

My stomach lurches. "Survivors?"

He nods quickly. "Not everybody died. And some of the people they found were people who'd been underground but who left out of fear as Michael's influence grew."

My head is spinning. I set a hand to my cheek, shaking my head. "Did you see who was there?"

Bear frowns deeply. "I'm sorry. I didn't see Jamie or Vic. But they have Leighton and a few others I can recognize. But it doesn't matter. They've been sentenced to death. There's to be a mass hanging tomorrow afternoon in the town square."

I nod, expecting nothing less. "We have to go."

He nods. "I know."

I let out a breath, shaking my head. "I thought I would get more of an argument."

Bear sighs. "Since when has arguing with you ever changed your mind?"

"Touché."

"So what are we going to do?"

I watch him, taking a deep breath. "We're going to stop it."

"*How*?"

"Well, first of all, what kind of weapons do you have around here?"

Bear takes a deep breath, and the corner of his mouth twitches up in a tiny smile. "I'm kind of a hoarder."

"Excellent."

When I finally make my way out into the world again, I'm dressed in normal street clothes, my hair is braided down my back, and my eyes are both dark brown. I hate the contacts, but Bear wouldn't allow me to go out otherwise. At least he didn't make me dye my hair. My wings are put away, and I'm focusing all of my attention on forcing my grace away so I won't stick out to the angels in the crowd.

I'm packing a compact assault weapon beneath my jacket, a hunting knife in my boot, and a glock strapped to my side. Bear has more. We were nervous about stuffing more weaponry beneath my clothing while I'm already looking heftier than usual with pregnancy.

Both vials of grace pulse against my chest, tucked safely away beneath my clothing. Their presence is calming, even as I worry about my friends. It allows me to think clearly enough to be able to do what needs to be done.

Bear is wearing sunglasses. His hair is tucked beneath his hat. He holds my hand tightly in his own, as though he's afraid I'm going to run away. I probably won't, but neither of us know that for sure.

The crowd surrounding the gallows in town square is enormous. It makes it difficult for me to breathe. I stare around, searching for familiar faces. I can see no one.

We're here early, just like everyone else. Michael has yet to show himself, and the prisoners are nowhere to be seen either. It'll be another hour before the event begins. I take a deep breath and look up at Bear, squeezing his hand.

He squeezes back and glances down at me. "Remember to keep your emotions in check. You can't seem upset," he murmurs quietly from the corner of his mouth.

I nod once and lay my head against his arm. "Of course not. Hangings are my favorite spectator sport," I mutter dryly.

He lets go of my hand in favor of sliding an arm around my shoulder and hugging me to his side. "You sure you want to be here?"

I nod.

"Don't do anything reckless."

"I *know*. God."

"Sorry." A pause. "We have to be careful. Everything has to happen at the right moment."

"Yes, *Father*," I tease, looking up at him.

He takes a deep breath, eyes tense, but a shadow of a smile makes an appearance on his face. "Can't blame me for being nervous."

"I know. I know." I pat his arm and take a deep breath.

We stand together, arm in arm. I lay my head back against his shoulder as I survey the crowd. I'm trying to appear as innocent as possible.

Bear stiffens suddenly, holding my arm tighter. He swallows audibly, and I turn to see what's triggered his response, but a knife at my back has me standing soldier straight. I inhale sharply, eyes widening.

"Don't make any sudden movements," a voice growls against my ear. "Turn to your right. Keep going through the alley until I say you can stop."

I nod, turning with Bear. He doesn't look at me, keeping his gaze forward. I swallow hard as we walk slowly to the alley, flanked closely by two hooded figures. I focus on controlling my breathing, never letting go of Bear's arm.

"Stop." The man behind me pulls on the back of my elbow, and I obey.

Bear's breath hitches beside me.

"Turn around."

I close my eyes for a moment and then turn with Bear, looking up at my kidnapper's faces. My eyes widen in tearful recognition and my knees feel immediately weak. "Jamie! Vic!"

Jamie drops her knife and jumps on me, knocking me back against the dirty alley wall. She kisses me eagerly until we're both breathless, and then pulls back minutely, looking up at me. "How are you?! Are you okay?"

I make a sad attempt at a confirmation, too in shock to reply with words. Instead, I wrap my arms around her and pull her closer, setting my face in her shoulder.

"God. I thought you were dead..." I manage after a few moments of controlling my breathing. Now is not the time for a breakdown.

"I know. We thought you had died, too. I was so afraid. Matthew is alive, too. A little worse for wear, but alive."

"Shit. Oh God, thank you!" I whisper, turning my face up toward the sky.

Jamie smiles and sprinkles kisses along the side of my face. She drops a hand to my belly and strokes it gently. "How's the little one?"

"She's good." I try to smile. Shit. I can't believe they're both here. Both alive. I look toward Uncle Vic. He's glaring at Bear, arms crossed over his chest.

Jamie steps back and follows my gaze, sudden anger hardening across her features. "You stupid son of a bitch."

I take her hand and shake my head. "He's harmless."

"Harmless? Maxwell, he sold out the entire fucking community! He's the reason your father is dead!"

I swallow hard and look down. "He wasn't alone in it, and believe me, I'm angry as all hell. But he's different now. He's changing. He fell."

Jamie wrinkles her nose and glares at Bear. "Why'd you fall?"

Bear swallows hard and gestures toward me. "Wanted Max to have my grace. So she can defeat Michael when it comes down to it."

Jamie stares at him and then looks back at me. "What?"

I nod, a hand going to my chest, where the vial rests between my breasts. "He's telling the truth."

Uncle Vic scowls at Bear. "You'd better watch your step, you little asshole. Try anything funny, and you're dead."

Bear nods, looking pained.

Uncle Vic steps away from me and grabs me into his arms, hugging me tightly. "Glad you're alive, kiddo."

I smile just a little and close my eyes. "I'm glad *you're* alive. I can't believe it."

"Believe it." He steps back and winks. "Takes more than a little explosion to off a former arch and his sidekick," he says, wrapping an arm around Jamie's shoulders with a smirk.

I laugh as Jamie rolls her eyes, shaking her head.

She looks up at me and smiles. "So you're here."

I nod. "Couldn't let this happen."

She nods. "What were you planning?"

"Uh…" I shrug. "Brought a few guns. Lots of ammo. Couple of knives."

She shares a look with Vic, and they both laugh.

I scowl, looking at them. "What's so funny?"

Jamie grins. "Amateurs."

"I can't believe you thought you were going to be able to stop a hanging with two people and a couple of guns," Jamie says, shaking her head as we make our way back into the big crowds. "Weapons are nothing with so few people."

"Yeah? What are you going to do?"

Jamie takes a deep breath. "Weapons, violence. People have seen enough of it. If we want to be known as the good guys, if we want them to help us out, if we want the prisoners to go free, we need to prove to them that we are who we say we are. We have to ruin the image that Michael has created of us."

I nod slowly. "How do we possibly do that?"

She smiles and shrugs. "We recreated our override system from when you were broadcast over Michael. It's the only way we can reach everyone. But this time, instead of projecting ourselves in real time, we've set a timer for a holovideo."

"You recorded a speech earlier? That's smart," I say softly with a nod.

She shakes her head. "Not exactly. We've taken holographic video footage from different days. Some of it may be hard for you to watch. Vic had stuff from years ago, from before we were even born. There's so much there. But it'll have an impact."

I swallow hard and nod. "Okay. I believe you."

She nods and takes a deep breath. "I just hope to God that it's enough."

Vic looks over at us and raises an eyebrow. "It should be. Unless the people have been robbed of every last ounce of humanity they once had, they should get angry. The hope is that an angry mob will be enough for some of our guys to duck in and save the prisoners' asses."

"Shouldn't we get ready to run in then?" I ask.

"Oh no. Not you. Especially not you. That belly would only serve to further frighten Michael. An elioud is a game changer. And if he finds out you're still alive, well..."

I *hate* being left out, but I know he's right. I need to be careful for my daughter's sake.

"Remiel is to remain with you at all times. We can't have Michael finding out that he fell. He'll be even more upset."

I nod once more and take Bear's hand tightly. I feel him squeeze my hand once, and it serves to calm my queasy stomach.

"Jamie and I are going to go hide under the gallows. You okay?"

I nod quickly. "Yeah... Just please be careful, okay?"

Vic nods and pulls me into a tight hug. "No matter what you see in that video, you have got to hold it together, okay, kiddo? Everything is going to work out just fine." He pulls back and stares at Bear. "You keep her safe. If shit hits the fan, you get her out of here real quick. You got it?"

Bear nods dutifully and slides and arm around me. "I promise."

"Good. We'll see you when it's over."

"Okay." I let out a shaky breath and turn to Jamie. She gives me a reassuring smile and bounces forward to kiss my mouth softly. She pulls back and gives me a wink. "Love you, Max," She reminds softly.

I try to smile through my anxiety, but I can feel my lips tremble with the weight of it all. "Yeah," is all I manage.

She grins and then hurries away with Vic.

I look up at Bear, who is very obviously avoiding looking at me. His cheeks are flushed, and he's worrying at his lower lip.

He clears his throat after a moment and looks down at me. "You and Jamie, huh?"

Oh, for the love of all things holy. I roll my eyes. "I don't believe in labels."

"Oh."

"Yeah."

We fall silent as we wait. It doesn't take long before a line of prisoners are marched to the gallows. There are only six nooses set up in the gallows, but there have got to be at least thirty people in line. I scan the line for people who I can recognize.

Leighton is there, head hung low. His face is red and puffy. It makes me sick. He's so fucking young. I spot about ten other people from my time spent below the ground, but the rest are all strangers to me.

Bear holds me tighter, and it's only then that I realize my breathing has picked up considerably. My knees are shaking, and he has to hold me up against his side to prevent me from sliding to the ground. I hate hangings. I hate them. I hate them. *I hate them.*

Michael appears, projected into the sky. The coward can't even show up for face-to-face time with the people who he's about to have murdered. He smiles brightly into the holocam, but then he disappears and is replaced with a new image.

Vic sits with a little girl in his lap. She's got to be about four years old. Her hair is up in two light brown pigtails. She giggles delightedly as he sings to her. He leans down toward her and covers her face in sloppy kisses. She shrieks and pushes at his bearded face. *"Daddy!"* she squeals. A woman behind the camera laughs quietly.

The image changes. I have to blink a few times to understand what I'm staring at. It's Gabriel. He's dancing with my mother. She's young. About my age. Her belly is swollen, and I realize she's carrying me. She laughs delightedly as he spins her around and then dips her low. They stare into each other's eyes, and it's obvious to anybody watching how completely and devastatingly in love they truly are. My mother turns to the camera and laughs. *"Put the camera away, Uriel. God, I'm enormous..."* she complains, grinning.

Now I'm staring at myself as a toddler. I'm gripping my mother's fingers in my chubby fists and grinning at Gabriel. He holds his hands out to me. *"Come here, Maxwell. I know you can do it, my sweet girl."*

"Go to daddy, Maxie. Go on, sweetie..." Mom lets go of my hands and I toddle rather ungracefully over to my dad. I trip over my own feet when I'm almost there, and my wings fly out to try to catch

me. They flap uselessly. He catches me before I hit the ground, and he laughs. *"Good job, little one!"*

It switches again. It's my parents again. My mom is laughing delightedly, filming my dad as he scowls at the camera. *"Aubrey…"* he complains. She laughs and sets the camera down. It catches a sliver of their faces as she pulls him in for a kiss.

Now I'm staring at a woman who looks very similar to Jamie. She has the same long, brown hair and big green eyes. She's curled up with Michael, her arms encircling his neck. She stares up at him in adoration and presses a kiss to his mouth.

He smiles and holds her closely. *"Remind me why it's necessary to film this…"* he teases, pressing a line of kisses down the side of her face.

She grins. *"I have something to tell you."*

"Yeah? What is it?"

The woman sits up straighter, excitement obvious on her face. *"I'm pregnant!"*

His eyes widen in surprise, and he chokes out a laugh. He sounds delighted. It sends chills down my spine. He stands, picking her up and spinning her around.

Wherever Michael is, I'm sure he's pissed. I can't imagine him this way with anyone. Even seeing it now, it's hard to accept. He's so cold. So devoid of emotion.

The image changes again. This time it's eerily familiar. A broadcast image of my mother and father standing at the gallows, nooses around their necks. I see myself fighting to get to them, screaming at the top of my lungs. And then I see my mother pleading to a man in the crowd. It's Gabriel. He scoops me up and fights through the crowd, trying to take me away before I can see them die. But I see everything.

And now I'm seeing it all again. Bile rises in my throat.

The atmosphere in the crowd is beginning to change. People are shifting uncomfortably, muttering beneath their breath. A couple of people have begun to leave, visibly shaken by what they're viewing. I know my mother and father's case was extraordinarily sensitive to the public in the first place. There had been a small riot after the hanging, though I hadn't stuck around to watch it. The crowd had pushed the gallows over and retrieved my parent's bodies, ensuring we would be able to have a proper burial.

The image changes. I see a version of myself from only a few months ago. I'm laughing at some unknown image that's off-screen, eyes bright and happy, despite the darkness that has overtaken my life. I hadn't been aware that I was being filmed. Jamie is there, too. She's staring at me with nothing less than love in her eyes. It causes a warmth to bloom in my stomach. Gabriel steps in, grinning and shaking his head.

Now I'm staring as a black-haired woman looks into a camera, dark eyes wide and troubled. *"My name is Ananael,"* she whispers quickly. *"It is December 24, 2147. I have just taken a child from Michael's human lover, Adelaide. She did not survive. He became very distraught at the news of her death, and his reaction was an instinct to kill his daughter. I told Michael that the child perished as well. I thought it best to remove her from the situation. She will grow up knowing her nephilim status and what it means. From Michael's reaction, I'm sure it will be very dangerous if he ever finds that she lives. I will raise her as my own, secure and loved.*

"Our Father has spoken to me. He told me she was special. I'm to keep her safe. There's another coming. I'll need to pay attention. The nephilim are to be protected if humanity is to be saved." Ananael shakes her head and worries at her lower lip. *"Change is coming, and I fear that everything will get much worse before it can even begin to get better."* Her lips tremble and she looks away.

Bear makes a soft noise of surprise, and I'm pretty sure that I do, too. This is all new information to me. It's an overload.

The image changes again.

It's me. I'm standing protectively over Emily and holding her son carefully. My face is wet and distraught. I look down at Zachary and then back at the silent crowd. *"You let this happen,"* I say. *"This is on you. And we can't save you if you allow things like this to happen."*

I kneel back beside Emily and ask her what her name is.

She lets out a long sigh, closing her eyes. *"Emily."*

I nod and gather her in my free arm. *"I'm going to take you home now, okay, Emily?"*

The image fades into one of my father. It's the film that was broadcast during his execution.

"Citizens. Brothers. I am brought here before you because I care too much about humanity. Because I wanted to raise my daughter and be a part of her life. Because I fell in love with her mother and created a life and fell in love with being human. Because I chose free will."

Michael kicks him in his side, forcing him to sway. He lets out a cry of pain and grits his teeth.

"Michael will tell you that the nephilim are dangerous. They are powerful, it's true. But they are uninterested in hurting you. Instead, they want to save you.

"And what Michael doesn't want you to know, is that he too has a nephilim daughter. Her name is Jamie, and I am confident that she will be his downfall because of his plan to exterminate humanity. She wants to save you. All of you. She cares about all of you."

Michael's fingers claw into his back, and my father tips his head back, letting out a cry as Michael forces his wings into view.

My father squeezes his eyes shut, breath hissing from between his clenched teeth. *"They will destroy you, Michael. Your reign will end soon enough, and God help you when he finds what you've done. You will burn in Hell for your crimes to the innocent people of this world. For your crimes against your own brethren!"*

The last image to appear is news footage of "rebels" being lined up and shot in the street by soldiers. An angel is standing beside them, leading them. His ivory wings are enormous and beautiful, but speckled with blood and gore as he commands the murder spree.

The film ends. I take a deep breath and stare around at the crowd, which is now restless in its combined anger.

I hear a familiar voice begin to speak from the gallows, and I turn my attention to Leighton, who is standing, hands now freed by some random stranger who has climbed on stage and begun to pick the locks on the prisoner's cuffs. Others in the crowd form a wall against the line of soldiers, who aren't even fighting back. They mostly looked confused. Their leader is nowhere to be found, and they aren't sure what to do. None of the angels have bothered to show face. They're either too scared or too cocky to be willing to deal with the crowd.

Leighton stares out at everyone, head and shoulders raised straight and defiant. "Michael is wrong. About everything!" he yells, the only way to be heard over the noise. "He's a liar! A murderer! You may think he just wants to kill the rebellion, but after he's finished with us, he'll turn on you!"

A single shot rings out from an unknown location, and Leighton drops like a weight, dead in an instant.

I cover my mouth with my hands, forcing back a scream. He'd betrayed us before, but he was still just a kid. And a good one at that.

The crowd goes crazy. They're falling over themselves to get to the prisoners and free them. Jamie and Vic are standing at the gallows, freeing as many as they can as quickly as they can.

Michael's hologram appears, and he looks furious. "Kill them all," he spits to his men. "Except for the two leaders. They are to be brought to me."

"NO!" My stomach drops, and I shake my head quickly, taking a couple of running steps toward the gallows as the military men open fire, peppering the prisoners and their saviors with bullets.

Bear grabs my arm and hauls me back quickly. "Max, *no*! Remember what you were told."

It's a bloodbath, and there's nothing that I can do. I can feel my body temperature rise as my grace threatens to leech out and give us away. I fight back another yell as I see Jamie and Vic tackled and bound. They remain surprisingly calm, both keeping their gazes forward as they're tugged away from the crowd of people still under fire.

Bear begins towing me away, toward the alley that we came from. I can't believe all of these people are dying, and all I can do is watch.

Only a few agonizing minutes later, Michael relaxes, and he takes a deep breath. "That's enough for now," he says. And then "stand down!" as the bullets continue being fired. The men gradually step back, lowering their guns.

The survivors of the massacre are a wreck, leaning over loved ones who are full of bullet holes, or wailing in pain.

Michael raises his eyebrows, surveying the scene through his own cameras. "I hope you've all learned a valuable lesson today. Obedience is key to the utopia that we are striving toward together. I will not hesitate to destroy anyone who jeopardizes it." He disappears.

I run away with Bear, feeling like a traitor as I allow myself to be towed along. I'm supposed to be their leader, a source of hope. And now all I've led them to is agony and death.

"Maxwell Odyssey. I know you're out there, alive and listening to me now."

I stare at the television as Michael stands, a hand on the back of Jamie's chair. She stares up at the camera, green eyes exhausted, but head held high. I can see similarities in their appearance now. She's inherited Michael's cheekbones and also his poise.

I set a hand to my mouth, shaking my head.

Bear stiffens beside me, reaching for my hand. I push him away with a shake of my head, leaning forward to catch every liquid word that drips from between Michael's lips.

"I hoped it wouldn't have to end this way, Maxwell. But you have refused my terms again and again. I can see now that I'm going to have to up the stakes a little higher.

"Now I'm sure as your father's daughter, you're a selfish little girl. Only worried about your own self-preservation. I saw you run from the crowd yesterday afternoon. You didn't fool me for an instant. I hope whatever straggling followers you have left can understand what a coward you are. However, I have higher hopes for you than you probably deserve. I'm hoping this new ultimatum causes you to consider your friends over yourself."

I scowl at the projection, hands balled into fists. I don't understand how he can stand there so fucking calm over his daughter...the daughter he conceived with someone who he was obviously in love with and attached to. Jamie looks just like her. It's a wonder he's able to hurt her at all.

Michael sets his hands on Jamie's shoulders and leans down to press a kiss to the top of her head. Jamie keeps her head held high, but her nose wrinkles in disgust.

He looks up at the screen and grins, and I know that this truly is a show just for me. "Tomorrow at noon, the gallows in city square will be replaced with big, old-fashioned burning stakes. Jamie and Uriel will burn. The only way to stop it is to turn yourself in. Tonight.

Before the evening curfew. If you're not at city hall cathedral before then, you can forget about saving them."

Jamie rolls her eyes. "She's not stupid enough to fall for that," she spits, not bothering to look up at Michael. "We all saw what happened when you promised Gabriel that his followers would go free if he turned himself in."

Michael scowls and slams a fist into the side of her head, snapping her head sideways. She gasps and hangs her head, closing her eyes for a moment.

"I don't recall asking for your opinion, you little traitor," he scolds, grabbing her by her hair and pulling her head back against the headrest of the chair.

She lets out a shaky breath, looking back at the camera. "We die either way, Max. There's no winning this round. You've got to wait for the others. They're coming. I promise. You just have to wait it out. They're coming!" she speaks quickly through trembling lips. She opens her mouth to say more, but Michael cuts her off with another backhand across her face.

The crack of the connection of skin on skin is sickening and loud in our otherwise silent apartment. I can feel my heart beating out of control. Blood drips from Jamie's nose and upper lip.

I want to kill him for causing her pain.

Michael turns his attention back to the camera. "Maybe they die, and maybe they don't. I guess you'll never know if you don't try." The hologram vanishes abruptly.

I don't remember standing or upturning the couch. I don't remember putting my fists through the wall or destroying the coffee table into splinters. I don't remember breaking the living room window or trashing the rest of the room. I don't remember screaming myself hoarse.

But when I finally turn to look at Bear, knuckles and arms bruised and bleeding, the room is destroyed, and my voice is hoarse when I speak.

"We have to go tonight."

He nods, getting to his feet. His brows are drawn together as he frowns, eyes tight and worried. "I know."

We walk together, hand-in-hand. The only way this plan will work is if I am able to speak directly with Michael before he attempts to kill me. If we're gunned down before I'm even able to see him, it will all be a waste. Bear is pretty confident that I will be escorted directly to Michael. He believes that he'll want to have a few choice words with me before he decides to off me. Maybe a little torture. Makes for a lovely scenario.

We move through the city square, still filled with the dead from the earlier massacre. I can't believe that all of these bodies still remain. Michael must have stopped the others from cleaning up the mess. Another warning. I suppress a gag. The flies are already buzzing.

As we approach the cathedral, I'm reminded of how terrifying it seemed to me even as a child. It looms over the city with a promise of hope and peace and love, but it seems to only bring hate and fear into its people's hearts. Portraits of Jesus Christ bleeding on the cross have always brought me more fear than appreciation. Suffering is the worst sort of way to go.

Now the cathedral is even more horrifying. A pair of wasted black wings are nailed high above the main entrance. My father's wings. A reminder to all that Michael is in charge, and that it is him who makes all decisions. I have no idea what they've done with his body or if he was even buried. It wouldn't be beneath Michael to just let him rot somewhere. I cringe at the thought and look away as we get closer. I can't stand to see them up close.

Military guards are stationed in front of the cathedral. I lift my head and glare at them, saying nothing. They step away to allow us access into the building. We walk up the main staircase and inside. I can't resist a pained glance up at the only remaining pieces of my father. It's a horrific kind of curiosity, and I immediately hate myself for looking.

Bear squeezes my hand tightly, and I take comfort in the gesture as we enter. My chest hurts. I'm scared. Terrified, even.

I'm afraid of the loss that could incur at this point in my journey. I've already lost Bear several times, my gran, my mother, my step-father, my father. I could very well lose Jamie tonight. And Uncle Vic. Bear. Everybody I have left. Hell, it's probable that I'll die tonight, too. But there's nothing left to be done. No more decisions that need to be made.

This is it. It feels so final.

And again, I am *so fucking* scared.

An angel dressed in a fine black suit leads us forward into the main room.

Michael is waiting for us there. His loose white clothing and bare feet are reminiscent of the image I always imagined angels to be, but it looks all wrong on him. Too white. He should be covered in blood. There's certainly enough of it on his hands.

2164

"TODAY IS THE DAY," Maxwell muttered to herself, head bobbing in time with the music playing in her garage as she finished wiping down her baby, a beautiful, sleek, 2091 Nova Dawn hover bike. They weren't made like this anymore. They were smaller, more compact and quieter, but Maxwell loved the noise.

Her fingers ran over the black paint that covered the body. She grinned to herself and patted the seat lovingly, the comforting scent of engine oil fresh in her nose. "It's been a long process, baby, but I think you're ready for your debut."

She rolled the craft slowly out of the garage after cutting the music, and she propped it up on its kickstand in the driveway before running to the backyard where Gran was hanging laundry to dry with Jamie.

"Gran!"

Gran looked up from the towel she was hanging and smiled over at her granddaughter.

Jamie grinned when she saw Maxwell. "You look excited."

Max shot her a wink, lips stretched in an excited grin. She turned her attention back to her gran. "The Nova is ready. Can Jamie and I test it out? Please?"

Her gran pretended to think on it for a moment, bringing a wrinkled hand to her mouth. "Hm... I don't know, Max. There's an awful lot of housework to be done before dinner."

Maxwell grabbed Jamie's hand and pulled the girl toward her. Both girls faced their gran, lips sticking out in sync as they pouted. "Please?" they chorused.

Gran laughed and reached out, patting each girl's cheek at the same time. "Go on. Be careful, though. Promise me, girls."

"We promise!" Maxwell pulled Jamie quickly to the driveway and handed her a helmet from the seat of the porch swing that hung from a beam connected to the garage. "We'll take her to the field."

Jamie nodded and followed along as Maxwell pushed her beloved hoverbike along the path to the field just outside of Gran's home, past the megachurch and to the end of town lines.

Sweat pooled at the base of Max's back as she pushed the heavy machine through the long grass. The sun shone brightly above, burning her already tanned skin. She squinted against the brightness and looked back at Jamie, almost quivering with anticipation. "Are you excited?!"

Jamie laughed, head tipping up toward the sky. The bright sun brought out some lighter tints in her dark brown hair. Her always pale skin shone with a light layer of sweat. "Not as excited as you, you little grease monkey."

Max grinned back at her and then stopped, stepping back from the bike to put her hair up in a messy bun. She looked back at her friend. "Put your helmet on. And hold tight when we ride, okay?"

Jamie rolled her eyes, still smiling. "Yes, *Mother.*"

Max wiped her sweaty palms on her jeans and then swung her leg over her bike, settling onto it comfortably. Her hands found the handles, and she flipped the switch on. She hit the ignition button and smiled as the bike roared to life beneath her. She looked back at Jamie. "Climb on."

She looked back down at the bike when she felt Jamie's weight settle against her back, the other girl's arms wrapping around her middle to hold on. Max grinned and flipped on the switch for the turbines, watching as the long grass around them began blowing around in the mechanical wind. "Come on, baby," she murmured, giving it a little gas.

The hoverbike started forward abruptly, still grounded. Its wheels bumped along over the uneven ground, getting ready for takeoff. These days it was uncommon for hoverbikes to have wheels. They lifted from the ground easily. But the Nova Dawn was older and needed a running start on the ground before it could lift off. It was actually one of the things that Max appreciated about it. She loved that she could choose to fly around on the ground or in the air.

She increased the gas and speed of the turbines. She focused her attention forward, watching as the field came to a river. She sped toward it, leaning forward.

Behind her, Jamie tightened her grasp on Maxwell. "Max! We're not going to make it!"

"Yes we are!"

"Are you *crazy*?! Gran said to be careful!"

Max didn't respond, leaning forward further, brow furrowed in concentration. The river came steadily closer, and just as it seemed the girls would go tumbling into it, the hoverbike lifted from the ground. Max crowed in excitement, fist pumping into the air.

Jamie let out a little cry of disbelief and then began to laugh, raising her hands up in the air as the girls traveled higher, flying through the summer breeze.

Maxwell laughed happily and closed her eyes for a moment, her hair whipping back around her face. She let go of the handlebars and held her arms out, the sensation of flying the most liberating and exhilarating thing she had ever experienced.

2165

HE SMILES WHEN WE ENTER, shaking his head with a tutting noise. He lets out a heavy sigh. "You've caused so much trouble for me. This was supposed to be so easy." He looks toward Bear. "And *you*. Remiel, you have disappointed me greatly."

Bear holds his head high, glaring at him. "You've almost single-handedly destroyed one of our Father's most treasured creations, Michael. There is a special piece of Hell reserved for you."

Michael tips his head back, laughing. "You give me too much credit. After all, you were quite a help to me."

I squeeze Bear's hand, shaking my head at him. I don't want him to get into a verbal brawl with Michael if it isn't necessary. There's more than enough drama to come without worrying about that.

"Where is Jamie? Vic?" I ask, wanting to cut out all the bullshit.

Michael looks at me and smiles. "So impatient. Just like your father." He rolls his eyes and turns to his guard. "Go and fetch them for me."

The guard nods and walks away.

"After everything in that film, I'm surprised you're able to hate your daughter so much," I say, staring up at him.

His smile falters, and he shakes his head. "She is no daughter of mine."

"But she is. She looks a little like you. More like her mom, though. They could be sisters."

His eyes flash angrily. "Don't speak of this to me. It doesn't matter."

"Oh, but it does." I cock my head to the side, narrowing my eyes at him. "What would Adelaide say? If she could see how far you've fallen?"

"Shut up," he growls, taking a step toward me.

"She would be disgusted by the monster you've become. To hurt your own *daughter*, your brothers..."

"Do not *speak* of *monsters* to me!" He yells, gesturing wildly as he steps closer. "It is because of *her* that Adelaide is *dead*! Nephilim are evil and must be eliminated from the Earth! It has *always* been so!"

I open my mouth to snap a reply, but I see Jamie being pulled in beside Vic, who looks dead on his feet. Jamie's face is swollen from where she took a beating earlier, but her legs and arms seem to be working fine, whereas Vic needs to lean on her to get anywhere. Neither of them are visibly tied or chained.

Jamie shakes her head miserably when she sees me. "You shouldn't have come," she murmurs miserably.

I try to smile at her. "Couldn't let you burn."

"He's going to kill us anyway. Max..." her voice breaks and she looks away. "There's nothing we can do. My magic is bound. I can't run. I can't move unless I'm directly told to."

I swallow hard and step forward to hug her, but Michael steps between us, shaking his head. "This reunion is all very touching, but we have a whole manner of things to speak about before I kill you. First of all, how about we discuss the abomination that grows in your womb." He looks from me to Bear. "You know how dangerous elioud are. Tell her."

Bear shakes her head. "Michael, we haven't had an elioud in centuries. Who's to say the child would be a monster?"

"The last one in existence destroyed a number of villages before we terminated it. You know this, Remiel. You were there, just as I was."

"Yes, but it knew it was being hunted! When someone is being hunted, they're far more likely to act out! They can't be expected to just sit back and die quietly."

I stare between the two of them, hands traveling protectively to my belly.

"It wouldn't stand a chance. Even if it *was* allowed to be carried full term. Elioud are uncontrollable. Wicked above all others and with the strength of *gods*." Michael stares at me. "It would not matter how well the child was brought up. It would be a monster. A disgrace. Nephilim are unnatural, so an elioud, well, you can imagine."

"It's funny," I say dryly. "I really can't imagine."

He scoffs and shakes his head. "I'm doing you a favor by ending the both of you. Another thing, Maxwell..."

"Yes?" I cock my head to the side, glaring at him.

"I just thought it could be important for you to know the truth about your father. Gabriel. He's not the saint you seem to have painted him to be."

"I haven't painted him in any particular way."

"Oh, but you have. You think he was such a great man. A devoted father. He wasn't. He came every time I called."

My blood begins to boil. I can't believe he has the nerve to talk about my father this way. "He came because you would have hurt him otherwise."

Michael shrugs. "He could have stayed. He could have disobeyed. Uriel did." He gestures toward Uncle Vic, who is slumped against a wall. The sight brings a stinging of tears to my eyes. I've never seen him this way before. I shake my head and look away, glaring up at Michael.

"Nothing you say about him will change who he was to me."

He only scoffs, turning away for a moment before looking back at me. "What is it about you that causes such destruction?"

I wrinkle my nose. "Excuse me?"

"There are a thousand different things that have gone wrong in your family, in your life. You were born, you suffocated your mother. She had dreams that far exceeded the likes of you. When she finally got to accomplish them, she was put to death, along with your stepfather. Your brother was sent to war. Grandmother dead. You made friends with the rebellion and now most of them have died. Your father is dead. Remiel will never be allowed access back into Heaven. Neither will Uriel. I'm sure you can figure out the common denominator in all of these situations."

"Were you never taught that it's rude to play with your food before you eat it?" I spit back, tired of playing games. I don't want to hear about all of the people who I've fucked over. I haven't done any of it on purpose.

He laughs, cocking his head to the side as he watches me, hands rubbing together in front of him. "It only bothers you because it's true. You know, I'd heard the rumors. You and Jamie were supposedly going to rid the world of angels so the nephilim would rise to power. But look at you. You're both here. At my mercy."

"What are you looking for out of this?" I ask quietly, staring into his cold blue eyes. "You think you're going to destroy all of the people of the world and then take your feathery ass back upstairs and everything's going to be the same? You think God is going to let that fly?"

Michael sneers, lips pulling back from his teeth. "Let me let you in on a little secret, Maxwell. My Father is *gone*. He abandoned you. He abandoned *all* of us. You want to know what God is going to think? Look at *me*. Because I'm it now. And you'd better show your respect by bowing to me."

I'm immediately, painfully brought to my knees. It's so sudden that my teeth crack together grotesquely. I glare up at him.

He grins. "There. That's better. You, too, Remiel."

Bear falls to his knees with a curse, head bowing low.

I don't look at him. Instead, I focus on Michael as he walks to Jamie, pulling her close. He shoves her to her knees in front of me. I can't move my arms or legs. I'm bound tight.

Jamie watches me, eyes sad. She swallows hard and shakes her head. "We tried," she whispers. "I'm sorry."

Michael slides forward and takes Jamie's chin in his hand from behind. "You were never worthy of your mother's sacrifice," he mutters, before taking a step back. He glares at Bear. "Get to your feet."

Bear stands on command, and I know there's nothing that he can do to stop it.

Michael puts an ornate, silver dagger in his hand. "Kill her."

"Bear, don't!" I plead quickly, shaking my head. I look up at him and then back at Jamie, who looks terrified, but dry-eyed. She's keeping it together a hell of a lot better than I'm capable of right now. "Michael, *please*!"

Michael arches a brow, smiling sadistically. "Groveling isn't very becoming of you."

Bear lifts the dagger, closing his eyes as though in pain. He whimpers. "Please, Michael."

"Do it *now*!"

It's all so fast.

I'm screaming, stunned at how swiftly a life can bleed away. How quickly things can change forever.

Jamie gives a little gasp before she slumps forward against me, body warm and bleeding.

Bear lets out shaky sob and drops the dagger. It clatters to the floor. He shakes his head back and forth quickly. "Max. Max, you have to do it."

Something snaps inside of me. I shoot him an apologetic look, saying it all in my eyes. How sorry I am for doing this. How I wish things could be different. How I wanted to keep him safe.

247 ❧ T.W.R. SHELTON

PART V

2165

MAXWELL ROSE IN THE AIR as the boy beside her fell forward. Her head snapped back, eyes and mouth filling with a light that overwhelmed her.

Vic stared up at her through eyes so swollen that they only opened in tiny slits. His heart raced as he realized what was happening. She was absorbing grace. He could remember showing Gabriel how to separate a piece of his grace and give it to Aubrey to keep her safe during her pregnancy. He must have given it to Max for safe keeping.

But something else was different, too. There was far too much grace to just come from Gabriel.

Then he noticed Remiel had slumped forward, and he realized that he'd sacrificed his grace to her. In that moment it finally clicked how much of an impact the relationship between Remiel and Maxwell had had on his brother. For Remiel to sacrifice Heaven after realizing what he'd been missing for so many years, he had to really love the girl. Had to care deeply about her cause.

Vic hadn't given him enough credit. He felt a temporary sorrow for his lost brother, but it was gone as quickly as it came because Maxwell's light was still building, spilling out into the room and beyond.

She looked positively terrifying.

Her wings spread wide, knocking chairs over and paintings from walls. They seemed bigger than normal, glowing with an excess of grace.

She turned her gaze on Michael and grinned a toothy smile. It made Vic shiver. It was very out of character.

Vic looked toward his brother. Michael looked absolutely stunned. He stared up at Maxwell, eyes wide in the closest emotion to fear that Vic had ever seen on him. He took a step away, his own wings flaring out.

"Impossible," he spit. "My brothers wouldn't be so stupid."

Maxwell only laughed. She closed her eyes and tipped her head back for a moment, clenching her hands into tight fists.

Vic swallowed hard and looked down, eyes traveling to his adopted daughter, Jamie, who lay on the ground. Her eyes fluttered open, and she locked gazes with him as she gasped for air. Blood trickled from the corner of her mouth. His eyes widened as much as they were able, and he crawled to her, pulling her up into his arms and away from the feuding angels.

Maxwell landed on her feet, taking a step toward Michael.

He took a step back, shaking his head. "Don't you dare come any closer to me. I am a *God*!"

She cocked her head to the side. "You are so fucked," she murmured, always an artist with her words.

She grinned, and then plunged her hand into his chest.

Michael howled, dropping to his knees as she dug around inside of him, searching for the piece of him that meant the very most.

She withdrew her arm slowly. It was soaked in blood. Inside her palm was a glowing light. It pulsed erratically, agitated at having been removed so forcefully from its host.

Maxwell stared at Michael's grace for a moment before sniffing, obviously unimpressed. She closed her hands around it and stared at Michael as she threw it toward the ground.

It hit the floor with a crack like thunder, and the light blitzed through the room with an enormous pulse, knocking Vic and Jamie backward and throwing Michael to the ground.

In the end, Maxwell was the only one left standing.

Michael clutched at his chest, bleeding out.

Maxwell leaned down and set her hand to his forehead, healing him.

He gazed up at her, eyes wide with shock and full of tears. He let out a gasping sob and shook his head. "You would grant me mercy?"

"Mercy? Oh no. What I have planned for you is much better." Maxwell wrinkled up her nose, jerking him to his feet. "I don't want to kill you. That's too easy. There are, however, several others who I know would love to see you dead."

Vic watched, wide-eyed as she pulled Michael across the room to the window that overlooked the city square. He got to his feet, pulling Jamie up with him. They stumbled slowly across the room, curious as to what she had in mind.

He was immediately horrified at what he saw through the open window. An army of dead were standing beneath the window, reaching with greedy hands toward the skies. Vic barely recognized Leighton, the blood coagulated all over his face. The boy moaned and reached impatiently toward the window.

Michael shook his head quickly, trying hard to pull away. "No!"

Maxwell laughed and shook her head. "The people want what the people want," she said, shrugging. "And right now, they want you. It's what you always wanted, right? The spotlight is on you now, Michael. Your people are calling your name."

Jamie let out a quiet sob beside Vic, shaking her head. "This isn't her," she whispered to him, clinging to his arm. "This isn't her. This is wrong."

Michael fell to his knees in front of Maxwell, sobbing at her feet. He shook his head quickly. "No. No, *please…*"

Maxwell smiled, lifting him by his shirt collar. "Groveling isn't very becoming of you," she whispered, before throwing him out the window and to the hungry crowd below.

Vic winced as he listened to his brother scream. He held Jamie close, shaking his head quickly.

Jamie pulled away, shaking her head. "Maxwell! Max, you have to stop!" She stopped in front of her friend, taking a bloody hand in her own. "Maxwell, you have to let those people rest! Let them go!"

Maxwell stared down at the crowd as they ripped Michael to pieces. His screams gradually died down to nothingness. She didn't react as if she'd heard Jamie at all.

"Maxwell, look at me!" Jamie took her friend's face in her hands and forced her gaze upon her. She stared into her eyes, pleading with her the best way she knew how. "They need to rest. You need to let them go. Please."

The light slowly drained from Maxwell's eyes. She blinked, a crease forming between her brows. A flicker of confused recognition crossed her features. "Jamie? You're alive?"

Jamie let out a sob and nodded. "I'm alive. Yes, I'm alive."

Blood dripped from Maxwell's nose onto her swollen belly. She gasped and pitched forward, falling dead to the world.

An army of corpses fell to the ground with her.

EPILOGUE

2168

I STAND BETWEEN UNCLE VIC AND JAMIE, looking down at our new group of trainees. They look rough around the edges, as per usual. Like I imagine Jamie and I looked when we first realized what our role in the rehabilitation of our precious planet was.

They vary in age, some as young as five, and some far older than Jamie and I. They come from all walks of life around the world. But each one of them has the similar scared-out-of-their-wits expression on their face. It makes me smile out of fondness for them all.

It's been almost three years since I woke after Michael's defeat. The months that followed were some of the hardest I've ever lived through, but I'm only stronger for it.

When I woke, I learned that because Jamie wasn't completely dead when I raised an army of dead, she'd only been healed when I'd performed the necromancy in my rage. I also learned that because Bear's grace had fully been passed to me, he was gone for good. It was hard to accept. I learned that Nicole and the others were only days away and ready to help clean up our mess.

What made the transition just a tiny bit easier was the little girl that I got to meet when I woke. She came early, but she was strong. She was already a few days old when my eyes finally opened. Theo has been my little light. An absolute gift. She looks just exactly like her daddy.

Except for her eyes. Oh, and her beautiful, charcoal wings.

She's dancing around with Matty to our left, arms wide open as she spins around and around in circles. She giggles delightedly and falls over, her wings fluffing out just before she hits the ground. Matty laughs and scoops her up, holding her to his chest. He's a really great uncle. Takes the role pretty seriously. Vic does, too. They're both always begging to spend time with her. I'm glad. She needs a couple of good men to look up to.

I smile at them and then look toward Jamie, who is addressing the crowd. She's talking about our journey so far and how important it is for them to take their jobs as nephilim seriously. We are protectors of the Earth and the humans who inhabit it. We rise to the occasion to take care of them in their time of need.

And we never, ever abuse our power.

At least... we try really hard not to.

I don't remember raising the army. The last thing I can remember from that day is seeing Jamie bleeding on the ground. And then feeling an overwhelming burning throughout my entire body. It was like passing through the gates of Hell.

And then there was nothing.

When I woke, I spent a lot of time mourning. But I've realized something.

Every one of us has a story. Big or small, long or short, each person plays a part in how our world works. The measure of who we are, what we're worth, sometimes we don't realize how important we are in the universal scheme of things, but it comes from our interactions with each other and what we do to make a change. Sometimes we don't think we're worth the excitement or the trouble that it takes for our stories to play out, but we are all important. It's impossible to take down the bad guys if your rebellion only consists of yourself.

We're doing better now. We still haven't figured it all out, but our students are learning how to better protect their cities. How to form steady relationships between both angels and humans. How to keep the peace.

Jamie speaks kindly, but firmly to our audience, words of encouragement and praise spilling from between her pink lips. They're feeding into her energy, all excited for their new adventures. She catches my gaze from the corner of her eye and smiles, reaching down and taking my hand in hers. She squeezes it gently. It's a firm reminder that I'm home. That this is my life now. No more running. No more fear.

As for God, well, we haven't heard from him yet.

But maybe that's the beginning of another story.

ACKNOWLEDGMENTS

I am forever grateful to my sister, Hayley, for her undying support and continuous excitement about the stories I want to tell; to my mom and dad, for always loving me and encouraging me to pursue my dreams; to my brother, Zachary, and his beautiful fiancée, Cortney, for always being amazing; to my grandparents, for providing undying support and love in my life; to Siara, for helping me work out the kinks and for staying patient; and to my friends, Sam, Hayley, Emily, and Nicole, for being awesome and reminding me to never take myself too seriously.

ABOUT THE AUTHOR

T.W.R. Shelton is currently a student at Western Washington University, studying to achieve her teaching certificate in Secondary English Language Arts. She is obsessed with the night sky, the ocean, and all other things great and wondrous. She lives in Washington with her quirky cat, Eleanor. This is her first book. For more information, visit twrshelton.wix.com/bluesirensbooks.

www.ingramcontent.com/pod-product-compliance
Lightning Source LLC
Chambersburg PA
CBHW050726180626
46814CB00002B/631